GREAT LONESOME

GREAT LONESOME

JOHN D. NESBITT

FIVE STAR

A part of Gale, a Cengage Company

GALE
A Cengage Company

LIBRARY OF CONGRESS CATALOGING-IN-PUBLICATION DATA

Names: Nesbitt, John D, author.
Title: Great lonesome / John D Nesbitt.
Description: First edition. | Waterville, Maine : Five Star, a part of Gale, Cengage Learning, 2016.
Identifiers: LCCN 2019041804 | ISBN 9781432868321 (hardcover)
Subjects: GSAFD: Western stories. | Mystery fiction.
Classification: LCC PS3564.E76 G74 2020 | DDC 813/.54—dc23
LC record available at https://lccn.loc.gov/2019041804

First Edition. First Printing: May 2020
Find us on Facebook—https://www.facebook.com/FiveStarCengage
Visit our website—http://www.gale.cengage.com/fivestar
Contact Five Star Publishing at FiveStar@cengage.com

Printed in Mexico
Print Number: 01   Print Year: 2020

For my mother, Elizabeth

CHAPTER ONE

Reese Hartley drew rein at the crest of a low hill, and his horse settled to a stop. The sorrel relaxed its muscles and let out a long breath. Hartley tipped his hat up on one side to let the faint breeze play across the dampness. Here in the midst of a vast, treeless grassland, beneath an endless sky and a hot, pale sun, the only shade to be found would be the shadow cast by his horse. But Hartley did not dismount. Heat was rising from the earth at this time of day, and he had not stopped to loiter.

Half a mile to the northeast, an object crawled across the drying rangeland. Hartley recognized it as a threshing machine, which jerked and wobbled as a large team of horses strained together to pull it. Hartley counted the horses, all dark against the light green background. Twelve. On the far side of the machine, a man rode alongside on a white horse. Two men rode on the thresher, a rigid, unyielding, rust-colored behemoth.

Hartley regarded the sight as something at once familiar and alien. He had observed threshing machines at work and in expositions, but this was the first one he had seen since coming to Wyoming. Most threshers were stationary, and the workers had to carry the shocks by the wagon load to feed the beast. Many of the stationary harvesters were horse powered, with teams walking in a circle, but some were steam powered. They were the true monsters. To move one of them from one location to another required a team of thirty horses or more, plus additional teams to haul the trap wagon and the parts that could be reassembled. This horse-drawn thresher, by comparison, was modern, compact. and mobile, yet it lumbered across the prairie like a giant mechanical dung beetle.

Hartley reflected on the date. June 28. In the last couple of days as he had ridden out to check cattle, he had seen a couple of wheat fields to the north. The stalks and heads of the wheat were turning yellow, with streaks of green fading. Now that the weather was heating up, harvest would begin before long.

The thud of hoofbeats on dry ground caused Hartley to shift in the saddle. Dick Prentiss, the foreman, was slowing his long-legged bay horse from a lope to a trot to a fast walk. He braced himself in the stirrups as he pulled on the reins and stopped the horse. His dark brown, wide-brimmed hat cast his face in shadow.

"Pretty sight, ain't it?" Prentiss motioned with his hat brim.

Hartley, accustomed to Prentiss's sarcasm, gave a straight answer. "To a wheat farmer, maybe. Not so much in my eyes." He watched the horses turn with the slope of the land. Smooth motion rippled across the dark bodies. "That's a complete harvester. Not just a header, or mowing machine, like you usually see, or the thresher by itself that sits in one place. This one moves through the field, cutting and separating at the same time."

"All the same to me. Hate every one of 'em."

Hartley maintained his steady tone. "I don't care for machines myself."

"Them and the men that run 'em. Come in an' ruin the country for everyone." Prentiss spit to the side.

"They seem to make it work for them."

"I mean for the ones that was here first. These nesters and grangers come in and cut up the range. Fence it in."

"I think the rule here is that they have to fence out the livestock."

"Same thing. They ruin it."

Hartley did not answer. He watched the machine tip and settle as it crested the hill.

"You sound as if you're stickin' up for these punkin-rollers."

"I don't have an opinion about them yet. It's their machines that I don't care for."

Prentiss shifted in the saddle. He was above average height, with rounded shoulders; mounted on a tall horse, he had a superior position that allowed him to glare down at Hartley. "You need to get a clearer way of lookin' at things, and not bite the hand that feeds you. This is cattle country. We got to stick together. Not just one outfit, but all the cattlemen. These flea-bitten dirt-grubbers can't half of 'em make a livin' out here anyway, and the more we can push out, the better."

Hartley frowned. "The government encourages them to take up land."

"Sure it does. And what's good for the goose is good for the gander. That's why Earl needs to take up all the land he can get."

An image of the big boss passed through Hartley's mind— lean, dark-haired, and reserved, puffing on his pipe.

Prentiss continued. "There's more of them than there is of us."

"I know that. I don't know how you can change the numbers."

"Don't act like a dummy. Everyone who works for the Pick is expected to file a claim, and when he proves up, he sells it to the company."

"That's news to me."

"You been workin' here long enough, I thought it was time someone told you. Seein' them farmers made me think of it."

"This goes for everyone?"

"What I said."

"What if a man wanted to do something on his own?"

9

Prentiss rolled his head from one side to the other. "I thought you'd learned more by now. A cattleman like Earl doesn't want anyone workin' for him who's got his own place or his own brand. It's just common sense. Let some yap have a brand, and see how his herd'll multiply. So a man either works for the company, or he doesn't."

Hartley gave a slow nod. "Gives me something to think about."

"Sure. And as far as thinkin' goes, I wouldn't worry so much about machines themselves." Prentiss motioned again with his hat brim in the direction of the threshing machine in the distance. "You can hate them things all you want, but you got to take the bitter with the sweet. If we didn't have machines, we couldn't have trains, and that's what gives us our cattle market. That's where our bread is buttered."

Hartley drew his brows together in thought. Trains also brought out the barbed wire, prairie plows, and seed planters that were helping the dreaded nesters and grangers cut the open range into pieces.

The aroma of fried beef lingered in the air of the bunkhouse as the hired men rolled and lit cigarettes. The big boss, Earl Miner, sat back from the table and pressed tobacco into the bowl of his pipe. In Hartley's perception, Miner had an aristocratic air about him. The man was slim, with well-trimmed hair graying at the temples. He was clean-shaven as always. He wore a dark suit and vest with a white shirt. His silver watch chain made a near match with the chromium or nickel-plated perforated cap on his shiny black pipe. Approval showed in his dark eyes as he lit the tobacco, blew a cloud of smoke, and flipped the cap onto the bowl. With the match still lit, he drew flame through the perforations and puffed another cloud.

Hartley's eyes moved to the brand that was burned into the

wooden wall. At first glance, it resembled a "T" with a rounded head, but closer observation showed it to be a miner's pick. Hartley appreciated the symbol. While the boss would have little sympathy with the labor unions that were forming in various parts of the country, his brand expressed work and strength.

Prentiss sat across the table from the boss. With his rounded shoulders, he seemed bent to the task as he rolled a cigarette, and his light brown eyes were intent on his work. He had large hands, but he made a neat job of rolling his pill. Lifting the globe on the kerosene lantern, he tipped his head to the side and lit his cigarette with the lamp's flame. He drew back, straightened up, and blew out a stream of smoke.

"I told Hartley it was time he thought about filing for a land claim."

Miner puffed on his pipe. "Is that right?" He brought his eyes to bear on Hartley.

"He mentioned it, sir. I don't know if it's a condition of employment."

Miner shook his head. "Oh, no."

"But he said everyone else has done so."

Miner glanced around the room. "Everyone here."

"I see. I'm thinking about it, of course."

"Sure." Miner leveled his gaze at Hartley. "I wouldn't want you to think I did things this way just for personal gain. It's bigger than that. We've got to work together and hold our ground. We were here first, and we can't have these other types come in and take our livelihood out from under us. So if someone works for me, he's got to be on my side."

"All or none, you might say."

"Those are your words, but they don't disagree with my thoughts." Miner made a wave with his hand and said, "Like you say, think about it."

Hartley nodded and withdrew. He made his way to the end

of the bunkhouse where the cots stood in a row. He didn't care for tobacco smoke, or close company with ongoing chatter. At this time of the evening, Prentiss and the other three hands often settled into a game of pinochle, and Hartley had achieved an understanding with them that he would not feel left out if he was not invited, even on those nights when not all four of the regular players were present. They could play pinochle three-handed.

At his bunk, he reached into the upright apple crate and drew out a ball of jute twine. With his pocketknife, he cut three lengths of about six feet each. After tying the strands together at one end, he secured the knot on a nail head that stuck up from the apple crate, and he began to practice braiding. Once he fell into the pattern, his hands moved by themselves. He did not allow himself to be in a hurry. He did not need the braid for a specific use or by a certain time, and he wanted the overlaps to be neat and consistent.

As his hands worked, his thoughts wandered. By turns, he recalled the machine he had seen on the prairie, the admonition he had received from Prentiss, and the toned-down exchange he had had with Miner. He was glad not to be one of the men working on the thresher. He enjoyed some parts of his current work of cow punching, but he did not like the expectation that he would file a claim and turn it over to the boss. He wanted to have land of his own, but he needed to earn some money in order to make his plan succeed, so he didn't want to lose his job.

He continued to braid right, left, right, left, with each strand by turn becoming the left, the right, and the middle strand. Some day he would try this with three colors of ribbons or cloth strips, to see the strands moving back and forth.

When he had finished the braid and tied off the loose ends, he unhooked it from the nail and laid it across the apple crate with the previous braid he had produced. This one looked a little smoother, a little more even.

He knew that men made cinches, halters, and lead ropes out of material like hemp and horsehair, and they made lariats out of strips of rawhide. Developing those skills took time, patience, and dexterity, plus aptitude. He would find out if he had it in him. Two brothers could grow up side by side, and one could have a natural talent for machines, from sewing machines to bicycles to steam engines to these new gasoline engines, while the other might have it in him to draw, paint, write, or sing. Since coming west, Hartley found himself on easy terms with wooden-handled tools like a hammer, a pitchfork, and a shovel, just as his hands seemed at home with cords, ropes, and leather straps. Somewhere inside, he felt the stir of wanting to make something. Having his own place would help.

He cast a glance around the room. Having had some time to himself, he thought it wouldn't hurt to make himself sociable and not give the impression that he didn't want to get along with others.

As he approached the table, a couple of the card players glanced up but kept their attention on the game. Earl Miner had set his dark pipe aside and was scraping the ends of his fingernails with a penknife. He paid no attention to the players, who sat cockeyed at the mess table in order to play across with their partners. Hartley took a seat a ways down the table so as not to give anyone the feeling that he was looking at cards.

Miner paused in his work and said, "How do you like braiding?"

"It's something to try."

"Some men get pretty good at it."

"That's what I've heard."

"Braidin' horsehair is one of the finer arts."

"I would imagine."

13

"Takes time." Miner paused. "They say men at the peniten-
tiary develop that talent. That's one thing they've got, is time."

"I've heard that, too."

"Tom Horn took it up while he was waiting in jail in
Cheyenne. But he came by it honestly."

"Oh?"

"He used to braid lariats and quirts out of leather, and hacka-
mores out of horsehair, when he worked on ranches. Pass the
time in the long days and nights of winter."

"Did you know him?"

"Sure. I met him a time or two. You can hear plenty about
him, both good and bad. But I'll say this. He did his work."

Prentiss spoke over his shoulder. "Puttin' cattle thieves out of
business."

"When that was his work," said Miner. "Protecting the
property of honest men. But he was a good horseman as well,
and as good at roping as any man you'll see."

"Well, he died at the end of a rope," said Prentiss.

"Like I said, you'll hear both good and bad."

"They say he didn't kill that kid down at Iron Mountain, but
he deserved to hang for all the men he did kill."

"I'll say this. He helped men hold their ranches together, and
he put the fear into cattle thieves."

"He did that."

Miner leaned back in his chair, took out his silver watch, and
opened it. "Time for me to go back to the house." He put away
the watch and reached for his black pipe with the shiny metal
cap. His eyes met Hartley's, and he gave a faint smile.

"Good night," said Hartley.

"Same to you." Miner stood up, took his hat from a peg near
the pick that was branded into the wall, and put on the hat as
he walked out the door.

Prentiss's voice rose on the air. "Bedpost queen."

14

Hartley frowned in puzzlement, then recalled that the queen of spades was an important card in the game that the men were playing.

"Damn the bitch," said Buck Whittaker.

Prentiss sniffed. "What did you expect, pot hooks?"

"No, they're all out."

"Ha-ha. This is just about game anyway." Prentiss scraped the cards toward him.

The game ended before long. The four men stood up from the table and yawned and stretched.

Prentiss turned toward Hartley and said, "What did you learn from the boss?"

"You might say I understand his philosophy."

Prentiss, still stretching with his elbows as he held his fists closed, took a couple of steps to loom over Hartley. "It's not hard to understand. You've been in this country for a while."

Hartley did not answer.

"Well, it's past ten, and daylight comes early. This old hoss has got to go to bed. See you in the morning."

"Good night."

Hartley sat across from Ben Stillwell at breakfast. The young man had a fresh shave and was wearing a clean, light-colored cotton shirt with a full row of buttons. His wavy hair, between a dark blond and a light brown, was combed into place, and his blue eyes brightened with his smile.

"Odom's got flapjacks on the way," he said.

"That's good."

"Here's bacon." Stillwell held a tin plate forward.

"Thanks." Hartley took the plate and served himself three strips. Looking down the table to Stillwell's left, he saw that Buck Whittaker had a short stack of two hotcakes with bacon strips on top and molasses oozing off the bacon. Hartley preferred to eat his bacon separate, so he picked up a piece and took a bite.

Stillwell said, "You seem unsure about taking up a land claim."

"I hadn't thought about it in those terms until yesterday."

"Ah, I wouldn't worry about it. You can prove up on it in a couple of years, and then when you sell it, you're free to do something else. There's plenty of time."

Odom, a lean, balding man with a fringe of brown hair, moved like a ghost in a white apron. He held forward a plate with four hotcakes. Stillwell and Hartley took two each.

"I suppose there is," said Hartley. "What happens if you quit working for the ranch?"

"That's between you and the boss. I think some fellas see it as a way to be kept on in the winter."

"And braid leather?"

Stillwell smiled. "That, or go out and brand mavericks. Some outfits still pay five dollars a head for that, on the *q.t.*"

Whittaker paused with his elbow on the table and his empty fork in the air. He had blond hair, bulging blue eyes, a flushed face, prominent yellow teeth, and a sparse mustache and chin beard. Although he looked as if he was ready for a dispute, his voice was calm. "There's nothin' to it. Takin' up land, that is. Like Ben says, you've got plenty of time ahead of you to do something else. Meanwhile, you help the outfit grow, and everyone helps each other."

"I thought the Pick was already a good-sized outfit."

"It is. But nowadays you need to have more deeded land. That's why Earl's spread out the way he is, got men at his different line camps."

"Do they stay on the places they've claimed?"

"They're supposed to, but it doesn't have to be that way. I just about never see the place I filed on, but someone would have to contest it for anything to come of it."

Hartley turned to his right to speak to Tobe Lestman. "How about you?"

"Same as what Buck says. Don't matter much to me."

"What if you met a woman and wanted to settle down for yourself?"

Lestman had straight brown hair, a bristly mustache, dull brown eyes, and a muddy complexion. He raised his eyebrows and peered at Hartley. "I guess that would be a problem, until you sold your land. I wouldn't want to live on one of these claims anyway. When I settle down, I'm gonna get a job in a town."

Whittaker's teeth showed as he said, "So you can go poke the old lady at noontime."

Stillwell gave a short laugh.

Lestman said, "Don't you worry about me. Maybe it's so I can keep an eye out for fellas like you."

"Me?" Whittaker stretched his face downward, with his mouth closed, so that his eyes feigned an expression of surprise. "You treat me like I'm some kind of a claim-jumper."

"Ha-ha," said Lestman. "When I get married, I'll make sure I live a long ways away from you."

Whittaker wagged his head back and forth. "Might be the best thing you ever do."

Hartley dismounted in the same place where he had stopped two days earlier to observe the harvester. The horse he had saddled after noon dinner today, a solid brown animal that needed to be nudged every minute or two, hung its head. Hartley took off his hat and wiped his brow with the cuff of his shirt. The day seemed like a replica of the day before—warm, with a wide, blue, cloudless sky. The prairie showed no signs, at this distance, of having had twelve horses and a clumsy machine

17

cross over it. Yet Hartley remembered it in some detail, a rust-colored land craft with two men aboard. He wondered where it had come from and where it was headed.

He took a broad view around him at this area called Decker Basin. A few miles south lay the town of Jennet, the only town he had known in the past few months. He understood that several wheat farms had taken hold close together in an area less than ten miles east of Jennet. Some twenty miles to the north and a little ways west of where he stood, a small town called Winsome served as the center for the surrounding wheat farms and cattle ranches.

He guessed that the harvester was making its way to the concentration of wheat fields near Winsome. He knew that as a general rule, wheat ripened from south to north, so workers who followed the harvest could start in the southern plains of Kansas and end up in Canada. But not every field ripened in order. In an area like Decker Basin, about twenty-five miles from north to south and close to thirty from east to west, wheat in one locale could be ready for harvest sooner than in another area a few miles south.

Decker Basin, to some extent, was an area unto itself. It had its clearest border on the west side, where Decker Rim ran in a broad arc, not quite a semicircle, from the southwest to the northwest. Grassy hills ran across from the northwest to the northeast. The basin was not as defined on the east, where it faded into rolling hills. Across the eastern half of the southern edge, however, a row of bluffs and mesa land marked the border. A large gap, about ten miles from the end of the bluffs on one side to the end of Decker Rim on the other, opened the vista straight to the south. If a man wanted to ride to Cheyenne, he followed the trail that ran along the western edge of the gap, close to the mountain-like end of Decker Rim.

With the exception of the wheat country east of Jennet,

Hartley had seen most of the basin during spring roundup. But he was new to the country then, and much of his attention was focused on the details of his new work, not least among them staying in the saddle when a horse cut to one side or the other. Hartley had become familiar with most of the range within ten miles of the Pick headquarters, and he was looking forward to learning more of it in closer detail as his work took him farther out. They had brought the herd to the home range after roundup, but the cattle drifted out again—a little farther each day, it seemed.

He knew where he was at the moment, and he had a good idea of how long it would take him to ride back to the ranch. He did not have a foreman looming over him today, so he could take the route he pleased. He cast a glance at the sun, checked his cinch, swung aboard, and headed his horse toward Jennet.

To avoid other travelers who might want to stop and talk, Hartley stayed a half-mile west of the north-south trail and rode into town from the northwest. By this route he did not pass by the Strong Water Saloon, which was all for the better. Earl Miner did not have any strictures against going through town during the workday, or against stopping in at a business, but he did have a rule about drinking anywhere when a man was on the job or on the ranch. Saloons and roadhouses did not exert a pull on Hartley as the sirens and mermaids tempted sailors in the old stories, but he found it better to steer wide anyway. In addition, he did not run the risk of seeing the horse of one of his fellow punchers tied up outside.

Hartley turned left on a quiet cross street and rode two blocks to the center of town, such as it was. Jennet was strung out along the wide north-south road, with a crossroad at the south end of town. At that point, a trail came in from the west, where Miner's ranch was located, and went out to the east toward the wheat country Hartley had heard about. He rode to the northwest corner of that intersection and dismounted.

The second-to-last business in the long building had a medium-sized plate-glass window with the words "Great West Grain and Livestock" painted in gold lettering. Hartley loosened the cinch and tied his horse to the hitching rail in front of the window. As he headed for the door, a bell tinkled, and the door opened. A man stepped out, leaning his head forward as he put on a hat with four dents in the peak and a round, flat brim. As he straightened up, Hartley recognized the full, rosy face, bushy mustache, and constant smile of Mike Ackerman.

"Good afternoon, Mike."

"Well, hello, young friend. How are things on the range?"

"Normal and quiet."

"Glad to hear it. Are things drying out?"

"Somewhat."

"Just as well. We could always use a little rain, of course. Not too much right now, because of the wheat, and I sure hope we don't get any hail." Ackerman rubbed his hand up and down on the surface of his full waistcoat, as if he was drying his palm of perspiration, but he did not reach forward to shake. He raised his hand to chest height, palm outward, and said, "I'm going to check the mail. Did you need me for anything?"

"Oh, no."

"Well, go on in. Don't stay too long and keep her from her work."

Hartley accepted the comment as a light touch with some humor. Ackerman, being a buyer of cattle and sheep as well as a grain broker, was a friend of Earl Miner. Even if he had the freedom to go for the mail and to drop into the Strong Water Saloon every day at five, his niece was a working girl, and Hartley was on company time.

Inside the office, as the doorbell sounded behind him, Hartley blinked to adjust his eyes from the bright afternoon outside. Bess rose from her chair and walked around the oak desk to greet him.

"Good afternoon, stranger."

His eyes were adjusted well enough to take in her light brown hair, blue eyes, fair complexion, and pleasing shape. She wore a white blouse and a light blue skirt with a narrow, dark blue sash.

He remembered to take off his hat. "And good afternoon to you."

"Are you working nearby today?"

"Not far. A gentle wind blew me this way."

"It's warm, isn't it? Not a breath of air in here." She fanned the space in front of her.

"There's no breeze to speak of outside, either."

"Are you on your way back to the ranch?"

"In a few minutes. I wouldn't want to take up much of your time. I saw your uncle outside, and he told me not to."

Bess smiled.

"I didn't have anything particular in mind. Just thought I would drop in."

"And work is going well?"

"Oh, yes. It's not very demanding right now, as far as time goes."

"That's good."

Silence hung in the air for a few seconds. "There is one thing," he said. "You've been here longer than I have. Maybe you could give me your view of it."

She tipped her head and gave a half-smile. "I can try."

"Maybe it's me. I know I can be hardheaded. But there's something I can't quite go along with."

Bess nodded.

He hesitated, recalling that her uncle and Earl Miner were

friends. "It goes like this. Maybe I'm being too finicky. But it seems as if the boss expects everyone who works for him to take up a homestead claim and then turn it over to him—after proving up on it, of course, and getting the title."

Bess raised her eyebrows a quarter of an inch. "I've heard of that. I think it's common. And it's not illegal."

"Oh, no. And the fellow who does it gets paid for the land."

"Then I suppose it's a matter of whether you want to do something like that. I have the sense that you don't."

Hartley took a breath to keep himself from saying too much at once. "Well, it's not what I came out here for. I came to make a new start. Part of that idea includes having my own land. So I don't care for the prospect of claiming land and then turning it over to someone else. The other hired men, who have all agreed to it, tell me not to worry. They tell me I can go on and find my own land afterwards. They say there's plenty of time. But you never know. Time goes on and can pass you by."

He felt a moment of mutual comprehension. He knew that she knew that he was about thirty years old, and he was sure that she assumed that he had her age figured pretty close to twenty-five.

She tipped her head again. "What does it take—two years?"

"On the average. They give you five. But that's not my only objection. I don't like the idea of going along with this . . . practice. That is, a man using other men, who are at a level below him, so he can take everything he can get. Oh, he's got a good reason for it. He wants to solidify his ranch holdings. I can't blame him for that. But it's the means by which he hopes to achieve his end. Then he wants to try to push out smaller landholders—nesters—who come here to claim land under the same law."

"You don't have to be part of that."

"Not directly. But I might be contributing to it. Still, I'll go back to the first part. Even if it's legal, I don't care for the scheme of gathering up land that way." Hartley smiled. "You look at me as if I'm missing something."

"Oh, no. It's your choice. But I wonder why someone would go along with it unless there was something in it for him."

"Well, yes. I didn't touch upon that. I understand that it keeps a man on good terms with his boss, and he can be sure of his job."

"Then it's not all bad. A man in that situation can cooperate with a plan that favors him."

"That's a way of looking at it."

"And I would expect him to be paid a fair price for the land, not just a token amount."

"I would think so."

Bess smiled. "It's your choice, of course."

"Sure. I just wanted to sound it out with someone other than the men at the ranch."

She laughed. "And I qualified."

"Well, not just any old someone." To himself he reflected that he had wanted to know her opinion, and now he had it. She would want him to go along.

The sun was beginning to slip in the west as Hartley took up the trail that led out of town. The clock on the wall behind Bess had read ten past five, so he hadn't lost much time. Once he was out of town, he could lope the horse. For the time being, the animal seemed to have grown more torpid in the short while it had been tied in the shade, but he could get it moving.

Hartley had his head tipped forward to block out the sun, so he did not see very far ahead. When the brown horse snuffled, Hartley raised his line of vision.

Two hundred yards ahead, a wagon drawn by two horses was coming his way. A blocky man rode alongside on a stout dark

23

horse. Hartley moved to the side of the trail and rode on. The wagon rumbled, and the traces rattled. Closer, he heard the labored breathing of the horses.

The man driving the wagon was slender and hunched. He wore a dark, short-brimmed hat with a rounded crown, dented on each side. The man had dust on his hat, hair, mustache, and clothes. He had a sad cast to his eyes as he looked up at Hartley and away.

The horseman wore a brownish-black hat, also dusty, with a tall, rounded crown and a wide, flat brim. He was broad-faced, thick-featured, above average height in the saddle, broad in the shoulders, and heavy in build. As he rode past Hartley, he gave an appraising glance with his dark brown eyes and said, " 'Lo."

"Afternoon," said Hartley. With the men past, he observed the load in the wagon. It consisted of a heap of dusty, chunky rocks, all of a size that men could lift into a wagon. Unlike smooth river rocks, these would have come out of a quarry or fallen off of striated bluffs. Hartley imagined the men had picked up the rocks somewhere along the base of Decker Rim. Of the various ways of making a living that he did not envy, he could add one more.

Hartley was brushing the horse he planned to use for his morning ride when Dick Prentiss appeared and stood within two feet of him. The foreman's face was stubbled, as he shaved but once a week, and his jaw had a firm set to it.

"I imagine you've thought some more on what we talked about," he said.

Hartley felt a nervousness creep through his upper body. He had known the moment would come sooner or later, but he hadn't expected it this morning. "Somewhat," he said.

"Somewhat. That's not very clear. You need to be more definite." Prentiss stood with his chin raised and his large right

24

hand on his hip. "Look straight at me when I talk to you."

Hartley quit brushing and turned to face the foreman. He thought Prentiss was in a good position to punch him if he wanted to. Hartley kept his eye on the man's right hand and caught a view of his leather vest and his gray wool shirt with its pointed collar and full row of buttons.

"Look at me."

Hartley met the man's light brown eyes that bore down on him.

"We don't do things halfway here. None of this one shoe on and one shoe off. You're either with us, or you're not."

Hartley took a breath to steady himself. "I asked Earl if it was a condition of my employment, and he said it wasn't."

"I heard him. And it isn't. But I don't think you'd be happy here if you didn't go along with the way everyone else does things. So tell me which way it'll be."

Hartley moistened his lips and swallowed. "I've decided I'd rather not."

Prentiss raised his hand to scratch his chin. "That's fine. It's your decision. I'll tell Earl, and he can figure your pay."

"In other words, you don't fire me. You let me quit."

"It's easier that way. No hard feelin's, no talkin' behind someone's back."

"No blacklisting."

"We don't do that."

Maybe not on paper. "Then I suppose I should put this horse back in the corral."

"Might as well."

Hartley carried his bedroll and duffel bag from the bunkhouse and set them on the ground by the hitching rail. He led his own horse, a sorrel with white socks in front, from the corral, then brushed and saddled him. As he tied his gear onto the back of the saddle, Prentiss stepped out of the ranch house into the sunlight.

The foreman did not waste one last chance to crowd into Hartley's space as he handed him the packet of paper folded around the short roll of coins.

"Thanks." Hartley took the money and put it in his pocket without opening and counting it. He checked his cinch by putting two fingers between the webbed fiber and the horse's ribs. Finding it snug enough, he stuck his foot in the stirrup and swung his leg up and over his gear. He caught the other stirrup and settled into his seat. As he turned the horse around, he raised his free right hand and said, "So long." With a touch of the spur, he rode away.

CHAPTER TWO

With no time constraints, Hartley took an unfamiliar route into town. He stayed about a half-mile south of the trail that led from the Pick into Jennet. He rode through patches of sagebrush and yucca, saw the pale mounds of a prairie dog town gleaming in the morning sun, and exchanged stares with a band of four antelope. Not far from town, he came upon a low area where a grove of cottonwoods must have grown during a few wet years. More than a dozen trees, none of them fully developed, lay spilled over and decomposing. Cottonwood was not good firewood to begin with, and these trees must have fallen and gone soft before the first tents of Jennet sprang up on the plain.

Hartley caught a good view of the town as he turned onto the main thoroughfare at the south end. The buildings were wooden now, most of them made of lumber but a few small structures built of logs. Notwithstanding a quantity of whitewash and painted lettering, the town gave an overall impression of dry lumber and dust. What few trees there were had not grown as high as any of the walls of the buildings, and daylight showed between their leaves.

Recalling the dead trees he had observed and seeing a low stable made of logs, he decided to take a look at something he had noticed in the past. He detoured one long block to the west and turned north at the corner. In the middle of the block, also a long one, he approached a small sawmill on his left.

The machine consisted of two parts—a stationary steam

27

engine on a heavy base and a saw blade on a metal stand, the latter secured by iron stakes and powered by a dark belt that connected it to the engine. Both parts sat under an open shed with a tin roof that was dented by hailstones. Drifts of sawdust lay all about, and a stack of scrap lumber, which he assumed was used to fire the engine, had a layer of earthen dust on it, with bits of sawdust hanging in cobwebs.

One detail took him by surprise. A pile of new logs lay on the north side of the firewood. The logs were about twelve feet long, each from a single tree, and none of them much larger than a foot in diameter at the thick end. They looked like jack pine, and Hartley imagined they came from one of the bigger canyons along Decker Rim. He appreciated the neat ax cuts on both ends as he rode on.

At the end of the block, he turned right. When he arrived at the wide main street, with the Strong Water Saloon across the way and to his left, he turned right again. A few doors down, he turned in and dismounted in front of the post office. Leaving his horse tied with all his worldly possessions in the full morning sun, he walked in through the open door.

Ned Farnsworth, who ran the post office as an adjunct to his pharmacy, appeared at the postal window. He took off his spectacles, held his blue eyes steady, and smiled.

"Well, hello. It looks as if you're going somewhere."

Ned was a pale, indoors fellow with trimmed, light brown hair and a clean shave. He wore a gray suit, white shirt, and darker gray bow tie. Though he was cordial by habit, Hartley found him inquisitive, as postmasters and postmistresses were known to be. But because he was about the same age as Hartley and seemed to value the friendship of another educated person, Hartley did not mind his questions. Over a period of months, Ned had asked him what he liked to read, what he liked to see at the theater, and whether he played any musical instruments.

An indirect question, based on the horse with bundles standing outside the door, did not strike Hartley as prying.

"At this point," said Hartley, "it's not so much where I'm going to as where I'm going from."

Ned's eyes widened. "Oh. Are you leaving us?"

"Not quite. I'm just leaving my job at the Pick."

"Oh. No trouble, I hope."

"None to speak of. It was my choice."

"Do you have another situation to go to?"

"Not yet. I think I'll look around in this area before I go on to a place I don't know anything about."

"Sounds like a good idea. There's work to be found, at least at this time of year. You won't be needing your mail forwarded, then?"

"Not now. I don't suppose there's any waiting for me today."

Ned turned to look over the pigeonholes, though Hartley was sure he knew the answer already.

"None at the present." Ned brought his gaze back to Hartley and smiled.

"Thanks. I guess I'll move along."

"Good enough. If I hear of anything, I'll let you know."

"I appreciate it. I'll drop in every few days anyway."

"That'll be fine." Ned raised his spectacles but did not put them on. "Good luck."

"Thanks."

Outside, Hartley paused at the hitching rail. Across the street, Mike Ackerman walked in the shade of the buildings and turned into the Owl Café. Hartley pursed his lips and decided on his next stop. He untied his horse and led the animal down the street to the office where Bess worked.

As he tied the sorrel to the hitching rail, he wondered if Bess saw him or was busy at her work. When he opened the door and walked in, he was surprised to see Ben Stillwell sitting in a chair in front of Bess's desk. He had his right boot hiked up onto his other leg, and his hat was perched on his knee.

Stillwell turned in his chair, raised his hand in greeting, and said, "Howdy, Reese."

Bess sat up with her hands together on the desk and a half-smile on her face. "Good morning."

"The same to both of you." Hartley took off his hat. In a quick succession of thoughts, he realized Stillwell had been dressed for town that morning at breakfast and must have ridden out of the ranch while Hartley was packing his gear. Whatever Stillwell's business was in town, he hadn't wasted time.

Speaking to Bess, Hartley said, "I didn't mean to interrupt anything, but I thought I would drop in and share a bit of news." He nodded toward Stillwell. "Maybe Ben has already mentioned it, but I'm not working for Earl Miner anymore."

Bess raised her hand as if to cover her mouth, then laid it against the top of her blouse, below her throat. "No, he didn't. I had no idea. You weren't . . . dismissed, were you?"

"No. I was allowed to make the choice myself." Hartley turned again toward Stillwell. "Sorry to interrupt your conversation, but Bess and I had been talking about this yesterday. About the boss expecting me to file on a homestead for him. So I was giving her the latest."

Stillwell shrugged. "I'm not much for someone else's business. I'm sorry if it ended up costing you a job, though."

"It might be all for the best. You never know." With a motion of his hat as he held it by his side, he said, "I suppose I'll move along. Good seeing you both."

Stillwell rose and shook Hartley's hand. "Good luck, Reese."

"Yes," said Bess. "We wish you all the best."

"Thank you." Hartley turned and walked outside, putting on his hat as he stepped into the sunlight.

Across the street, a man in a skull cap and leather apron was standing in the shade of the blacksmith shop and staring in the direction of the grain and livestock office. Hartley frowned until he realized that the blacksmith, Jock Mosby, also served as town marshal and was regarding him as someone passing through.

Hartley untied his horse and led the animal across the street. As he drew near the marshal, he raised his hand in greeting. "Good morning."

Mosby had a pair of brown leather gauntlets in his hand, and he raised them in response.

Hartley stopped a few yards from the man and squinted with the sun in his face. From past impressions and his present view, he guessed the marshal's age at about thirty-five.

A husky voice came out of Mosby's dark bushy mustache. "What can I help you with?"

"My name's Reese Hartley. I don't think we've met. I've been working for Earl Miner."

Mosby's dark eyes moved to the horse and back to Hartley. "On your way out?"

"Not really. I plan to stay around the area and see what other work there is. I thought I would let you know."

"It's a free country. All I do is keep the peace when I have to."

Hartley smiled. "I hope not to give you any work in that area."

"A little thought ahead of time never hurts." Mosby raised the gauntlets in a slight gesture of dismissal. "I've got a fire to tend to," he said.

"So long." Hartley turned to the left, and with his horse in tow, he walked northward in the wide, quiet street. He passed up the Owl Café and wondered if Mike Ackerman saw him. Within a few minutes, he found himself approaching the Strong Water Saloon. Even on a warm afternoon, he could resist the

31

temptation to go in, and at this early hour, he felt no attraction at all. He knew that a saloon was a good place to hear about a job, but he also knew it was a good place to lose a job, get into a fight, or fritter away money. He was not afraid of such places, and he was familiar with this one, but he could wait to visit it again.

By now he had an idea of where he might go. Rather than spend money on lodging, he would find a place to camp. It would have to be on public domain, which meant he might have cattle or riders wandering through. He recalled an area about five miles north and five miles east, about seven miles in a beeline, that he had seen in the outer reaches of spring roundup. Not many of the Pick cattle, or riders, drifted that far. He would stay out of the way, mind his own business, and ride into town when he felt the need.

He passed up two possible sites that offered shade. One had a short file of chokecherry bushes, and the other had a grove of box elders. Both were located in dry creek beds, which meant possible danger in the event of a flash flood, and both were littered with cow pies. Flies and gnats added to the atmosphere.

He also passed up the shelter of a lone cottonwood. It grew in a hollow, the upper end of which was dotted with a hundred prairie-dog holes marked by mounds of light-colored earth. Hartley had heard that prairie dogs carried fleas, which in turn carried plague-like germs.

At last he found a cutbank on the east side of a hill. Shadows were beginning to stretch in early afternoon, and the only insect he saw was a red velvet ant crawling away into the sagebrush. Except for being exposed to the elements, and perhaps being a haven for rattlesnakes, it looked like a good place.

By the time he had set his camp, put his horse out on a picket, and gathered enough dry sagebrush for a fire, the sun was slipping in the western sky. Odom the cook would be peeling potatoes. Mike Ackerman would be checking his mail and wetting his whistle. Hartley made himself picture Bess sitting by herself at her desk, tending to her work. She was all right. She just had more of a conformist outlook than he did.

This camp was all right, too. He might get rained on or pummeled by hail, but he was not someone else's serf or vassal.

The morning sun warmed the campsite early, and the flies would not leave Hartley alone. He had slept well, but now he was perspiring, and the flies kept buzzing around his face and landing on him. He wouldn't have minded lying in bed a little longer, but he gave up and rolled out.

Thirty yards away, his horse snuffled. Off and on in the night, as he had heard the shifting of hooves and the drag of the picket rope, he found the animal's presence reassuring. Now as he sat up and saw the large figure of the horse against the rising sun, he appreciated the quietness and simplicity of being alone on the rangeland. He had slept on the ground for more than a month during roundup, but the camp had noises at all hours. Men snored and mumbled in their sleep, night riders came and went, and the cook was banging pots and pans at four in the morning. This was the bliss of solitude, as he recalled the phrase.

He shook out his boots and pulled them on, then listened to his surroundings again. The swish of the rope across the low brush, the stamp of a foot. The silver tones of a meadowlark floating across the prairie. He expected to hear the mooing of cattle, which was always in the air, during daylight hours at least, at roundup camp. All he heard now was the five notes of the meadowlark, time and again.

He recalled a cloudy day during roundup when the sound of the herd grew loud. A puncher from another outfit complained about the noise, and his boss said, "That's the sound of money."

33

Hartley had heard a similar defense when someone complained of the odor of crowded corrals. It was the smell of money. Hartley assumed he would go back to working with cattle, but for the time being, he did not miss the sound and the smell of money, which was someone else's, anyway.

After building a small sagebrush fire, he boiled coffee in a can. Taking stock of his provisions, he figured he would go through the grub Odom had given him—biscuits, cold meat, and raisins—by the end of the day. He counted back and confirmed that today was Saturday. If he went to town in the afternoon, he might stay until evening and see what knowledge he could pick up about available work

A mile away from town, Hartley began to hear the *chug-chug* of a steam engine. The sound was not strong enough for a locomotive, and he knew there was no railroad for miles. For as much as he preferred to avoid machines, he thought he should find out about this one. He remembered the sawmill, the new logs, and the scrap lumber, and he imagined puffs of smoke from a beast that ate its young.

Closer to town, he placed the noise as coming from the east side, which was not the location of the sawmill. Turning his head, he caught the sound of another racket as well—a grinding, crunching sound. He wondered if something had broken inside the machinery, but it chugged on.

He followed the sound to the first block east of the main street. On a large lot not far from the metal boneyard in back of the blacksmith shop, Hartley saw what at first reminded him of a stonecutter's yard. But instead of slabs of marble waiting to be made into headstones, a few piles of rough rock lay about, and dust floated in the air. Two workmen moved back and forth from a rock pile to a large hopper that Hartley recognized as a rock crusher. The hopper was made of heavy iron and was secured in place by iron stakes. Like the sawmill, it was powered by a belt that ran to a steam engine, also secured, about twelve feet away. Each time a man tossed a rock into the maw of the crusher, the machine sent out the horrible grinding sound against the constant noise of the steam engine.

Hartley slowed his horse but did not stop. As he rode by, he recognized the rocks as being the same kind as he had seen on the wagon a couple of days earlier. He also recognized the slender, older man wearing a short-brimmed hat with a dent on each side. As before, the man's hat and clothes and mustache had a layer of light-colored dust.

Hartley shifted his gaze and picked out the second worker. He was slender also, with a cloth hat and slanting brim that looked like a bottle cap. He wore a neckless, sleeveless shirt. His upper arms were dusty, and his lower arms glistened with sweat in the warm afternoon as he hefted the rocks. He showed a toothless mouth as he spoke to the other man, but the machine drowned out all other sound. Hartley had seen the second man before, and now he placed him. His name was Cletis, and he worked as a swamper in the Strong Water Saloon.

The crusher clattered and crunched and gnashed. Hartley cast a final glance but did not see the blocky man who had been riding the stout horse a couple of days earlier. The two drudges worked on, moving in the strange silence created by the deafening machine.

Out of curiosity, Hartley directed his horse to the other side of town where he had seen the sawmill. From two long blocks away, he could hear the rock crusher, but the noise was not so loud as to drown out sounds on this side. He heard the clucking of chickens from within a henhouse, and a dog barked about a block away. The sawmill gave forth no noise, however, and as it came into view, Hartley made out the partial figure of a man sitting in a chair in the shade of the roofed structure. A tan hat and tan vest struck a note of familiarity, and as more of the man came into view, Hartley recognized Ben Stillwell. The young man appeared quite relaxed in the shade, smoking his pipe. Seeing a passerby, he raised his hand and waved in an automatic sort of way.

Hartley turned into the lot and came to a stop by the shelter. He swung down from the saddle and stood by his horse's shoulder.

"The people you meet," said Stillwell. "I didn't recognize you at first. I didn't know you were still around."

"I found a place to camp a few miles out of town."

"Which way?"

"North and east."

Stillwell blew out a small stream of smoke. "No harm there, I hope."

"None that I've seen so far." Hartley glanced at the equipment, which had been dusted off. "I'm surprised to see you here."

"Just work, is all."

"Is this a new job for you, or does this place belong to Earl?"

"New job, same boss. Earl bought it a while back, but he waited until after roundup to get it going."

"Do you know how to run this machine?"

"A fella's supposed to come and show me."

"You're not going to move those logs by yourself, are you?"

"Nah. I'll have help."

"That's good. Do you expect to be busy? There's not that much timber in this country, is there?"

"They get what they can. Every little bit helps. Freighting lumber in costs money." Stillwell puffed on his pipe. "Have you found work?"

"Not yet."

"You know, wheat harvest will start pretty soon."

"I hadn't thought of that."

"Used to be, there wasn't much to be found between spring roundup and fall roundup, but now there's more work all the time."

Hartley heard the *chug-chug-grind* of the rock crusher, but he did not make a comment. Instead he said, "Well, I'd better be going."

Stillwell smiled. "Maybe we'll see you in the saloon tonight."

"I had thought of that." Hartley led his horse out a few steps. He checked his cinch and swung aboard.

"Good to see you, Reese."

"Same to you, Ben. Good luck."

Hartley stood at the bar in the Strong Water Saloon and pondered the painting that hung above the mirror. To the right of center, a shapely woman in a blue dress looked out from a garden upon a field of wheat. Her dress, of royal blue, was full-length, long-sleeved, and close-fitting. She wore a chaplet of red roses, and her hair was the color of the wheat. The background of her profile consisted of bright green fruit trees with golden fruit, which Hartley imagined were either apricots or peaches. At mid-level, purple grapes hung from vines with leaves a shade lighter than the fruit trees. At ground level, small red fruit like strawberries shined amidst dark green leaves. The wheat field was ripe, and the blue sky in the distance was adorned with white, fluffy clouds. The woman held her hands together at waist level, and her lips were parted as if she were singing or speaking.

"Another?"

Hartley came out of his reverie to focus on the bartender. The man could have been Odom's younger brother—lean, balding, with brown hair and a pale face, a white shirt instead of an apron. He was pointing at Hartley's glass, which had about a teaspoon of whiskey in the bottom.

"I suppose so." Hartley had made the first glass last for half an hour, and he did not want to seem in a hurry to drain it. As he was about to reach for it, the bartender took the glass away.

Hartley frowned. It wasn't enough to say anything about. He had expected the bartender to pour the new drink into the same glass, but the bartender had his own plan. With a flourish, he produced a clean glass and set it on the bar with his left hand, while his right hand tipped the bottle forward, went up and down like a machine, and tipped the bottle back.

"The other one had a bug in it. Don't know if you noticed."

"No, I didn't."

"Tiny little thing like a gnat. They get down inside the glass, and the fumes overwhelm them. It would be like you or me being trapped in a vat of formaldehyde or chloroform."

Hartley blinked. "I hate to think of it."

The bartender shrugged. "You kill bugs when you don't want to, and they get away when you try to swat 'em."

"That seems to be the case."

"How many times have you tried to kill a fly with a newspaper, and he got away?"

"Too many."

"It's because you push air at him. You help him escape."

"I never thought of that."

"It's a fact. I'm working on a device that won't push air."

Hartley raised his eyebrows. "Really? What does it look like?"

The bartender screwed up his mouth. "Can't tell ya."

"Oh, I understand. What's your name, by the way?"

"Tinker."

"Did you paint that painting?"

The man laughed as he turned and looked up. "No, that was done by a professional artist. I just tinker around."

"Well, I hope you make a million with your invention."

"I'm no Benjamin Franklin. But I'm more like him than Eli Whitney or Elias Howe."

"In what way?"

"They used movable parts."

"Oh, yes. And interchangeable."

"What'll it be?"

The bartender had not shifted his eyes. Hartley made a half-turn to his right, where Buck Whittaker and Tobe Lestman stood back a step. Hartley thought they might be uncertain about talking to him, so he said, "Hello, boys."

Whittaker said, "Hullo," and Lestman nodded. They stepped forward to the bar, and Whittaker said, "Whiskey."

With a flourish of both hands, the bartender set two glasses on the bar. Squinting with one eye as if he was pointing a pistol, he held the bottle at arm's length and poured the whiskey.

Whittaker tugged at his chin beard as he watched the work. When the glass was free, he settled his thumb and first two fingers upon it. He drew himself up to his full height, lifted the glass, and downed the contents. Stretching his lips back and revealing his yellow teeth in a kind of death grin, he let out a long "Ahhhh." He fished into the pocket of his buckskin vest and brought out a white bag of cigarette makings. With a slow turn of the head, he regarded Hartley and said, "Find another job yet?"

Hartley shook his head. "Not yet."

Whittaker set his hat back on his head. It was light brown, sun-bleached to a yellow on the ridges of the crown. He peered at the little cloth sack as he opened the drawstring. "There's work. You just have to look for it."

"I'm thinking of becoming a sack-sewer."

"Wheat sacks?"

"Just an idea. It's something I'm suited for. Nothing complicated. No moving parts. Just a big needle and a roll of twine, throw a row of stitches across the top of a burlap sack."

Whittaker raised an eyebrow. "You might meet girls that way. Some of your sack-sewers are women."

"Another good idea."

Whittaker began to roll a cigarette, showing some dexterity with the yellowed fingers of his right hand. "Back home, the men and boys did all the fieldwork, and the women and girls did the cookin' and brought out the grub. In this country, you see women doin' all kinds of work." Whittaker cocked his head. "Well, that, too."

"I always liked the stories about the girls who brought flagons of ale to the men when they were cutting grain with their scythes."

"Them, too. Workin' girls. I don't like some woman who thinks she's the Queen of Sheba."

"Like her?" Hartley motioned with his head toward the painting.

"She might be."

"She's not Ruth, gleaning in the fields."

Whittaker lit his cigarette and leaned his elbow on the bar, turning his back on Lestman. As he did so, his low-slung revolver came into view. "I know you didn't get along with the boss, but he's right about one thing. We gotta stick together if we're gonna hold out against these nesters."

"I didn't have much of a quarrel with Earl. It was Prentiss who kept pecking at me until he got me to quit."

"Well, he works for the old man. He carries out the orders." Whittaker took a long drag, and as something caught his attention, he stood up. In a raised voice, he said, "Hey, here's Ben. Come on over, boy, and have a drink with us."

Ben Stillwell moved forward into the lamplight. He was wearing a clean shirt, and his boots were buffed. He smiled and said, "Good evenin', boys. Are you here to cut your wolf loose?"

Whittaker tipped his ash on the floor. "Not me. I'm as gentle as a lamb."

Stillwell waved his fingers at the bartender. "One for me."

Tobe Lestman moved around so that the men formed a quartet. Standing next to Stillwell, he made a contrast. He wore a dark, dusty hat with a flat crown and a flat, circular brim that cast his muddy complexion in shadow. A cloth vest hung loose over his three-button shirt, and his denim trousers were stiff and grimy. He wore his pistol in cross-draw position, while he carried a sheath knife on his right hip. He lifted his glass of whiskey and took a sip. He nodded his head, blinked his dull brown eyes, and said, "What's new?"

Stillwell smiled. "Just church and work."

Whittaker tipped his head toward Hartley. "Reese tells us he's gonna go work with the wheat farmers."

Stillwell raised his eyebrows. "Is that right?"

"Just a fanciful idea," said Hartley. "I said I might learn to sew sacks. I doubt that I would have thought of it if you hadn't mentioned wheat harvest earlier in the day."

"I guess I did. Just a thought at the moment."

A fifth person joined the group, pushing in between Stillwell and Lestman. In a loud but not very clear voice, he said, "Can anyone spare a dime for a glass of beer?"

Whittaker said, "I will." Speaking over his shoulder, he said, "Give me a beer for Cletis, and another whiskey for myself."

Hartley shifted half a step in order in order to catch a better view of the man he had seen earlier at the rock crusher.

Cletis was no longer wearing the cloth hat. His hair was cut short all over, and as it was thinning on top, his light-colored scalp showed through. He appeared to have rinsed off the rock dust, but he was still wearing the neckless, sleeveless, sweat-stained shirt. Veins showed on his lean, muscular arms. His prominent neck reminded Hartley of a prairie dog looking up out of its hole, and his face had a blank expression. He took the glass of beer with both hands, and his toothless mouth opened as he said, "Thanks, boss."

"You're welcome." Whittaker squinted as he took a drag on the snipe of a cigarette he had left.

"Saw you workin'," said Stillwell.

Cletis nodded and began to raise the glass, but Whittaker's voice stopped him.

"Did you play with yourself last night, Cletis?"

Hartley felt as if time had stood still.

The older man's face went sullen as he said, "No."

"Oh, come on. I bet you did."

"No, I didn't."

"I know you do. Just about every night. You told me before. You did it last night, didn't you?"

Cletis took a swallow of beer and did not look up.

"You can't lie to me, Cletis. And besides, I just bought you a beer. So tell the truth. You did it, didn't you?"

Hartley searched his mind for a reason to leave. He wanted no part of making fun of a drunk.

Whittaker's voice was insistent. "Didn't you, Cletis?"

The answer came out low and muttered. "Yes."

Lestman tittered, and Stillwell smiled.

"It's all the same to me," said Whittaker. "But for tellin' the truth, I'll buy you another beer." He raised his finger without looking in back of him. "Tinker. Another glass of beer for Cletis. Anyone else care for a drink?"

Hartley drank his whiskey in a burning jolt and set his empty glass on the bar. "Not for me. I've got a long ride back to my camp."

CHAPTER THREE

Hartley awoke at sunrise, but he did not feel like rolling out of bed. The whiskey from the night before left him with a faint dullness in the head. He had thrown the blankets partway off because he was too warm, but when the flies began to pester him, he covered up. Now he was restless.

Images of the bartender came back to him. If the man's device did not have movable parts, it would not kill many flies at once. Hartley recalled a story the teacher had read in school. A man who was eating jam with his bread killed seven flies in one blow. Impressed by his own deed, he made himself a belt that proclaimed the feat. As he wore the belt on his travels from town to town in his part of Europe, he astounded people, for they thought he had killed seven men. Hartley could not remember how the story ended, but that was the way with some of the old stories. They were improbable and did not have much of a point.

He did not think he had ever heard the story of the Queen of Sheba. To him, it was just an expression that people heard and repeated. He was sure it came from the Bible, but he had gotten it all mixed up at an early age because so many of the stories and sayings had something to do with sheep. He had pictured her as some kind of a sheep queen, with golden ringlets, a crown, a shepherd's staff, and ten thousand sheep behind her. Years later, he saw a painting of her in a museum, and he learned she was Ethiopian. Yet he had gone back to the idea of her being blond when Whittaker said her name in the presence of the woman in the painting.

Hartley was beginning to perspire now, with the covers on him, and the flies would not leave him alone. He gave up, threw back the blankets, and sat up.

He reviewed the plan he had put together the day before. He would look for land as he looked for work. The idea of having his own acreage was predominant, yet he knew he could not make the necessary improvements on a hundred-and-sixty-acre claim without working on the side. If he could find land, he would take whatever work he could get. If he found agreeable work first, he would continue to look for a place to settle. He had heard that when the government let out a large tract for homesteading, most of the claims, and all of the good ones, went right away. The tracts in Decker Basin had been let out a few years earlier, so most of the available land now would be parcels that people had given up on, or relinquished. He would keep an eye out for something like that.

For breakfast he ate part of a loaf of bread he had bought in town, and he boiled coffee in a can. The song of a meadowlark carried on the air. A thin black wasp hovered and darted low to the ground between the bed and the firepit. Hartley appreciated being close to the natural world, but he knew that sooner or later, he was going to need a shelter. He shook the grounds out of the bottom of the can and pushed himself up from his seat.

As Hartley rode out into the countryside, he saw that the area east and north of his campsite had been pieced into a large number of homesteads. Most of the settlers here were what the cattlemen called nesters—people who fenced in or otherwise cut up what used to be open range. They had cattle or sheep as well as horses, and they often had chickens in the front yard.

Hartley saw crops as well, such as eighty acres of wheat or smaller patches of potatoes. Near the houses he saw corn and pumpkins. He understood the idea behind these smaller, diversified operations. If the potatoes failed or too many sheep died, the family might still make money on eggs, milk, or vegetables. They did everything on a small scale, in contrast with the cattlemen. Hartley had seen big outfits that had nothing but cattle, horses, and dogs.

In this district he also saw standing water in an occasional slough or ditch, as well as in broad, shallow ponds with sparse grass all around. Whenever he was near water, he felt humidity building as the air warmed up, and clouds of gnats and flies swarmed around him and his horse.

In late morning he changed his course, heading south for a ways and then west. He came to a broad, higher area, a swell of land that overlooked an open plain stretching south for several miles. The plain ended at a row of bluffs that marked the southeastern edge of Decker Basin. Below him, gleaming in the sun, lay the wheat country he had heard about. More than half the area was in wheat, with ten or twelve parcels together in some places. These people would be grangers, or farmers. Hartley imagined they worked with unity, sharing equipment and labor. He did not think he would want a piece of land in their midst, even if there were a claim available. He would have the feeling that he was surrounded, not only by sameness but by machines that would devour the plant life all around him—machines that also drove out or killed the smaller animals such as rabbits and grouse. He knew these farmers needed efficiency, but he had come to this part of the country for a different way of life.

He touched a spur to his horse and continued west, following a trail between section lines, with the expanse of wheat fields on his left and the more varied nester holdings on his right.

Grasshoppers skittered away in front of his horse's hooves. Two hundred yards ahead, a doe antelope materialized out of a dip in the grassland. It was walking toward the southwest, where the wheat country gave way to open pasture.

Ahead on his right sat a homesteader's shack. Like many he had seen, it was built near the road. The parcel was not fenced in yet, and the remnants of a previous year's garden lay weathered and deteriorating behind the building. The shack was a common twelve-by-twelve structure, which met homesteading requirements, and it looked as if it was holding together all right. The gray lumber had not begun to split or lift off.

He wondered if the place was abandoned, and if so, what its status was. If he could find out the name of the homesteader, he might be able to make an offer on it. He did not see the location as ideal, as he could imagine being snowed in for miles around during a blizzard, but its eminence offered a good view of the bluffs to the south and of the eastern end of Decker Basin, some fifteen miles away.

His horse stepped along, hooves on dry ground, as Hartley considered the ways by which he could find out about this property. He could ask neighbors, but he did not like to tell strangers his business, and for all he knew, they might covet the property. He could ask someone in town, like Ned Farnsworth.

His thought broke off at the sound of a human voice. Someone was singing. A woman. The melody was so familiar that he did not have to hear all of the words, but he heard enough that he could follow it.

> My grandfather's clock was too large for the
>   shelf,
> So it stood ninety years on the floor.
> It was taller by half than the old man himself,
>   Though it weighed not a pennyweight more.

Without seeing the singer or anything more than the weathered shack, Hartley summoned up an image of old Miss McMahon thumping on the piano as he and all the other children in the classroom sang. He went along with the next stanza.

> It was bought on the morn
> Of the day that he was born
> And was always his treasure and pride.
> But it stopped—short—never to go again
> When the old man died.

No dog came out to bark; no children peeked around the corner of the shanty. Yet he was sure the place was inhabited. Ghosts did not sing schoolroom songs at midday.

Hartley loosened the reins, and the horse picked up its pace. After coveting the property himself, Hartley felt embarrassed. He made himself keep his eyes straight ahead. The song went through a third verse, then the chorus, and ended with the old man dying.

Hartley took a measured breath and kept riding. As he came abreast of the little gray house, the woman's voice sounded again. He stopped the horse in order to hear her plaintive voice. He recognized this song as well, an old ballad about a girl who tells her lover not to sing love songs, for it will wake her mother, who cautions her that all men are false. At the end of the second stanza, the horse snuffled, and the music broke off. A woman's form appeared in thin shade on the west side of the house, twenty yards away.

"Oh," she said. "I didn't know someone was here."

"I'm sorry. I didn't mean to startle you, and I'm sorry for interrupting. But I couldn't help stopping to listen to your song."

"I'm the one who should apologize. Making other people listen to my notes of lament and sorrow."

47

"Quite to the contrary. I thought it was beautiful. And the song before, it reminded me of my childhood."

The woman stepped into the sunlight. She held a dark mandolin in her left hand, and she shaded her eyes with the right. "How long have you been here?"

"I stopped just a few seconds ago. I was riding by."

She laughed. "And you could hear me from a mile away."

"There's no other noise out here."

"That's true. Sound carries. Sometimes I forget." Her eyes moved as she took in his horse. "Do you have a place nearby, or do you ride for a cattle outfit?"

"Neither at the moment. I was riding for Earl Miner and the Pick, over west a ways, but I'm on my own now. I'm on the lookout for a place to settle on, and I hope to find work so I can pay for it all."

As he spoke, he noted that she had dark hair drawn together in back and a tanned complexion. She wore a plain, sand-colored dress that did not conceal her pleasing figure, and her leather shoes were suitable to a land of coarse grass, low cactus, and bugs. He guessed that she was about his age, not young and pristine but with an aura of energy suggesting that she had not been worn out and beaten down by the chores of a homesteading wife. He took a chance. "And yourself, Miss—?"

"Dulse. My name is Muriel Dulse. I live here by myself, but I have plenty of people to look after me. My cousins, the Hudsons and others. They live back thataway." She pointed over her left shoulder, in the direction of the area where he had seen the aggregation of nester claims.

"I don't know them."

She shrugged. "And your name? I could tell them, in case they ask me who came by."

She had such an airy way of referring to her cousins that he thought she might have her own interest in knowing his name.

"Hartley," he said. "Reese Hartley." He had the presence of mind to take off his hat, though the action felt out of place as he sat on his horse in the broad sun of noon.

"Don't let me keep you," she said. "Unless you'd like to water your horse. I don't know how long you've been riding."

"For a few hours." He put on his hat and swung down from the saddle. "I thank you for the offer."

"Around this way." She motioned with her arm toward the side of the house where she had been standing. "Watch your step. I've seen a couple of snakes while I've been here."

As he followed her, he kept his thoughts proper and his eyes above waist level. Her dark hair lay in a single thick braid and swayed from side to side.

In the backyard, Hartley loosened the cinch on his horse as Muriel uncovered a wooden water barrel and dipped a tin pail into it.

"He can drink out of this, can't he?" Her gray-green eyes met his.

"Oh, yes. And thank you again. It looks as if I'm using up your supply of water. Do you have to haul it?"

"The cousins do."

He took the pail from her and held it so that the horse would not knock it over.

"This place belongs to a member of the family. He's a little older than the rest, and as they say, he did not shine at farm work. His wife did not like living in the country, so they moved to town. He works for them there." She glanced around the wasteland of old vegetable vines and weeds. "He didn't have much drive, and this is all he could get planted, not the percentage that the homestead conditions require."

"I'm sure it was hard enough if he had to haul water."

"I'm not a farmer, but the Hudsons say he could have done more. Plant a dryland crop."

49

"Are you holding it down, then, or are you taking it over for yourself?"

She made a matter-of-fact expression. "The Hudsons want to keep it."

"I see. I've heard of other women taking up land by themselves, and I didn't know if you were inclined to that sort of adventure yourself." He lowered the empty pail and took it away from the horse's muzzle.

"I would be. And that's why I came out when they invited me. But before long, I learned that they wanted to hang onto it, and they wanted my help."

"Oh, I know that strategy. They want you to get a clear title to it and then turn it over to them. For a fair price, I hope."

"That's one way. The other is to take it by marriage."

His spirits fell, and she must have caught his expression.

"The way the rules are written," she went on, "if a woman files for land and then marries before she proves up, she is no longer the head of the household, and the property goes to her husband." She paused. "You might think I'm too modern in my outlook, but I'm not going to go along with that. I'm not going to be used."

"I don't blame you. I've been through something similar myself. I parted company with Earl Miner because I didn't want to file on a claim and then turn it over to him. He wants to build up his holdings, of course, and I imagine your cousins want to do the same thing."

"Similar, at least. They have five claims all together. The other four make up a section, and they work it like a cooperative. This one is a couple of miles away from their other holdings, but they want it to be a part. And they would like to get their hands on anything else nearby. On top of that, they have a rock-crushing enterprise in town. That's what Al Wisner went to when he left this place."

"I've seen it, and I may have seen him. Older man, not very big, with a gray mustache?"

"That would be him."

"What do they used the crushed rock for?"

She gave her matter-of-fact expression again. "Railroad beds."

"Huh. It's a long way to any railroad line, and they won't build many miles of track with the little bit of rock that comes out of Jennet."

"From what I understand, the men who consider themselves civic leaders are always talking about bringing in a spur line to one town or another to bring goods in and to haul products out. Grain, for example, as well as cattle. And they've got to get the rock somewhere."

"I suppose."

"So that's the story on my cousins." She glanced around. "I always expect them to ride in at any minute."

Hartley cast a glance at the open land of the claim. "Too bad your arrangements couldn't be more agreeable. This wouldn't be a bad place to make a start."

"I have come to see that, but they don't think a woman should own land or run her own business affairs."

Hartley decided not to say anything stronger about people he didn't know. "That's the way things are, I suppose."

"How about yourself?"

"Oh, I tend to agree with you."

"No, I mean you—where you come from, and so forth."

Hartley was glad to change the subject, as he had begun to share her apprehension about her cousins dropping in. He also noticed that she was holding the mandolin upright close to her body. "I'll be happy to tell you," he said, "but would you like to put that instrument in the shade?"

"There's not much at this time of day. Let me put it inside."

With his horse trailing, he followed her around to the front of the shanty. She stepped inside and came out.

"Go ahead," she said.

"Well, I come from a little town not far from Mansfield, Ohio. Like a lot of other people, I came out here for opportunity. To get a new start. I'm not running from anything, but I wanted to get away from systems and machines."

She smiled in a way that he thought she might if he told her he was looking for buried treasure.

"I realize it sounds naïve and innocent to say that I want to escape machines. After all, even a clock is a machine."

She glanced at the rifle in his scabbard. "So is a gun."

He laughed. "Well, you're right. But I meant the loud, incessant machines that stamp and boom and hiss all day and night. Of course, I've seen machines like that out here, including the family rock crusher."

She smiled.

"At any rate, I came out here at the beginning of the season, went to work for Mr. Miner, and have learned a little bit about the ways of the country."

"I wouldn't have guessed you had been here so short a time. You seem to fit in much better than I do."

He met her gray-green eyes, and he saw that she wasn't bantering with him now. He said, "I think it's easier for a man. He goes to work, and he learns by doing."

"And you like it well enough to want to settle here."

"That's right." He wasn't sure how much to say, but he went ahead. "Maybe I sound old-fashioned again, but I believe in the value of having one's own land."

"So do I."

"And I believe that a person should be able to do that without having to give in to other people's material schemes. Speaking for myself, of course."

She held him steady in her eyes and said, "Oh, yes."

"And I know none of this is easy." He waved his arm at the countryside. "You can't expect to come out here and live off the fat of the land, milk and honey, fruits and berries, without confronting the system. Homesteading has rules. That's one system. Anything you can't raise or gather yourself, you've got to buy. Money and trade is another system."

Her smile returned. "I didn't think you had escaped from a utopian commune."

He felt himself being irked by her levity. "No, but I do believe in the common good. For as much as I want to go off by myself and avoid these men who want to take what they can get and make a fortune in one generation, I believe in being a good citizen and doing my part."

She regarded him with a serious expression again. "By that you mean paying taxes and, as a man, exercising your right to vote?"

"Women are allowed to vote in Wyoming."

"Yes, but not on a national level." She paused. "I'm sorry. You were talking about your good citizenship."

"I'm sure I went far enough."

She gave a slight smile. "I wouldn't want you to go away miffed."

"Oh, no. I won't. I don't know you well enough to be laying out all of my social and political beliefs anyway."

"It's good to know that you have them." With a light laugh, she added, "And it's good to know what they are. By the way, those are two of my cousins."

Hartley turned to follow the motion of her hand. Two horsemen came riding from the east, along the same trail he had followed. They were traveling faster than he had, for they raised a small cloud of dust that drifted to the north behind them.

Hartley waited without speaking. He did not think the cousins would be happy to meet him, but he did not want to leave and give them, or Muriel, the impression that he was afraid of confrontation.

As they drew closer, the two men showed a similarity in appearance. They both wore dusty black hats with curled brims, buttoned-up black vests, and gray work shirts. Their horses were both sorrels with no markings.

The riders drew rein, dismounted, and sauntered forth. Hartley continued to see similarities, as both men had straight, whitish-blond hair, narrow features, and close-set blue eyes. They did not show any friendliness beyond a brief nod to Hartley.

"Afternoon, Muriel," said one of them.

Her voice had a cheery tone. "Good afternoon, boys. Let me introduce a friend. This is Mr. Reese Hartley. He's originally from Marion, Ohio, but he's out here like the rest of us, in the land of opportunity."

The two cousins nodded.

Hartley said, "Actually, it's Mansfield, Ohio. A small town near it. Not that it matters much."

"Of course it does. Thank you." Muriel smiled. "These are my cousins, Arlis and Crisp Hudson."

"Pleased to meet you." Hartley stepped forward to shake hands with each of them, though he wasn't sure which was which.

"Arlis and Crisp are from the southern part of Missouri, near Arkansas. I'm from Columbia, myself."

Something in her tone struck Hartley as humorous, but the Hudsons showed no response. At length one of them said, "Stopped by to see if you need anything."

"Nothing at the moment," she said. "How are things over on the section?"

"Dryin' up."

Muriel spoke to Hartley. "They raise wheat and alfalfa, and

smaller patches of potatoes and turnips. What else, Arlis?"

"That's about it."

"Now I remember. Pumpkins. Al raised them here, too. That's all those long, dead vines."

Arlis nodded.

"Mr. Hartley would like to take up some land, if he could find a good parcel."

The other brother, Crisp, said, "Ever' one's lookin' for it." He made a small spitting sound, as if he was trying to get rid of a fleck of tobacco. "Thought we might do a coupla things while we were here."

Muriel's tone was not quite so airy as she said, "What do you have in mind?"

"Clean out them dead plants you mentioned."

"I'm sure there's no hurry. They've been here since last fall."

Arlis said, "Gotta keep down the fire hazard around the buildings."

Hartley figured it was their way of sitting in Muriel's lap until he left. To make it easy on her, and to let the Hudsons do work they might not have planned on, he said, "I'd best be on my way as well. I've got work waiting for me."

Crisp looked at him as if for the first time. "Where do you work?"

"I'm on my own right now, but I need to lay in some firewood." Hartley raised his hat and said, "A pleasure to meet you, Miss Dulse."

"And likewise."

"Good to meet you fellows as well."

The Hudsons nodded and muttered, "Same here."

Hartley led his horse out, tightened his cinch, and climbed aboard. He did not look back. He hoped Muriel Dulse appreciated his not mentioning her consideration for his horse, as the Hudsons might have begrudged him the water that they hauled.

He had not ridden half a mile when a rider appeared ahead on his right and urged his horse at a fast walk toward the trail that Hartley was following. Hartley assumed that the man wanted to intercept him, so he kept his horse at an easy walk and allowed the rider to turn onto the trail and head toward him. As the man came into view less than a hundred yards ahead, Hartley recognized him as the blocky man who had been riding alongside the wagon of rocks.

Hartley let his gaze wander, but he brought it back to the oncoming rider every few seconds to gather a full impression.

The man rode a tall, husky, white horse with dark gray flecks. He sat straight up in the saddle, which showed his height to advantage. As before, he wore a dusty, brownish-black hat with a tall, rounded crown and a wide brim. He had a broad face with heavy brows, prominent cheekbones, and thick lips. An unbuttoned, dull black vest covered part of his bulky upper body, and a dark-handled revolver rode on his hip. He wore brown leather riding gloves, which came into full view as he fiddled with his reins, adjusting them for length, pulling out the loose ends, and letting them fall by his knee.

He stopped the horse. With his lips set, he stared at Hartley with his dark brown eyes. "Afternoon."

"Good afternoon to you."

"Do you need help finding something? You seem like you're wanderin'."

"I'm out seeing the country. I was riding for a cattle outfit during spring roundup, but I didn't see much of this corner of the basin."

"Not much to see. Once you've seen pastureland and wheat, it doesn't get much different." After a pause with no response, he said, "I seen you stopped back there. I'm a cousin."

"Of the Hudsons?"

"And Muriel, too. We're all pretty close."

"I just met her as well."

"She's a widow and needs to be left alone."

Hartley found the man's heavy face impassive. "Huh," he said. "I had no idea. We didn't go very far in conversation."

"What's yer name?"

"Reese Hartley. And yours?"

"Doyle Treece." As he pronounced his name in deliberate syllables, he kept his gloved hands on his saddle horn and made no motion to shake hands.

"Do you have your place over that way?" Hartley pointed to the northeast.

"That's right."

"I was in that area earlier today. Good country. Looks as if you have plenty of potential here."

"Lotta work." Treece set his heavy lips in such a way that the corners of his mouth turned down.

"No doubt. But it looks as if there's more water than in some of these other places. I saw a couple of sloughs or marshes, and a few shallow ponds."

Treece kept the hard expression on his face. "That's from the late spring rains. This gumbo clay don't drain very fast. Most of these ponds, as you call 'em, will dry up by midsummer. You'll see nothin' but dried mudflats."

"I've seen a couple of ponds that look deeper. They're not so broad. I wonder if they're fed by some underground source, artesian-like."

"You could read about it in a book. Here's what I know. Water is where you find it, and it's not all good. And when it goes dry, you're out of water."

"That's for sure."

Treece's dark eyes traveled over Hartley and his horse. "Who did you work for?"

"Earl Miner. He has the ranch they call the Pick."

"I know."

Hartley looked up at the sun. "I should be moving along. And I'm sure you've got things to do."

"I always do."

Hartley said, "Pleased to meet you. By the way, we've crossed paths before."

"I know. The other day. You were riding a Pick horse." Treece nudged the speckled horse, and it took off at a fast walk.

CHAPTER FOUR

At his camp, Hartley ate a meal of bread, cheese, and dried apples. He built a small sagebrush fire, which sent off thick, pungent smoke and then burned quick and hot as he boiled a can of water for his coffee. He pictured the Hudsons, under the watchful eye of Treece, hoeing and scraping away dead pumpkin vines and leaves. He hadn't been lying when he said he had to lay in a supply of firewood, but he had in mind a small heap of dry, twisted pieces of sagebrush less than an inch in diameter.

Treece and the Hudsons seemed like a humorless bunch. Hartley wondered if they joked among themselves or sang songs. Now that he thought of it, today was Sunday. He tried to imagine them singing the song about the little brown church in the vale as they chopped with hoes and stabbed with shovels.

For his own part, thanks to Muriel, he had had the song about the grandfather's clock running through his head off and on since he had ridden away from the meeting with Treece. He wondered if he could drive out that tune with another. He tried a verse about the church in the wildwood. After the first four lines, he could not remember enough of the song to keep it up. Maybe another verse would come to him.

Hartley stood up straight and lifted his hat. A pool of sweat washed down his face. He had waited until later in the afternoon to gather sage wood, but stooping close to the ground was hotter than working on horseback, and when he was bent over, he felt no movement in the air. Now that he stood up and had his hat raised, he appreciated the faint breeze that drifted from the south and cooled his damp skin.

He savored the peaceful moment, alone on the plains, with life's needs reduced to picking up minimal scraps of firewood. He recalled characters he had read about, on the moors of England, or the heaths, where they gathered furze faggots. It seemed to him that the moors and heaths were always cold, windy places—like Wyoming just a couple of months ago. The people who lived there were provincial folk, not like the grandfather who had the clock. From a few words in the song, Hartley had derived a picture of him as a pleasant old chap who enjoyed his toasted muffin, tea, mince pie, and elderberry wine until one day he died.

A thudding of hooves caused Hartley to turn around. A man wearing a straw hat and denim overalls was riding toward him on a large sorrel horse. Hartley settled his hat on his head and waited by his small pile of branches. The man rode up to him with a swishing of horse hooves against the low-growing sagebrush. When he stopped, Hartley spoke.

"Good afternoon. What can I do for you?"

"Long ride." The stranger twisted in the saddle, grabbed the pommel with both hands, heaved his right leg over the horse's hips, moved his right hand to grab the cantle, and slid to the ground with his belly pushing against the horse. The sorrel let out a sigh as the man landed on his feet. He brushed the bib of his overalls and turned to Hartley.

He had a long, full face with small blue eyes and a sun-reddened nose. His heavy body sloped out to a large girth, and the legs of his coveralls ended an inch above his brogan shoes. He took a couple of breaths with his mouth open, held up his hand to keep the horse from pushing against him, and spoke.

"Mike Ackerman said there was a fellow camped out here

who might want to do some work."

"That could be me. What kind of work is it?"

The man raised his head and scratched his chin. "Buildin' pens. I can't do it all by myself. My wife was a little help on some chores, but the diabetes got worse and worse, and now she's gone."

"I'm sorry to hear that. What kind of pens?"

"Pigpens. My hogs need shade in this hot weather, and they need a shelter where they can bunch up in the winter. I've got the lumber and everything, but I can't do it all myself."

"I could lend you a hand. I assume you're willing to pay something in the way of wages."

"I can give you a dollar a day and a place to stay. I'll feed you."

Hartley met the man's small blue eyes. They looked like gemstones pressed into a ball of dough. "When would you like to start?"

"Tomorrow morning. You won't get drunk on me in the meanwhile, now, will you? I need to get this work done."

Hartley gave a small laugh. "No, I won't get drunk. I don't have a drop to drink here, and I won't be going anywhere to buy any."

"Good. Because I don't want it on my place."

"I can go with you now if you want."

"No, this is as much business as I want to do on a Sunday. You be there tomorrow morning, and we'll go to work."

"Just tell me where."

The man peered at Hartley. "Do you know where the Rooshians are?"

"No, I don't."

"Well, I'm on the other side of them. You go three miles north of here, take a section line east, and cross a dry creek. You'll see the Rooshians on your left. They've got their house dug into the side of a hill. I'm the next place after that."

"I should be able to find it. What's your name, by the way?"

"Eldredge."

"Mine's Hartley. Reese Hartley."

"That was my mother's name. Hartley."

"Oh, where was she from?"

"Missoura."

"That's where the Hudsons are from. I don't think they're very far from you."

Eldredge's mouth tightened. "I know who they are. We can leave them out of this."

The sun had crested the hills to the east when Hartley crossed the dry creek, saw the Russians' dugout on the hillside, and had his first view of Eldredge's place. A hundred yards off the road, three or four piles of salvaged lumber provided a backdrop for a pigsty and a twelve-by-twelve shack covered with tar paper. Half a dozen white chickens scratched in the yard, and the odor of swine carried on the cool morning air.

Sunlight fell on the front door of the shack, which faced south. As Hartley rode into the yard, the door opened and Eldredge stepped out. He put on his hat and closed the door behind him.

"I see you made it. We'll find a place to put your things, and we can go to work."

Eldredge walked around to the side of the shack. The chickens moved out of the way, and the pigs in the board enclosure began grunting.

"Sup, sup," said Eldredge. "In a little while." Behind the shack, he pointed to a bare spot on the ground. "You can leave your traps here, and you can stake your horse out anywhere on the grass."

Hartley stacked his gear against the rear wall of the shack

and put his horse on a picket. When he returned to the yard, Eldredge had a hammer, a crowbar, and a saw ready. He handed them to Hartley.

"We've got to clean up this lumber first. I was lucky to get it as cheap as I did. You'll need to pull out all the nails, and anything that needs to be trimmed, cut it off with the saw. I'll bring you a bucket to put the nails in."

For the next five hours, Hartley worked his way through a stack of lumber, first pulling the nails and sorting the pieces, and then cutting off all the rotten ends of posts and the broken ends of boards. The sun had passed the high point in the sky when Eldredge appeared and told him it was time to eat.

Inside the dark dwelling, Hartley squeezed into a chair and sat at a narrow table. Eldredge moved around the heaps of clothing, blankets, tools, harness, and riding gear as he served up three cold flapjacks and a jug of syrup. He served three more flapjacks for himself and sat down.

"Made these this morning. It doesn't do to make three fires at this time of the year. One in the mornin', one in the evenin'."

The syrup was thinner and sweeter than molasses. Eldredge was not stingy with it for himself, as he sopped at the pool with the pieces of cold hotcake and cleaned the plate with his spoon.

"Hope you don't mind cold coffee."

"Not at all."

As the week wore on, Hartley made progress with the building project. When he had the lumber cleaned up, he began to build the shelters as Eldredge directed him. He dug holes and tamped in posts, then nailed on the boards. Some pieces were too short and had to be spliced, while others were too long and had to be cut, often less than a foot away from a cut he had made before. Anything longer than a foot was set aside for splicing. All the shorter pieces went on the scrap pile with the rotted and broken ends he had cut off earlier in the week.

Hartley slept outside each night, which he would have preferred even if he had his choice. For each meal, he crowded into his seat at the table inside. Eldredge served hotcakes at breakfast and at noon dinner, and he fried bacon and potatoes each night for supper.

One evening he said, "I had to buy this bacon. Hate to do it. In another year, I hope to be sellin' bacon and ham."

Hartley expected the man to talk more about his hogs, about his plans, or even about his deceased wife. Eldredge had seemed like a talkative sort at their first meeting, but he did not speak much beyond the work or the grub at hand.

Hartley pushed himself to finish the sawing and hammering by Saturday evening. Eldredge seemed satisfied with the end product but did not offer praise.

"It looks all right," he said. "It should do."

He paid Hartley six silver dollars and did not invite him to stay for supper. Hartley figured the man had to save a nickel wherever he could, so he went about packing his gear onto his horse.

As he shook hands in parting, he wished Eldredge well.

"Same to you. Don't know how good a friend you are with the Hudsons."

"Nothing to speak of. I met them once in passing."

"Just as well."

Hartley awoke to the silence of his own camp as the sky grew pink in the east. He recalled the grunting of Eldredge's hogs, and he hoped they were happy in their new shelter. For his own part, he thought a bath would do him some good. The day being Sunday, he hoped he could slip into town, pay for a bath at the Argyle Hotel, and leave without having to engage in any conversations.

★ ★ ★ ★ ★

At his camp once again that afternoon, Hartley wished he could have prolonged the effects of a clean bath, but Jennet was not a mountain resort where a person could bathe in the hot springs and then relax in the shade of the murmuring pines. When he finished his bath, he rode out into the hot sun. Still, he had soaked in a tub and had put on clean clothes, and although he had sweated a bit on the return ride and was going to have to gather more firewood, he felt free of the residue of old lumber, rusty nails, and swine. He would take his time and not exert himself too much.

Out on the rangeland away from his camp, he bent now and then to pick up a dead branch of sagebrush. He straightened up each time and lifted his hat in order to feel the breeze and not let the sweat collect. As he meandered, his thoughts went back to the Sunday before. He recalled another verse about the little brown church.

He began to sing the song, to see if more verses would come to mind. There was so much repetition that he had to sort out the lines. He started over, but before he made it through the first verse, the drumming of hooves on dry ground caused him to leave off and look around.

Two horsemen were riding his way from the direction of his camp. He recognized them right away as Buck Whittaker and Tobe Lestman. He waved to them as they slowed from a lope to a trot to a walk. When they came to a stop, Hartley spoke to them in a raised voice.

"Afternoon, boys. Out for a ride?"

Whittaker's prominent eyes, bloodshot, showed no trace of merriment. "This is no holiday for us," he said.

Hartley glanced from Whittaker to Lestman. "Something wrong?"

"Ben's missing," said Whittaker.

Hartley knew Whittaker well enough not to take his flushed face for anger, but he detected at least a level of insistence. "He's been staying in town, hasn't he? And if he's got today off, he might be spending it with his girl."

Whittaker huffed out a breath. "No one has seen him in town since last night. And they found his horse wandering around out this way."

"Hmmm. What time did he take his horse out of the stable?"

"No one saw him take it. We stopped in there when we were asking around town."

Hartley glanced toward Lestman and back to Whittaker. "Did you boys spend the night in town?"

"We stayed at the Argyle."

"And Ben? Was he staying at the hotel as well?"

"He had a room at the boardinghouse."

Hartley reflected. "Not far from the sawmill. Or the saloon, for that matter."

Whittaker took a deep breath, which Hartley interpreted as impatience.

"Well, I sure haven't seen him out here. I went into town myself for a short while. Took a bath at the hotel, as far as that goes. I made it back to camp at about one or so."

"I doubt you'd see him if he wasn't on his horse."

Hartley gazed out across the landscape to the northwest. "Do you need some help looking for him, then?"

"If you want. If not, we'd better get goin'."

"Let me put away my firewood and saddle my horse."

The grassland they searched was not unknown to Hartley. The crew had come this far on roundup, and some of the Pick cattle had drifted back this way again. The land was higher and broader than the nester area that Hartley had observed in the last week, but it still had a thousand dips and rises. The men spread out a mile apart from one another and rode back and forth. Hartley took the sweep on the far right. Sometimes he lost sight of Whittaker, who rode in the middle, and most of the time he did not see Lestman.

Shadows began to stretch out from the clumps of sagebrush, and Hartley felt the air a little cooler in the hollows that lay in shade. From the high points he saw the sun making its daily descent toward Decker Rim in the west. Dots represented small groups of three, four, or five cattle. At this distance, their heaving and lowing made no sound.

Hartley drew rein at the top of a hill that offered a wide panorama. Silence held over the rangeland, as this time of day had a peaceful quality of its own. For a moment he forgot his mission and took in the tranquility.

A gunshot cracked in the air less than a mile away.

His horse flinched, and he tightened the reins. He began to count. The three of them had agreed that if someone found something, he would fire a shot in the air, count to sixty, and fire again.

Hartley had counted to fifty-six when he heard the second shot. He placed it better than the first one and rode toward it, heading southwest.

Whittaker and Lestman were standing by their horses when Hartley found them. They blocked his view until he rode around and came at the scene from the north. On the short grass of the open range lay the body of Ben Stillwell, facedown with his arms spread out and his hat several yards away.

Hartley dismounted, took off his hat, and led his horse the last few steps.

Whittaker and Lestman took off their hats as he approached. Whittaker seemed more agitated than before, while Lestman had a subdued air.

Hartley said, "Do you think his horse threw him?"

Whittaker shook his head. "Might be made to look that way, but he's got bruises on his throat."

CHAPTER FIVE

Hartley expected the town to be buzzing when he rode in the next morning, but the wide, dusty street had only two horses standing hipshot in front of the Owl Café. He thought he might learn the latest news there, but he did not want to go in and share his story with Mike Ackerman and others. Also, for the time being, at least, he preferred to leave Bess alone. If she was grieving, she did not need him, and he would not want her to think he was taking an opportunity. There would be time for condolences later.

He tied his horse in front of the post office and went in through the open door. Ned Farnsworth appeared at the postal window and took off his spectacles. He was clear-eyed, freshly shaven, and dressed in his suit and tie.

"Good morning," he said in his cordial tone.

"Good morning. I thought I'd drop in and see if I have any mail."

Ned put on a thoughtful expression as he turned and nodded at the pigeonholes. "None today." Returning to Hartley, he smiled and said, "How are things going for you?"

"All right, I guess, with the exception of helping to find Ben Stillwell yesterday."

Ned drew his brows together. "Oh, that's terrible, isn't it? And no idea of why somebody would do something like that."

"I hope someone finds out."

Ned spoke in a more amiable tone. "Have you found any work?"

"For a while. All of last week. A man named Eldredge, over east, had me building some pens."

"Oh, yes. I know him. Poor fellow, he's had a hard time. His wife died, you know."

"He told me." Hartley paused, and when Ned did not say anything, he continued. "He knew how to find me. Mike Ackerman sent him. The Pick riders knew how to find me as well. All I had to do was tell one person."

"I suppose that's to your benefit."

"So far. Anyway, I'm still in the market for work. And at the same time, I'm on the lookout for a piece of land. If you happen to know of a homestead claim that's available, I might be interested."

"Here or elsewhere?"

"Well, here, to begin with. But I would be willing to look at prospects somewhere else."

Ned put on a mild frown. "Places around here are, how shall I say, being competed for, it seems. But if I hear of something, I'll let you know. The same with other regions. The government sends out notices when they're going to open up another area."

"That would be fine. I would appreciate it."

Ned's light blue eyes widened. "Anything else?"

"Not at the present. I don't need any camphor or strychnine today."

"Heh-heh. When you do, ask here first."

"I'll do that. Thanks, Ned."

"The same to you. Good luck."

Hartley broke off a chunk from his new loaf of bread and ate it with a piece of ham. Now that he was back at his camp with an empty afternoon ahead of him, he told himself he needed to be more willing to go out and ask about opportunities. He needed to earn more wages, and work wasn't always going to come knocking on his door. If there was no land to be found in this area, he should be thinking about where to go next.

Now that things had slowed down again, or come to a standstill, he could see that sitting around his camp in the full sun was going to bring him an increasing sense of restlessness. He should go somewhere and do something. He had already gone to town. It was too late in the day to ride out to any of the ranches he knew in the western half of Decker Basin. He had seen enough of the nesters for the present, and he did not want to ask for work with people like the Hudsons. Muriel, on the other hand—he could pay her a visit, and with a little luck, the Hudsons would all be busy working.

He took the route he had followed the week before when he left Muriel's place. The countryside emanated heat in the mid-afternoon, but the air became drier when he reached the swell of land where the homestead claim was located. He rested his horse on a high spot as he surveyed the nester claims in the near distance and the wheat country beyond. He picked out Muriel's place and headed toward it. As the relatives had not fenced the hundred-and-sixty acres but had piles of rocks on the corners, he saw no harm in riding across the property.

The land had not been plowed or planted. Like the rest of the range, it ran to grass and sagebrush and a thin scattering of prickly pear. As he rode onto the northern edge of the quarter section, a ditch-like depression on his left gave rise to a species of brush he did not have a name for. It grew about two feet tall and had flat, round, dull-green leaves. The little thicket would be a good hiding place for a deer, but he had not seen a deer in this area, only antelope.

A pale splotch of color appeared as a figure sprang up from

the brush and spooked his horse with a cry of "Haah, haah, haah!"

Hartley pulled on his reins and settled his horse down. He turned the animal around to see a girl stepping out of the hiding place.

She had whitish-blond hair and a slender shape, and she wore a dress made of flour sacks. Hartley guessed her age at about seventeen. She walked with exaggerated quarter-turn steps, as if for comic effect, then stopped and brushed back her hair with both hands.

"Ha-ha-ha," she said. "Scared you, didn't I?"

"You shouldn't spook a horse. Someone could get hurt."

She made an eighth of a turn and said, "You're going to see Muriel, aren't you?"

He thought she was practicing being coy, with her motions saying, "Look at me." He decided not to play along.

"Might be," he said.

"They call her a grass widow."

He shrugged.

She put her finger against her cheek. "What's your name?"

"Hartley. What's yours?"

"Nancy."

He noted her hair again. "Are you related to Muriel and the Hudsons?"

"Might be." She drew out the two syllables. "But my last name is Wisner."

"You must be part of the family that used to live here."

"Yes, but we moved to town. I got tired of eating pumpkins."

"Are your folks there now?" He motioned with his head toward the homesteader shack.

"No, they're over at the section."

"You shouldn't be wandering around by yourself. You could get bit by a snake. Or catch a heatstroke."

She raised her chin, and he saw that she had the close-set blue eyes of the Hudsons. "I can get around by myself," she said.

"You'd better get back to your folks." As he adjusted his reins to turn his horse, Nancy spoke.

"She thinks she's the Queen of Sheba."

He stopped and looked at her. "What do you know about that?"

"Nothin'."

He wanted to tell her again to move along and not to be spooking horses, but he thought he should not prolong their conversation. He was glad he had not stepped down from his horse. Turning now, he said, "So long."

In what he took to be one last attempt to attract attention, she said, "Fare-thee-well."

Conscious of being watched, he decided to keep to the western edge of the quarter section. When he arrived at the trail, he turned left and rode to the front yard where the gray shanty stood. He stopped with his horse facing the door and called, "Yoo-hoo! Anyone home?"

The door opened, and Muriel appeared, shading her eyes. "Oh, it's you," she said. She stepped into the sunlight, closing the door behind her. She was wearing a light-colored, blue-gray dress, and her dark hair hung loose at her shoulders. Shading her eyes again, she said, "Are you here on a dire errand, or is this a social call?"

"Just a social call, if you've got the time."

"I believe I do. Let's go around to the side. There's a bit of shade there."

Hartley swung down from his horse and followed. As he stood in the shadow of the small building, he put three fingers between the cinch and the horse's side, and he decided not to loosen it any more.

73

"Does he need water?" asked Muriel.

"We didn't ride that far. I can water him on the way back, not use up your water. Thank you for the offer, though." He met her gray-green eyes. "What kind of dire errand might I have been on?"

"Al and Betty Wisner dropped by, and they said a man was killed in town."

"He was found outside of town, but no one knows for sure where he died. Well, someone does." He paused. "Did they come all the way out here to tell you that?"

"No, they dropped off a roll of barbed wire. They were going on to the section to talk some kind of business there."

"I believe I met their daughter. She was wandering out on the range."

"Nancy," said Muriel. "She came with them and then left on foot. Said she'd meet them over there."

"Maybe it's none of my business, but I think she could use more supervision."

Muriel gave a light shrug. "I agree. But she's an only child, and I don't think they've ever been very strict with her."

"She said she didn't care for living here."

"She and her mother both. And as I said before, the family didn't do well at farming."

Hartley hesitated, deciding what to mention. "She says odd things."

"Oh, yes. Whatever runs through her head."

"She said she got tired of eating pumpkins."

Muriel waved her hand. "Well, as you know, pumpkins and potatoes are two things that keep through the winter. I learned not to complain about food."

"She bears a resemblance to your cousins the Hudsons."

"Her mother is a Hudson. She's an aunt to Arlis and Crisp and Brant."

"I haven't met Brant."

"He's quite a bit like his brothers."

"Do they make many friends?"

She laughed. "Did you feel left out? Please don't. They're that way with everyone. Clannish."

"I wasn't asking so much on my own behalf. I worked for a fellow last week who had to bite his tongue to keep from saying anything about them. Man by the name of Eldredge."

"Oh." Muriel pursed her lips.

"You know him—or know of him?"

"Poor fellow. His wife died."

"I understand that."

Muriel sighed. "He's had a hard time making improvements on his place. You know, there's a time limit, and people who don't get enough work done on their property can have their claims contested. And that's what my cousins have done. They've contested three or four claims. They also pounce on relinquishments. Whenever someone is ready to give up and seems desperate to sell, my cousins move in and try to buy it as cheap as they can. Steal it, for all practical purposes. They have a few deals pending."

"Sounds as if they're really trying to add to their base."

"They say they have to, or they'll be run over."

Hartley nodded back and forth. "Is Mr. Treece something like a partner or associate in all of this?"

"You met him, too, didn't you? Yes, he's right in there with them when it comes to making deals and putting leverage on people."

"Do you think there's anything to their claim that they have to keep from being run over?"

Muriel's eyes widened. "Oh, I know there is."

"Really? Has someone done something?"

She hesitated. "Well, yes. I don't know how much to say. I

think you've had an affiliation with them."

Hartley frowned. "Earl Miner? The Pick? I don't have anything to do with them now, although I did help a couple of them find the young man who died. But I didn't realize Miner or his men had come over this way."

Muriel nodded. "Primarily a man named Prentiss. I believe he's a foreman. He's come by with a couple of henchmen, and he's dropped in on his own."

"Pushing?"

"Yes. He's quite the one for argument. On one hand, he told me I should 'pull up stakes' here, not only to get out of the way of any trouble but because this claim is going to have to be given up. Then, when he came here by himself, he said I should find a better way of spending my time—with his excellent self, I understood."

Hartley let out a low whistle. "I heard he was looking for a woman, but I didn't know how he went about it."

"Not very well."

"And what does Mr. Treece think of this?"

"I didn't tell him about the personal attention. He would be furious. As for the more general intimidation, they've been pushing back and forth. My cousins make no secret about building up their holdings so they can resist the cattlemen, but then they whine about being picked on and being called land-grabbers."

Hartley thought for a second. "Do you think your cousins could have anything to do with this young man's death? He worked for Earl Miner, you know, although he was running a little sawmill in town at the time that he met his end."

Muriel shook her head. "I don't think it has come to that, though I am sure there are things I do not know." She regarded him with open eyes. "What do you think?"

"I agree with you, including the last point. I'm sure there are things that I don't know, either, and not only about Ben Stillwell's death." Hartley patted his horse's neck. "I wonder if I should be moving along. I don't want to take up too much of your time."

"It's one thing I have. But you might be right. Al and Betty were going to stop by here on their way back to town."

He met her eyes again. "Maybe we'll find more pleasant things to talk about next time."

She smiled. "We can try. It doesn't have to be all dread."

Hartley led his horse out into the bright sunlight, snugged the cinch, and climbed aboard. He held the horse in check as he tipped his hat. "So long," he said. "I'll drop by again when I've got time."

Muriel smiled as she shaded her eyes. "Do that."

The trail ahead was clear as he rode away. He would not have been surprised if Treece had emerged from the landscape or if Nancy had popped out of another of her hiding places, but the land stretched out on all sides with evidence only of sun and wind. Bits of plant life had blown up against the base of a short row of sagebrush on the right side of the road. A tumbleweed, which he assumed had been driven up the slope from the wheat country by the wind, had lodged between two taller clumps of sagebrush.

His thought skipped back to the visit with Muriel. She had spoken with openness about her cousins and their maneuvers, but she had not said much about herself. Then again, neither had he. If Treece and Nancy hadn't made their remarks about her being a widow, he would not have the feeling that she was withholding something. He would not know what he was waiting to hear about. As he imagined her view, she would not know he had heard anything, so she would not feel that she was holding anything back. He shrugged. He figured he would hear it from her at some point, unless their acquaintance did not go that far, in which case it would not matter anyway.

He turned his attention again to the country around him. People took it for granted and saw its sameness. Treece had said that once a person had seen pastureland and wheat, there wasn't anything new. But Decker Basin had more variety than that, such as the places where Treece harvested rocks and the canyons where Miner's men found trees to cut down.

Hartley passed an anthill on his right, a mound of mineral granules rising from a ten-foot circle of bare ground. Most of the anthills he saw were of that variety, but he had also seen colonies made of small bits of grass, twigs, and other plant life, such as pine needles or the spines of leaves. He had seen these nests in hilly, brushy country, and he might have concluded that each kind of colony was native to its own kind of terrain, until he discovered one of each within a space of a hundred yards. He imagined them as two towns, and from there he imagined a giant towering over Decker Basin, looking down on the towns of Winsome and Jennet.

Hartley recalled people saying of small towns that nothing ever happened there except the weather. Those generalities were as bland as Treece's statement about the landscape. In a town, as in an anthill, a great deal went on beneath the surface.

Hartley was leading his horse to camp from a water hole about a half-mile away when he saw three men on horses riding from the west. He did not recognize them from the distance. They dropped out of sight for a few minutes and reappeared on a closer rise of land. From their relative sizes and shapes, Hartley took them to be Prentiss, Whittaker, and Lestman. He hoped they had not come to tell him of another calamity.

He reached his camp and stood holding the lead rope of his horse as he waited for the three men. They did not seem to be in a hurry, as they slowed their horses and came in at a walk. Prentiss rode in the middle, with Whittaker on his left and Lestman on his right. Hooves fell on the ground with dull thuds, and bits of dry grass lifted on the light cross breeze.

The riders came to a stop about ten yards away and did not dismount. They kept their backs to the sun, so Hartley had to shade his eyes as he looked up at them.

"Good afternoon, fellas. Anything new?"

Prentiss said, "We came to talk to you."

Hartley felt a sinking in his stomach, and he had a quick recollection of Muriel's account. Unsure of what to say, he borrowed a phrase he had heard. "Light and set."

"We're fine where we are."

Hartley made a short swallow and moistened his lips. "Well, go ahead and tell me what's on your mind, then. You're in my camp, you know." He had heard of a code about how far out a man's camp extended and how it was impolite for someone to stay mounted. He thought it was a hundred feet, but he could not remember the distance for sure.

Prentiss put both hands on the saddle and rose to full height. "Here it is. We think you made a mistake."

Hartley frowned. "In what way?"

"In not stickin' with the boss and then comin' over here lookin' for land."

With a sideways tip of the head, Hartley said, "I'm interested in finding my own place wherever I can, provided it's the kind of land I'm looking for. As far as that goes, I understand there's not that much available over this way."

"Then what are you doin' over here?"

"It happens to be where I found a place to camp."

Prentiss's chest rose as he took a breath. "It happens to be in the vicinity of a bunch we don't care for." He held his hand out and upright, like a cleaver. "I already told you, those of us that have cattle interests have got to stick together and keep these nesters in their place."

"That's one of the reasons I came over here, to get out of your way."

"You'd be better off somewhere else."

Hartley shrugged. "I'm here right now."

"Yeah, neighbors with these land-grabbers. They're a bunch of snipes."

Hartley realized that Prentiss meant the Hudsons, not the nesters in general. He said, "I'm not friends with them anyway."

Prentiss spoke with his hand again. "I'm goin' to make you an offer. You either take it or leave it." He paused. "You can come back to the Pick and forget about taking up land either for yourself or for the company's benefit."

"What if I want to go over to Bordeaux or Uva and see about land there?"

"Oh, that's different. That's your business. Just don't do it in Decker Basin."

Hartley stared at Prentiss. "What if I do?"

"Like I said before, you're either with us or you're not. This is cattle country. If you settle here, you're in our way."

Hartley felt his temper rising. "Well, here's my answer. I'm not willing to do things your way, and I won't be pushed around just because I don't want to help someone grab land to feed a few hundred head of slobbering cattle. I've got my rights, and I'm going to stay here."

"You're making the same mistake as before. You know, I think you might not have the right outlook for getting along in this country. You'd be better off in another climate."

Hartley moved to his left so he would not have to look up into the sun. The men shifted their horses so that they continued to face him.

Prentiss cleared his throat and spit. "I'll tell ya, it's not good for a man's health to be fraternizing with nesters and grangers."

"I don't like to be threatened." Hartley glanced at Whittaker and Lestman to imply that they were witnesses.

Prentiss ignored him. "Especially after what happened to Ben. Your rival."

Time stood still for a moment. Hartley let his gaze travel back and forth between the men on horseback. "Do you think I had anything to do with that?"

Prentiss took on a matter-of-fact tone as he said, "Until yuh know, yuh can't rule anything out."

Hartley's eyes narrowed. He turned to Whittaker. "What do you think?" Then to Lestman. "And what do you think? Did I have anything to do with what happened to Ben, other than helping you find him?"

Lestman mumbled, while Whittaker said, "Well, no, but we wouldn't put it past the Hudsons or that pig of a cousin of theirs."

"Well, I'm not them."

Prentiss stepped down from his horse, handed his reins to Whittaker, and walked forward. He did not stop until he was a foot and a half from Hartley. His light brown eyes blazed. "You can talk all day, but I don't have time for it. I'll tell you right now, you'd do well to steer clear of all of this bunch. And if they knew what was good for them, they would pull in their horns. Or better yet, go find another climate for themselves. So that's the end of my offer."

Hartley felt as if Prentiss was giving him one last chance to go along. He said, "I've given you my answer."

Prentiss bore down on Hartley with his blazing eyes and stubbled face. "That's your choice. But if something happens, just remember, if you hadn't been with the crows, you wouldn't have been shot at."

Prentiss clenched his teeth with a menacing glare, and Hartley wondered if the man was going to punch him. Prentiss did not. He pivoted on his heel, strode away, and took his reins from Whittaker. He stabbed his foot in the stirrup and swung up into the saddle.

Whittaker and Lestman averted their eyes until their foreman turned his horse and said, "Let's git."

As the three horsemen loped away, Hartley found himself having to steady his hands. He did not think Prentiss would shoot him, but he felt that the big man would very much like to punch him more than once. Hartley realized he had never had to defend himself by physical means. If he was going to stay in this climate, he might have to work himself up to that level.

CHAPTER SIX

The town of Jennet lay quiet under an overcast sky as Hartley rode in from the north end. After passing the Strong Water Saloon on his left, he decided to take a side street. He turned right, in no hurry, and swayed with the motion of the horse as it clip-clopped along. The Weston boardinghouse came into view on his right, with empty chairs on the front porch and a spindly tree on each side of the walkway. Next came an empty lot with a broken-down ranch wagon sitting in a patch of weeds growing up to the level of the hubs. On the porch of the house ahead, a large black dog lay on its side sleeping. Hartley crossed to the other side of the street.

He passed two houses on his left, an empty lot, and a shed that had a post leaning against its double doors. Straw stuck out of some of the cracks between the boards.

At the corner, he turned south. He heard light, whopping sounds, and as he passed the next house on his left, he saw a stout woman with her hair tied and covered in a bandana. She had her back to him and was beating a rug that hung over a clothesline.

He rode a little further until he came to the sawmill. No logs were in sight, nor any lumber. Most of the wood scrap was gone—consumed, he imagined, by the machine that ripped the logs. A few unsplit thicker pieces lay around, but for the most part, the lot was bare, with drifts and patches of sawdust. The scene reminded Hartley of a cemetery, with the roofed shelter suggestive of a primitive chapel or a charnel house he might have seen in an illustration in a Gothic novel.

Past the sawmill and the lot, he heard sounds of life again. Chickens clucked in a henhouse. A horse in someone's backyard whinnied to his, which snuffled in response. An awareness of the rest of town came back to Hartley, and he nudged his horse to pick up its pace.

The next cross street took him to that part of the main street where he faced the blacksmith shop. He did not hear any sounds of iron beating on iron, but the large front door was open. Hartley decided to ride close by.

He crossed the main street and drew rein in front of the shop. At that moment, his attention was caught by the sight of a man walking toward him from the direction of the Owl Café and the Argyle Hotel. The man was wearing a black, wide-brimmed cattleman's hat, a charcoal-gray vest, and a white shirt. Hartley observed the man's bushy mustache and dark eyes, and he realized the blacksmith was dressed for his marshal duties. Hartley dismounted and waited.

The marshal walked up to within ten feet of Hartley and stopped. He was wearing his badge and pistol, and his eyes roved over Hartley and his horse. "Is there something you need?" he asked.

"Not so much a need. My name's Reese Hartley. I introduced myself a while back."

The marshal nodded with his dark hat. "I remember."

"I was one of the three who found Ben Stillwell."

"Oh, yes. Too bad about him."

"And I heard a comment yesterday suggesting that I might have had something to do with his coming to an end. I was wondering if you had heard anything of that nature, because there's no truth in it."

The marshal's mustache went up and down. "It's not in my

jurisdiction, because they found him out of town. They. I should say 'you.' Now, if someone could show he was killed in town, that would be different. But it's not in my bailiwick at present."

"It could become that way. And I'm sure you've heard what talk there is."

"I haven't heard your name, if that's what you're worried about."

"That's not the only thing, but thanks."

The marshal brought his dark eyes to rest on Hartley and said, in a slow, casual tone, "What else is there?"

"Well, there's evidence that a crime was committed. Is anyone going to do anything?"

The marshal pushed out the side of his cheek from the inside. "I 'magine the sheriff's office 'll send someone out. But it's a long ways, and sometimes things move kinda slow."

Hartley expected the marshal to follow with something like "Just go on home," and he did not want to be brushed off. He said, "Excuse me for being forward, but I'm speaking as a citizen. We have some responsibilities here. We're a social body. We have towns and states and laws for a reason. Something like this affects all of us."

The marshal put his hands on his hips. "I know all of that. If this case comes back to me, I'll do something about it, believe me. I don't like it any better than you do. But I have to keep in my place. In a way, you can do more than I can, in the sense that I can't be pokin' into someone else's territory. All the same, I keep my eyes and ears open."

Hartley let out a long breath as he felt himself settling down. "All right. I think I understand. I don't mean to pester you."

"You haven't. If you do, I'll tell you." The marshal shook Hartley's hand and went into the blacksmith shop.

Hartley set out walking, leading his horse and keeping to the east side of the street. He wondered if Bess was at her desk and could see him. He resolved to drop in on her before long.

The words of the marshal came back to him. If he could do more than the marshal could, he would like to know what it was.

At the Owl Café he noted two horses tied in front. Still not in the mood for that kind of society, he crossed the street toward the post office.

He tied his horse and went in through the open door. He almost bumped into Ned Farnsworth, who was sweeping the floor. Ned was wearing a white apron as well as his spectacles, and he fulfilled the image of a pharmacist.

"Hello," he said. "I didn't mean to trip you."

"Not at all. I'm used to watching where I step."

"Ha-ha. Snakes do come into the buildings once in a while, you know."

"Oh, yes. Even in civilized places. My father killed one in the house with a hammer when I was about eight years old."

"In Ohio?"

"Yes. It was in the summer, as I recall."

"That's what I've heard. They say a hot, dry summer is the worst."

"Maybe we should hope it rains."

Ned smiled. "Rain, maybe. No hail. It would be a bad time for the wheat."

Having nothing to add, Hartley said, "No mail today, I suppose?"

Ned shook his head. "Nothing has come in at all. For anyone." After a pause, he said, "Anything new?"

Hartley had thought of asking Ned if he had heard any insinuations about Ben Stillwell's death, but his conversation with the marshal seemed adequate for the moment, and he did not know if he would be creating new gossip by asking a question. He said, "Nothing worth mentioning with me. I imagine this has been a hard time for Bess Ackerman."

"Oh, I'm sure." Ned held the broom still, as if he was waiting for more.

The sound of a steam engine rose on the air outside.

Hartley gave a toss of the head. "That's the rock crusher, isn't it?"

"I believe so."

"Here's a question I have that's related to it. I heard they were crushing rock for a railroad bed."

"I've heard that, too."

"But the nearest railroad line is over thirty miles away."

"That's right. They've tried to get a line into Winsome, and they haven't had any luck. This is even farther. But there's always a need for crushed rock. They use it in other building projects."

"You'd think it would be easier to dredge sand and gravel, but you need to find a river or an old riverbed, some kind of a gravel pit, for that."

Ned smiled. "Well, it's all business."

"I suppose it is." Hartley glanced at the broom. "I'll get out of your way and let you do your work. See you later, Ned."

"You too, Reese. Good luck."

Outside, the noise was louder. Although Hartley found it annoying, he thought he could tolerate it for the sake of having another look at the operation. If he was going to detest something, he should not be afraid to know more about it.

After checking his cinch, he mounted up and rode across the street on a diagonal. He turned east on the cross street between the café and the saloon. A block later, he turned right again and headed south as the racket of the machine grew even louder. Toward the end of the long block, the lot appeared on his left. As before, he saw piles of dull, soft-colored rock. A film of dust lay on the wagon, on the machinery, and on a rusty iron wheelbarrow. Two men moved back and forth, picking up rocks and heaving them into the hopper. Because of the noise, the men seemed to move and talk in silence, as if they were in another dimension. One man was Cletis, in his cloth hat and a long-sleeved shirt, and the other would be Al Wisner, wearing his short-brimmed hat and loose clothes that, like his mustache, were coated with a layer of light-colored dust. Hartley's sense of unreality and detachment was enhanced by the adumbration of an overcast sky and by a thin suspension of powder, the likes of which hung in the air of a flour or feed mill.

Through the haze, toward the back of the lot, movement caught Hartley's eye. A light-colored figure stood in the shade of a stable-like building. Hartley recognized Nancy by her whitish hair and a dress that looked like the same one she was wearing the day before. She was making theatrical movements as part of her conversation with a larger person dressed in dark clothes—a person who, as Hartley strained his eyes, proved to be Doyle Treece.

Hartley felt that the machine gave all four people the sensation of being isolated in their own world, for none of them paid attention to him as he rode by. Behind him, the racket rose and fell as the machine chewed the rocks that went into its gullet.

Within a few minutes, Hartley entered onto the main street again, at the corner where the blacksmith shop stood. Having made a full circle of town, and now facing the Great West Grain and Livestock office, he knew it was time to pay a visit to Bess. He headed his horse across the street, dismounted, and tied up. As a routine, he gave his saddle and saddlebags a quick glance to see that everything was in place. As he did so, movement from across the street caught his eye. Mike Ackerman had stepped out of the Owl Café and was putting on his hat.

Hartley took brisk steps toward the door of the office and tried the door. It opened, and the doorbell jingled. As he walked in, closed the door behind him, and took off his hat, Bess looked up from her desk.

Her face was dough-colored and puffy, and her blue eyes had a lost expression. Tears started in her eyes as she straightened in her chair and placed both hands on her desktop. "Reese," she said.

"Good morning, Bess. I stopped in to tell you how sorry I am for all you've been through. I know this is a terrible shock for you."

"It's been hard for me to accept or understand. It makes no sense. Ben and I were . . . getting along, you know."

Hartley nodded. "Yes, I know. If there was anything I thought I could do, I would do it. As I tried to tell the marshal, it's just not right that something like this happens. Somebody has to do something. I know that sounds vague, but—"

Her voice came near to crying as she said, "What can anyone do? It wouldn't change anything."

"I know. But as civilized people, we can't let things like this happen without trying to make someone answer for it." He waited for her to sob, sniffle into a handkerchief, and look up. "I'm sorry, Bess. I know we can't change what happened, but we should still be able to do something about it. Someone should."

She blinked her eyes. "The marshal says he can't. It's outside of his jurisdiction. And waiting for the sheriff is like waiting for rain." She sniffed. "As far as that goes, rain will probably come sooner."

"Well, I just wanted you to know that my thoughts are with you, and if there's anything I can do, I will."

She blinked again. "Thank you, Reese. It's kind of you."

The door opened behind him, and the doorbell jingled. Hartley's thought came back to the moment, and he turned to greet Mike Ackerman.

The owner of Great West Grain and Livestock took off his hat and smiled. His full, rosy face showed no worry or grief but rather gave off a glow of complacency. He brushed the palm of his hand down across his bushy mustache and said, "Good morning, young fellow. Did our friend Eldredge catch you by the toe?"

"Yes, he did, and I thank you for the recommendation. I worked for him all last week."

"Ah-ha. I'm glad it turned out well."

"Of course, I'm on the lookout for more work, or I wouldn't be in town on a weekday morning."

"Quite so. I thought that might be the case when I saw you pass by earlier. Have you tried the Sabine outfit? I heard a couple of men left there."

"I wouldn't have known to. I don't believe I've heard of them, and I'm sure I haven't met any of them."

"Originally from Texas, like so many of the folks in this country who settled here in the early days. Came up the trail with the cattle. Owner's name is Lawhorn."

Hartley nodded. "Where can I find them?"

"South of here and through the gap. Then to the east. Their buildings are on high ground, so you can see the headquarters from a few miles off."

"Thanks for the tip. It's early enough in the day that I could ride down there."

The broker smiled. "Doesn't cost anything to ask."

Hartley turned to Bess, who had regained some of her composure. "Goodbye," he said. "I wish you the best."

"Thanks, Reese."

He moved to the door and opened it. As he stepped outside and put on his hat, he almost ran into Earl Miner. The cattleman gave a curt nod as he moved sideways to the doorway. He took off his hat, brushed the front of his suit with his hand, and opened the door that Hartley had closed behind him.

Hartley heard the words "Mike" and "Bess," and the jingling door closed.

Hartley's trail took him through good grassland until the gap and then a greater amount of sagebrush as he rode east. The Sabine headquarters stood out, as Mike Ackerman had said, and the overcast sky was clearing up.

As Hartley traveled east, he was impressed once again with the distances at which a person could see objects in the wide-open spaces. He would ride for a mile, drop into a low spot, climb onto higher ground again, and have the impression that the object was not any closer than it was a half-hour earlier. By the time he reached the last gentle slope leading up to the Sabine buildings, he estimated that he had ridden more than five miles from the north-south trail.

Up close, he could see that though the buildings were whitewashed, they were not new. The wood was weathered and splintery, and the paint was flaking. As Mike Ackerman had suggested, the ranch had been in operation for many years—twenty to thirty, by Hartley's guess—and yet not a single tree grew around the buildings and corrals. Hartley had seen such bareness at several ranches and homesteads, and he wondered why people didn't plant trees, at least on the west side for shade in the summer. Maybe they did, and the trees didn't survive. Maybe the scarceness of water discouraged some people. And maybe some people did not see enough immediate or material gain in return for the effort. Whatever the case, the Sabine headquarters had the austere appearance of one more outfit that ran only to cattle, horses, and dogs.

A man appeared at the barn door and stepped out into the daylight. He was short and slender and walked bowlegged as he carried a coiled rope. A dove-colored hat with a round crown and a wide brim kept his face in shade. He wore a red bandana, a brown leather vest, and a dull white shirt. A pair of brown chaps matched his vest, and the toes of his black boots had the breaks and scuffs caused by contact with stirrups. He came to a stop, holding the rope at his right hip. A cigarette appeared in his left hand as he raised his elbow and took a drag. He turned his head to blow away the smoke, then fixed his eyes on Hartley.

"What can I do for you?"

"I dropped in to see if there are any prospects for work."

"Don't think so, not until beef roundup. But you can ask the old man, see what he says." The cowpuncher turned and walked away.

Hartley had grown accustomed to hearing the ranch owner referred to as "the old man," regardless of his age. Hartley swung down from the saddle and held his reins as he waited to see what this one looked like. The day was warming up with the afternoon, and heat rose from the dry, packed earth of the ranch yard.

After a few minutes, a bent-over man came hobbling out of the barn. He wore a black hat with the brim pulled down in front and back, and he held his head up as he peered ahead. He covered the ground in his own good time, without a cane or walking stick, and he did not show any danger of falling over, although he swayed when he came to a stop.

He had jug ears, a weathered face with pale splotches and dark spots, and washed-out blue squinty eyes. He moved his lips as if to get started, and then he spoke. "Jemmy says yer lookin' fer work."

"That's right, sir."

"Ain't got none. I just fired two, and I didn't need them."

Hartley was not prepared for the conversation to be over so soon. "Well," he said, "thanks anyway."

"Don't mention it." The old man made a half-turn, then

paused with his hand out in front of him. With a sidelong glance he said, "Next year."

The pause gave Hartley time to recover his thoughts. "Do you mind if I water my horse?"

"Nah. Go ahead." The old man turned the rest of the way around, shuffling his feet. As he began to walk away, he said, "Water's free."

The sun was descending in an orange sky beyond Decker Rim when Hartley rode into Jennet from the south. His horse was plodding, and he himself felt the stiffness and fatigue from almost eight hours in the saddle, plus the ride into town earlier in the morning.

He stopped at the water trough in front of the livery stable, sagged down from the saddle, and pulled the latigo to loosen the cinch. The horse stuck its muzzle in the water and made a light sucking sound as a swirl formed on the surface. Hartley took off his hat and dragged the cuff of his shirtsleeve across his forehead. He had gone on a long ride for nothing, it seemed, but he told himself he was doing what he was supposed to—get out and try to make something happen.

The horse lifted its head, and clear water drops fell to the murky green trough. Hartley waited, sensing what would come next. The horse held its head forward and shook its whole body, causing the stirrups to rattle and the saddle leather to rustle. The horse settled down and lowered its head for another drink.

When the horse lifted its dripping muzzle a second time, Hartley decided it was his turn. Leading the horse, he set out on foot toward the Strong Water Saloon on the north edge of town.

Several horses were tied up outside the roadhouse. Hartley did not take the trouble to look over the brands, figuring he would see soon enough who was in attendance. The sorrel fell into a relaxed posture as soon as Hartley snugged the reins to the hitching rail. After a glance at the setting sun, Hartley made his way inside.

He recognized most of the men as being either from town or from the ranches the Pick crew had cooperated with during spring roundup. Hartley crowded his way to the bar, and with a dryness in his throat from the day's ride, made ready to order a glass of beer.

He was met by a bartender who was shorter than average and had a red complexion and a low hairline. Wearing a loose white shirt and a white apron, he looked more like a butcher than a barkeep.

The man tapped the bar and said, "What'll it be?"

"A glass of beer."

"Coming up."

A minute later, the bartender set down a glass that had an inch and a half of foam. Hartley laid a silver dollar next to the glass.

"I'll collect later," said the bartender.

"Quite a few customers for the middle of the week."

"Yeah." The bartender moved his jaw sideways. "Had a burial this afternoon. Young fella they found dead the other day."

Hartley's eyebrows went up. Nobody had mentioned it. They must have thought he already knew. For a second, he wondered if Mike Ackerman had sent him out of town on purpose, but he doubted it. Mike would not have thought much about the funeral until the hour arrived, and even then, he might not have dwelled upon it.

"Did you know him?" Hartley asked.

"Nah. I just came here. There was work."

"Where's Tinker?"

"He went back to Kansas."

"Oh." Hartley wondered if he had missed an opportunity for

a job. He tried to imagine himself on the other side of the bar, but the idea was too improbable.

The bartender moved away to attend to other patrons. Left to himself, Hartley took a drink of beer. As he raised his head, he caught sight of the mirror behind the bar and of the bottom of the painting that hung above. He set down his glass and observed the whole picture. The image had not changed from the way he remembered it—an attractive woman standing in a garden looking out upon a panorama of golden wheat, blue sky, and white clouds. Her hair reflected the hue of the wheat. The other colors were rich as well—the red roses in the wreath on her head, the blue dress, the green foliage, and the golden, purple, and red fruit. He found everything clear and in place, with no hidden details—no snake in the undergrowth, not even a twisted branch suggesting a serpent in the garden. He noticed, as before, that her lips were parted, and he wondered if she was speaking or singing.

He thought that a serious artist or a critic might dismiss the painting with adjectives such as "naïve," "sentimental," or "shallow," terms that people used to describe the use of color or the arrangement of detail as well as the feeling evoked. Maybe the woman was idealized, but he saw no harm in that. At least she was not overdone with the tiara of a princess or the aura of a Madonna.

A man jostled him on the left, a man with no hat and tousled wavy brown hair. "Excuse me," said the stranger. "Tryin' to get a drink. This place is crowded. You'd think the circus was in town."

A familiar rough voice sounded from the other side of the newcomer. "We don't need a circus here, mister. We ride buffalo and milk wild horses."

Hartley placed the voice as Buck Whittaker's. He shifted a quarter-turn in order to avoid a confrontation, in case Whittaker wanted to carry out more of Prentiss's hostility.

To his right, Hartley saw Cletis approaching a group of men. Bare-headed, in his neckless, sleeveless shirt that displayed his muscular arms, Cletis again reminded Hartley of some kind of a creature—if not a prairie dog, perhaps some less specific being that had not arrived at the refinements of human clothing and behavior. Hartley saw him as a personification of the baser impulses of man, off the leash and running around.

One of the men in the group, a puncher named Dodd from the Delmore outfit, handed Cletis a glass of beer. Hartley saw but did not hear Cletis say, "Thanks." The Delmore riders went back to drinking and talking among themselves, and Cletis did not seem to mind being ignored.

Lamps had been lit all along the ceiling beams, and the glow was suffused through a cloud of tobacco smoke. A din of voices and laughter hung on the air as well. From out of the mélange rose a chorus of two or three voices.

On a flea-bitten mule with no mane and no tail
He rides to perdition on the lariat trail.

Hartley listened, but no more of the song came forth.

From the edge of his vision, he saw the hatless stranger leave the bar with his drink. Something curious caught his eye, and he turned to see the man carrying a pasteboard suitcase with his other hand. Beyond the empty space in the man's wake, Whittaker raised his glass in greeting. Hartley responded with a wave of the hand and directed his attention to the mirror, where he could watch the crowd.

A minute later, Whittaker and Lestman drew nearer. Hartley turned to nod to them. As usual, Whittaker took the lead in conversation.

"Well, we buried Ben today."

"That's what I understand. Had I known sooner, I would have gone."

"It was short and sweet. No one had much to say except the preacher. It wasn't like one of those times when a fellow dies from a fall from a horse or gets drowned in a river crossin', where you bury him there and anyone who wants can say somethin', and maybe you all sing a sad song or two."

"I happened to ride past the sawmill. It looked pretty vacant."

"For now. Earl's got some men to bring in more timber."

Hartley supposed that the word "timber" applied to small logs such as the ones he had seen. "Who's going to run it?"

Whittaker held his drink at chest level as he squared his shoulders. With his bloodshot eyes bulging and his nostrils opened, he said, "I guess I am."

Hartley glanced at Lestman and back to Whittaker. "I hope that works out all right for you."

"It'll be something different."

Lestman said, "Closer to the girls."

"What few there are." Whittaker took a sip of whiskey. "Did you see that dude with the cheap suitcase?"

"I noticed him."

"You wonder where they come from."

"Everyone comes from somewhere. Even old man Lawhorn. He's been here a long time, but he came from Texas."

"You know him?"

"I went out there to ask about work. He didn't waste time saying no."

Whittaker snorted. "Old skin flint."

Hartley thought it notable that Whittaker not only took the initiative to talk to him but also expressed something like a sympathetic point of view. He interpreted Whittaker's actions to mean that he had gone along with Prentiss only because he had to.

Hartley said, "I've got to go around and ask. The only work that came to me was building pigpens, and it didn't last but a week."

"There's wheat harvest. Don't know if you care for that. Now that I think of it, you said you wanted to be a sack-sewer."

"That was more of a joke."

Whittaker pointed sideways with his thumb. "Maybe that's what this traveler is here for. Workin' in the wheat."

"You could ask him."

Lestman said, "Here comes Cletis."

That didn't take him long, Hartley thought. *Must have been his first one.*

The swamper's toothless mouth opened as he said, "Can anyone stand me to a glass of beer?"

"I can," said Whittaker. He turned to the bar and called, "Hey, Fred!"

When the beer came, Cletis reached out his hairy arms and took the glass with both hands. His lips flapped and his gums showed as he said, "Thanks, boss." He did not take a drink right away but smiled and nodded to both sides. As he began to back away, Whittaker's voice stopped him.

"We were just talkin' about somethin', Cletis."

"What's that?"

"Have you ever seen a woman naked?"

Cletis put the glass to his mouth and tipped it without looking up. After a sip, he said, "Oh, yeah."

"How many?"

"Oh, I don't know."

"Have you ever done it with a woman?"

"I don't want to say."

Hartley felt a sense of dread creep through him and began to look for a way out.

Whittaker's rough voice rose. "Oh, come on, Cletis. You know if you did or didn't."

Cletis kept his head down, like a dog that expected a cuff.

"I bet you like to watch. That's what I think. You're a sly old dog, Cletis. You know a lot more than you let on."

Cletis's eyes narrowed, and he smiled like a fox.

Silence hung in the air amidst their group, though the hubbub of the saloon went on around them. Hartley again tried to see a way of getting out, but the space at his left closed off with the presence of a large, human form.

Doyle Treece laid his hand on Cletis's shoulder. "Don't drink too much, buddy. You've got work tomorrow."

"I clean up in here first, anyway."

"Doesn't matter. Don't drink too much."

Whittaker raised his chin and said, "I just bought him a beer, and I'd like the pleasure of his company while he drinks it."

Treece remained impassive with his heavy cheekbones and down-turned mouth. "I wonder about the company you keep."

Whittaker's face took on an insolent cast as his mouth opened. "Look here, mister—"

"Don't mister me. You know who I am, just as I know who you are. And I know this one." Treece pointed his thumb at Hartley. "You keep company with him, even though he had a jealous case against your late friend."

Hartley drew his brows together as he confronted the larger man. "I don't think that's a fair thing to say."

Treece faced him straight on with his hands at his side. He was not wearing a gun, but his hands hung like mallets. "If you want to make something of it, go ahead."

Whittaker said, "Don't pay him no mind. He don't cut no ice with us."

Treece wagged his head. "He don't cut no ice. Gimme that." He jerked the glass from Cletis and flung the contents at

Whittaker, who jumped aside in time to let the liquid sail past him.

A loud *crack!* sounded from the bar, and almost all the talk in the saloon died away. Fred the bartender held a .38 pistol with the handle resting on the top of the bar where he had slammed it.

"That's as far as it goes," he said. "If you want trouble, go look for it somewhere else. You're done here tonight, so you can leave."

Treece handed the empty glass to Cletis. "Like I said, don't stay up late drinkin'." Cletis took the glass with a forlorn expression on his face. Treece hitched up his pants and headed for the door.

The man with the pasteboard suitcase stood about a foot and a half from Treece's path and did not move. His head turned as he watched Treece's sulky process. As Treece came abreast of the man, he shot out his left arm and almost tagged the stranger on the nose. The stranger jerked his head back, and Treece did not break his stride as he walked out of the Strong Water Saloon.

CHAPTER SEVEN

Hartley stood on the back porch of the Weston boardinghouse and observed the rangeland as it stretched away to the north. The rain should have done it some good. After four days of clouds building up and dissipating, conditions had come together to produce rain. Each day as he had ridden out to a different ranch, he had watched the skies and had wondered whether he was going to ride through a deluge and find his camp soaked. He thought he had used good judgment in coming to town when he did, for the rain had come down in sheets as soon as he had gotten settled in his room. Now the sun was shining again, and the sky had cleared in the west.

He hadn't felt this clean and comfortable in a while. After a hot bath and a shave, and a breakfast of bacon, eggs, and potatoes followed by two cups of coffee, he felt energy running through his body. The midmorning sunlight and the clear, freshened air added to his sense of vitality.

In his room once again, he pondered the shirt that the landlady, Mrs. Mead, had washed and ironed for him. It would not stay fresh for very long in the heat, wind, and dust. He decided to fold it, wrap it in his jacket, tie the bundle to the back of the saddle, and put the shirt on before he reached Muriel's place. He did not expect to find a grove of trees or a screen of bushes, and it gave him a shy feeling to imagine changing shirts out in the big wide open. A fellow could ride for miles and miles and not see another person, but as soon as he needed a moment of privacy, someone was bound to show up—another rider, a wandering sheepherder, a bug hunter. He recalled Nancy hiding in the bushes, and he was glad he had not given her a peep show.

After riding seven miles east out of Jennet and turning north, Hartley found a low spot out of sight and changed his shirt. Back on the trail, he saw two prairie-dog burrows with their light-colored mounds of dirt shining in the sunlight. From each hole, a yellowish-brown rodent raised its head and craned its neck to watch the horse and rider. Two burrows. Hartley wondered how long it would be until a whole town ruined this piece of pasture. From somewhere in his reading he recalled an aphorism. "Two houses make a village." From the beginning of *Romeo and Juliet* he recalled the words "Two households." That was more like it in this country. Like Thoreau's battle of the ants. Miner's minions and the Hudsons.

He arrived at Muriel's dwelling before the sun reached its high point. He felt perspiration inside his clean shirt, and he hoped the shade would last.

Quietness prevailed to the extent that he could hear the door open from forty yards away. Muriel must have heard the horse hooves. He knew that the sound of hoofbeats traveled quite a ways in dry ground and was conveyed by the four walls of a house.

As Muriel stepped outside, her form caught the sunlight. She was wearing a straw hat tied on with a wide, light blue ribbon that matched the color of her dress. Hartley would have thought she was going somewhere except that she carried a hoe upright in her left hand.

"Hello," she said. "What a surprise."

He stopped his horse. "Good day to you. Are you on your way to doing some work?"

"No. I was about to go out to take a turn in the yard, when I thought I heard someone coming. I can spend only so much time inside until the walls begin to close in on me."

"And the weapon?"

"I carry it in case of snakes."

"Not a bad idea. I suppose I shouldn't interrupt you."

"Oh, my walk can wait. Pile off, as they say, and chin awhile."

Hartley laughed and dismounted. He took off his hat as he led his horse forward. She struck such a rustic pose with her straw hat and hoe that the poetic spirit moved him. "Happy is he who sees such grace."

Her smile showed from beneath the shading brim of her hat. "Much hast thou seen, and this delights thee?" She tapped the head of the hoe on the ground, as if she held a staff. "Stand not too long in the heat of the sun."

He put on his hat. "It doesn't look as if it rained much here."

"Very little."

"We had quite a rain in town. I had just taken refuge in the boardinghouse."

Her eyes traveled over him, as if she was noting his clean appearance. "Any news?"

"Not much on my part. I've gone to a few ranches to look for work, but everyone seems to have enough help right now."

"Something will come up."

"I hope so."

"My cousins are busy as the devil."

"I've seen Mr. Treece. He seems to get around more than the others."

"He does." She tipped the hoe handle to her left. "Shall we stand in the shade before it goes away?"

"A good idea." Leading his horse, he fell in beside her where she waited and turned.

They had not reached the corner of the house when a drumming of hooves caused them to turn around. Tightening his brows, Hartley made out two riders. The one in front was Dick Prentiss, and his companion was Tobe Lestman.

They slowed as they approached the yard, but they seemed to be in a hurry, as they did not slow down to a walk. They stopped in a cloud of dust. Prentiss dismounted, said something to Lestman, and handed him the reins. He strode forward with his shoulders rolling and his large hands open at his sides. His pistol swayed at his hip.

He stopped at about eight feet from Hartley and Muriel. He did not take off his wide-brimmed hat or make any other show of courtesy. Hartley noted, however, that the man was clean-shaven and wore a clean, light-tan canvas shirt with two chest pockets and a full row of buttons. Over the shirt he wore a brown leather vest, from the pocket of which a white tobacco sack with a yellow drawstring poked out. Slouching in a posture that relaxed his rounded shoulders, he rested his right hand on the dark butt of his pistol, while with his left hand he rubbed his thumb against his fingers. He fixed his light brown eyes on Hartley and said, "I thought you would have taken a hint."

"I've had several."

Prentiss straightened up and squared his shoulders. "About the climate."

"I told you I wouldn't be pushed."

"You don't decide that." Prentiss began to walk forward.

Hartley stood his ground.

Quick as a cat, Prentiss brought up both hands and pushed Hartley in the chest. Caught off guard, Hartley stumbled backward and lost his hat as he fell in the dirt at Muriel's feet.

She reached down to help him, and he waved her away. He rolled over, pushed himself up, and retrieved his hat. Seeing that his horse was standing still a few yards away, he turned to Prentiss and began to brush himself off.

"What did you gain by that?" he asked.

"Show you that I can push you when I want."

"See here," said Muriel. "No one asked you to come in here and act like a ruffian."

Prentiss raised his eyebrows and gave her a mild look. "It's for his own good. I've warned him about fraternizing, and I've told him there's talk about him having something to do with Ben Stillwell dying."

"This 'talk' sounds like hot air. What would he have to do with that?"

Prentiss shrugged. "You could ask him, but he might not tell you." After a smirk, Prentiss went on. "They were both payin' attention to the same girl. When he lost out, and then quit his job, he came over this way to fraternize."

"You seem to enjoy saying these things."

"I've tried to make things clear to him, for his own good if nothing else."

"Why don't you go away? No one asked you here."

Prentiss gave her an unguarded up-and-down look. "Does he need you to take up for him?"

Hartley cut in. "I can speak for myself. You know as well as your men do that I didn't have anything to do with Ben dying. He was my friend, and I helped find him. You're just trying to make trouble, and your own motives are self-interested. The lady has made it clear that no one invited you here, and she has asked you to leave." Hartley glanced at Lestman. "We all heard her."

Prentiss's face carried a sullen expression, and he had his jaw offset. "Sure. I'll go." He glared at Hartley with his light brown eyes blazing. "But I'll tell you one thing. You've had it easy up until now. You don't miss your water till the well goes dry." He stomped away, took the reins from Lestman, speared the stirrup with the toe of his boot, and swung into the saddle so hard that his horse flinched. In another five seconds, the two men were galloping away.

"He's quite a bully," said Muriel.

"Yes, he gave me an ultimatum the other day, at my camp, so some of this was repetition. I don't think he expected to find me here, but once he did, he tried to make good use of his time."

Muriel regarded Hartley with open eyes. "What's the basis of his implication that you had something to do with the young man's death?"

"I don't know where it started, but I heard it from Treece, too. I had visited this girl, Bess, a couple of times, maybe four or five altogether. When she said she thought I should go along with the boss's idea of taking out a homestead claim and turning it over to him, I could see that we had different views of the world. So we had an amiable parting before we ever got anywhere. I don't think Prentiss believes I had a hand in what happened to Ben. He more or less retracted it the other day. But it gave him something to say today, to discredit me in front of you."

"It wouldn't get him anywhere, even if you and I didn't speak again after today." Catching his expression, she added, "And it wouldn't cause me not to speak with you again. You look worried."

"Oh, I just feel unnerved. I don't get knocked down every day. I need to learn how to do more for myself."

She seemed to be giving him a calm appraisal. "You picked yourself up all right."

He laughed. "Thanks."

Silence hung for a few seconds until she said, "One other thing. He mentioned fraternizing, twice."

"Oh, yes. He used the word the other day, and I thought he meant I had come over this way to join forces with the nesters, which would mean your cousins for the most part, so I didn't put much stock in it. But as he repeated it today, I gathered that he also meant my dropping by here. So he must have known more than I gave him credit for."

"It suggests that either he or his men keep an eye on things."

"Yes, and they've got plenty to do elsewhere."

"Well, they're gone now," she said. "Shall we go back to the side of the house where we were headed? Or do you have time?"

He brushed his shirtsleeve. "Oh, I've got plenty of time. Let me get hold of my horse. Where's your hoe?"

"I set it against the house when they rode up. Next time, I'll keep it in my hands."

He fetched his horse and joined her in the shade. He waited for her to introduce a topic for consideration, but she seemed in no hurry. "Here's an idea I have," he said. "If you tell your story first, someone who comes along to make you look bad has a harder time of it."

"I think that's a good idea in general. Are you still brooding over what the bully said about you?"

"A little, maybe." Hartley waved his hand. "But I might as well tell you about another episode in my past, just to get my story in first."

She nodded.

"Before I came here, when I was still in Ohio, I knew a woman for a while. I knew girls before that, but nothing serious. But this person and I formed a mutual attraction, more than something frivolous. I would say that it was serious. Then it fell apart. It was a big disappointment for me, and it contributed to my decision to come out west and start over. It wasn't the only reason, and I wasn't running from anything, but as I say, it contributed. Anyway, that's my story, or a short version of it."

Muriel tipped her head. "Well, if it's over and in the past, you don't need to dwell on it."

"Oh, it's over, that's for sure." He felt lighter now. "And I don't mind having told the story."

"And no harm in it. Unless someone has lived in a convent or some other extraordinary conditions, just about everybody has a past at this point in life."

Having stood in the shade for a couple of minutes, and having let his sense of his surroundings settle down and broaden out, he had a clearer awareness of where he was, which in turn allowed him to see the details around him, such as her face beneath the hat brim, with some clarity. Framed by her dark hair, which hung loose behind her shoulders, her face had a pleasing, tanned complexion, and her gray-green eyes conveyed a depth of emotion that appealed to him.

He found words. "I agree, of course."

"I appreciate your willingness, and I might even say your courage, to bring out something on your own when you don't have to."

"I had help. And like I said, I believe in telling your story first. You not only establish what you think is the correct version, but you show you have nothing to hide. When I say 'you,' I mean a person. This is a general idea."

"Of course. As for the idea, not all people practice it."

"Oh, no," he said. "I've heard of men and women, either side, who were married for a while and then found out that the other person had been married before, maybe even had a child or two."

"Or had a criminal past."

"That, too. I'm sure some of that damage is hard to repair. That's why it's good to take care of it earlier. The question is in deciding when. That's how I had help today." He brushed at his shirt front.

"Also, if it's something that would make a difference in a

person's acceptability, it's good for the other person to know ahead of time. Saves a great deal of trouble."

"Yes. That's a practical aspect that I didn't mention, but it's part of the idea as well. It's better to know ahead of time that your intended has stolen sheep or robbed a bank. As you say, it saves time."

She gave a light laugh. "It was polite of you not to say what a woman might have done."

He smiled. "It's because I don't know of anything a woman might do."

Her eyes had a shine. "Are you pretending not to be wise to the ways of the world, or have I caught you being gallant again?"

"Pretending to be both. But let's just say that in present company, I believe in the proposition that nothing is ever a lady's fault."

She gave him a wry smile. "Well, you *are* being chivalrous, aren't you? Or let me see. We moved from 'woman' to 'lady,' didn't we? In other words, if she's a lady, then nothing is her fault. Does that apply to the washerwoman and the scullery maid?"

"Probably not in the chivalric sense, but in the democratic sense, I would think that being a lady is more a matter of character than station. But then in a democracy, where everyone is equal, it should be possible for a lady to be at fault. I'm afraid I'm digging myself into a hole. The term 'lady' is probably not democratic anyway. I was just being poetic, you know."

"It's just as well. I was worried for a moment."

"That I was floundering in ideas?"

"No. That I would be judged."

He met her eyes, which had lost their playful shine. "How so?" he asked.

"I have something of a past myself. Not criminal, I'm happy

to say, but not unblemished, at least in the view of most people."
She halted.

"I'm not scared yet."

"I was married once, and I left my husband."

He felt as if a five-hundred-pound weight had thudded on
the ground between them.

"That's why they call me a grass widow. I know they do. I've
heard them. And I think it's what gives men like Mr. Treece and
Mr. Prentiss some of their ardor."

Hartley made a slow gulp. He did not know if he was, in a
way, being included as well. He would like to say he had no
idea, but he couldn't. He said, "Is this man likely to follow you
here?"

"Not at all. I'm a regular kind of widow as well."

Hartley felt a small wave of relief. "I'm sorry for his sake, in
that he didn't get to live any longer."

Muriel took a deep breath. "It's nice of you to say that. I'll
tell you some of the story, as you say, to put in my version first."

"Go ahead."

"I was married at the age of twenty-two, not young and fool-
ish, but in for a few lessons nevertheless. Within a year, I learned
that my husband, who was in his early thirties, had been keeping company with a courtesan all along. When I confronted
him, he gave me to understand that he was the one who made
the money, and I could learn to live with those conditions. I
decided I was not going to be treated that way, so I left him. He
retaliated by cutting off all my money. I continued to live on my
own and took back my maiden name. It was not all that simple,
back and forth and tit for tat, but that's what it boils down to."

"Of course."

"A little more time went on, and one night he was shot while
he was waiting for a hack outside the house where his female
companion lived."

"It sounds almost like poetic justice."

"Like in a sentimental novel. *The Vicar of Wakefield* at the dawn of the twentieth century. It sounds that way, but as it turned out, he was killed because of crooked business dealing with a man named Fulton, whom I never met. Fulton paid an assassin, the law caught up with him, and all of my husband's assets were confiscated."

"And the husband's name?"

"Brewer. He would have been much better off if he had gone into the brewing business. Or the manufacturing of cooperage. But he thought he had a head for bonds and finance."

"I know nothing about that."

"Neither do I, except that it's more complicated than raising sheep. Or stealing them."

"At least you're done with all that. Or I assume you are."

Her eyes were clear and direct. "Oh, yes. But between leaving him and then coming out here to take up land on my own, I've earned the dubious reputation of being a modern woman." She blew out a light puff of air. "At least I don't have the stigma of a divorce."

Hartley winced at the word. "Well, you're in a place where people can make a new start."

"Biding my time until I can find a place of my own. But I don't mind. I find ways of passing the time. Reading, going on walks, playing music."

Hartley's mind lit up. "Oh, yes. That reminds me. You were playing music the first day I met you. I've wondered whether I might hear you play again."

"The grandfather's clock song? Da-dum, da-da-dum, da-da-dum, da-da-dum."

"As I mentioned on that occasion, it brought back a pleasant childhood memory. But I also enjoyed the ballad you played."

" 'Silver Dagger'? There are quite a few of those. Many of

them go back to the old country, you know."

"I'm familiar with a few. Do you know one called 'Bonny Barbara Allan'?"

"There are a couple of versions. When I play it, I do the version in which they are both buried, and the red rose and briar grow out of their hearts."

"And entwine in a true lovers' knot."

"That's it."

"Do you have time to play it today?"

"I think so. Let me go for my mandolin."

He stepped aside from the narrowing shade and let her pass by.

She returned in a couple of minutes with the dark instrument upright at chest level. Settling it into place, she picked a few notes and tuned the strings. With a nod, she began to play the music and sing the song. Hartley felt a glow of pleasure as he heard the familiar story about the Scarlet town where there was a fair maid dwelling, named Barbara Allan, and where, in the month of May when the green buds were swelling, a young man named Sweet William lay dying for love of the maiden. Both Sweet William and Barbara Allan died of sorrow, were buried in the churchyard and the choir, and gave life to the red rose and the briar. When Muriel finished the song, she lowered the mandolin and made a short bow with her head and shoulders.

Hartley applauded. "Wonderful song," he said. "It's been quite a while since I heard it. It's as beautiful as ever, especially out here, where there's not a bunch of carousers to drown out the sound."

"I think I heard a meadowlark answering back."

"I did, too, now that you mention it."

"Your horse didn't seem to mind."

Hartley glanced at the sorrel, standing in full sunlight. The shadow was moving closer to the house, and Hartley did not want to overstay his welcome. Tipping his head back, he squinted at the sun. "Time is passing. I should let you get along with your day." He lifted his hat. "It's been a pleasure to see you again."

Her eyes met his. "And a pleasure for me as well."

He held out his hand, and she laid hers upon it for a second.

"Have a safe trip back to where you're going," she said.

"Town, at present. And I wish you well here in the meanwhile."

CHAPTER EIGHT

Hartley sat on the front porch of the boardinghouse, gazing at the yard in front of him. The morning sun had not yet brought out the humidity, but the ground lay damp, and the weeds were growing. He hoped the recent rain was doing good to the two spindly trees.

A voice rose up from across the street and down the block. A small man with gray hair and no hat was running toward one of the houses across the street and not so far down. He was hollering, "Mother! Mother!"

In a moment, townspeople came out of the houses on both sides of the street. A woman with white hair appeared on the doorstep of the house that the man was running toward. He cried something indistinguishable, in a voice of pain and urgency. The woman shrieked and came down the steps to face the man. The other townsfolk gathered around them, and voices went up and down.

The small group began to move toward a shed close to the far corner of the block, on the other side of an empty lot. Hartley remembered having seen it, silent with a post against its double doors. Now the doors were open.

Something's wrong, he thought. He did not want to be part of a gawking crowd, but he wanted to be able to help if he was needed. Settling his hat in place, he made quick work of going down the steps, crossing the street, and catching up with the crowd.

The group stopped at the open doors of the shed, and the man and the woman went in. Loud, wailing cries came out, accompanied by the woman's piercing voice. "No! No! No!"

Hartley made his way around the crowd. He was afraid of what he might see, but he did not know if the group was immobilized and someone should be doing something.

The man and the woman were holding each other, sobbing on one another's shoulder. Beyond them, a female form lay in the straw. A dress made out of flour sacks lay wrinkled and folded above the knees of a pair of pale legs. Farther up the body, because of the position, the young woman's whitish-blond hair was visible but her face was not.

The woman standing inside sobbed, "Nancy! Nancy! Not my Nancy!"

The onlookers seemed rooted to the spot, held by the grief and agony of the two parents. Hartley said, "Someone needs to go for the marshal. Does anyone know where he lives?"

A man about thirty years old with dark hair and bloodshot eyes and wearing nothing but an undershirt and a pair of trousers said, "I do. Let me put on my boots, and I'll go find him."

Hartley scanned the rest of the crowd. About ten people had gathered by now. He wanted to ask them to leave, to give the family some privacy, but he knew it was not his place, and furthermore, some of these people might be witnesses.

Hartley walked to the back of the crowd and waited. He found it too painful to stand near the suffering parents, and the presence of the dead girl disturbed him in ways he had not known. As he stood by himself, he overheard people make remarks such as "Something like this was bound to happen," and "On a Sunday morning."

The marshal arrived within fifteen minutes. He wore his black hat, a gray work shirt, his vest with the badge, his pistol, denim work trousers, and heavy shoes.

"All right," he said. "I need to know the names of everyone here. Then you can all go home." He took a pencil and a small notebook, like a tally book, from his vest pocket and handed them to Hartley. As he did so, he stopped for a second look and said, "Were you here?"

"I was sitting on the front porch of the boardinghouse when the noise started. I came over to see if anyone needed help."

"Well, write your name down and pass the book along. And don't leave town until I've had a chance to talk to you." He studied Hartley for a couple of more seconds, then turned to walk to the shed where Mrs. Wisner was still crying.

Hartley wrote his name at the top of a blank page and handed the notebook and pencil to the next person. As he turned to leave, he almost bumped into a man who had just arrived. Drawing back, he recognized the man with no hat who had been in the Strong Water Saloon several nights earlier.

"Excuse me," said Hartley.

"What's going on?"

Hartley chose his words. "There's been a death."

"Is that right? Young man? Old man?" The stranger raised his head to look past the crowd.

Hartley took a measured breath. "A young woman."

"Oh." The man returned his gaze to Hartley. "I believe I saw you in the saloon the other night. When the honyocker pitched the beer at the cowboy."

"I was there."

"Name's Blue," said the man. "And yours?"

"Hartley." After a couple of seconds, he said, "I didn't know you were still around."

"Been lookin' for work. Tryin' to get to Sacramento. Got a good job waitin' for me there. Big farm with orchards."

Hartley took a quick glance at the man. He was wearing

inexpensive, lightweight clothes such as a person would wear in a city. He looked as if he had taken a bit of sun since he came to town, but he still had a pale cast to him, like a man who had just gotten out of prison. He seemed like a fish out of water, dropped on the sunbaked plains.

"Where do you work?" Blue asked.

"I'm on my own right now."

"Hard to find work. People aren't all that outgoing here."

"That's the way they are with newcomers."

"How long does it take until they see you as one of their own?"

"I don't know. Maybe ten years."

"Just thought I'd ask. I don't plan to be here that long."

"Even people who plan to stay sometimes pack up and leave."

"Does the unfriendliness get to them?"

"Not so much as the sun, the wind, the hail, the rattlesnakes, and the grasshoppers. Not to mention the freezing cold winters." Hartley realized he was speaking the idiom of the country and enjoying it.

"Grasshoppers?" said Blue. "Ah, the farmers. The honyockers."

"Them, too," said Hartley.

Hartley was sharpening his pocketknife in his room when a knock came at his door. He opened it to see the red face of Fred the bartender, who also stayed at the boardinghouse.

"What is it?" asked Hartley.

"There's a public meeting to take place in front of the post office at four."

"What time is it now?"

"A quarter till."

"I'll be there. Thanks."

Hartley finished with his knife and put things away. He

wondered if Muriel would be in attendance. He assumed that the Hudsons and Treece had received word and had come to town, but he thought it possible that they would leave women out of a public gathering where people might voice opinions.

A crowd was gathering when Hartley arrived, having walked the distance in five minutes. Shadows were stretching out from the square front of the post office and from adjacent buildings, and a few men stood with their backs to the businesses. In front of the door of the post office, Al Wisner had Ned Farnsworth on his left and the marshal on his right. A few paces away, in front of the barbershop, Doyle Treece stood with his arms folded. After him, three Hudsons loitered, also with their arms folded. All four men had pistols in view. Returning to the Hudsons, Hartley could not tell which two he had met.

Hartley took a place at the edge of the crowd and in back. He counted fifteen people in the group, all men. Fred the bartender, shorter than most, stood in front, while Blue, a little taller than most, stood in back, where he raised his chin and swayed his head.

The marshal stepped to the front of the crowd. He was dressed in full attire, with his black hat, charcoal-gray vest, white shirt, dark wool trousers, and knee-high black boots, plus his badge and pistol. He held up a small brass bell and rang it. The crowd quieted down. "It's time to get started," he said. "We all know this is a terrible thing that's happened, and we want to keep things in order. First, if there's any of you that put your name down and I haven't talked to you, I will." He turned aside and cleared his throat. "Meanwhile, if anyone has any information, and I mean any little thing, that will shed light on this, you have a duty to tell me." His dark eyes roved across the crowd. "Now, Mr. Farnsworth, the postmaster, has agreed to present a few words for the family."

Ned Farnsworth stepped forward, dressed in a black suit and

necktie and with a somber expression on his face. He began with a slight bow of the head as he closed and opened his eyes. He adjusted his spectacles and turned his head to each side, taking in the crowd. When he spoke, his light voice sounded in contrast with the husky voice of the marshal.

"Friends, we thank you for gathering here today. Mr. Wisner has asked me to speak because he doesn't know if he could hold up. But his message is brief, and it does not differ from the marshal's." He took a short breath and continued. "This is a terrible event, something that can never be undone. Whoever did it has broken the law of man and the law of the Lord. He has taken the life of an innocent young woman and has destroyed forever the life of a family." He paused again. "No punishment would be too severe. But first we must find out the perpetrator. Let us not be too hasty to point an accusing finger, but let us heed what the marshal has said. It is the duty of every citizen to share any knowledge that might lead to the discovery of the truth. On behalf of the family, and in the name of all that is just, I ask your help. Thank you."

Silence fell on the crowd as Ned Farnsworth stepped back into place next to Al Wisner, who turned to him and blinked away tears as he thanked him.

The marshal's voice took command again. "Thank you, Mr. Farnsworth. And now we open the meeting to anything that might be said from the floor. Also, let us bear in mind what the postmaster said, which I'm glad he mentioned. Let's not fling accusations on the basis of something you heard. Rumor runs rampant at times like this, and it may have already. But if you have information, something you know, don't be shy."

The marshal folded his arms and waited. Seconds ticked by until a voice near his shoulder caused him to turn.

Doyle Treece had stepped forward, apart from the Hudsons. His hands hung at his sides like two hams, and his face had a sallow cast in the shade of the building and his hat. He raised his right hand and turned it palm upward like a baseball mitt.

"With all due respect to what you've said, and as a member of the family, for those who don't know, I think I should say something."

"Well, go ahead," said the marshal.

"It pertains to something that was seen."

"To the point, man. Is this something you heard, or something you saw?"

Treece raised his head and tipped it to each side as he scanned the crowd. "It's something I saw, and something I believe others would have seen as well."

"Out with it, then."

"It pertains to a newcomer to this town, name of Blue, I believe. He's standing at the back of the crowd there."

Gasps and murmurs accompanied the shuffling of feet as fourteen men turned to stare at the stranger, whose eyes grew wide with surprise.

The marshal's voice prevailed. "And what witness do you bear against him?"

The crowd turned again.

Treece said, "When the saloon closed last night, he was seen walking the streets of town."

"Did you see him?"

"Yes, I did."

The marshal addressed the crowd. "Did anyone else?"

The man who had gone to fetch the marshal earlier in the day spoke up. "I did."

A few murmurs began until the marshal spoke again. "Blue. Is that your first name or your last?"

"It's my last name, sir."

"And what do you say to this report?"

"It's false to the extent that he said I was walking the streets,

plural. I walked on one street, this one, from the saloon to the
livery stable, the length of town. I've been sleeping at the livery
stable, as you may know."

"I may. How many drinks did you have?"

"Not many. Two, as I recall."

Treece cut in. "He only drinks if someone else will buy it."

"That doesn't pertain," said the marshal. Returning his dark
gaze to Blue, he said, "Did anyone see you go into the stable at
that time?"

"Not at that hour. I've been staying there almost a week, and
Ed Becker is used to my coming and going."

"I see. Did you know the deceased?"

"No."

"Did you ever see her before today?"

"I don't know. I didn't see the body, so I don't know what
she looks like or whether I happened to see her in passing."

"But you know where she lived. Did you ever walk past that
house before this morning?"

"In the course of my short stay in this town, I've walked up
and down all the streets. There aren't many."

"When do you plan to leave?"

"As soon as I can."

"Well, then, I'll ask you to come along with me. We don't
need you leavin' town until we've got an answer to this question."

"I'll tell you right now, I didn't do it."

"I didn't say you did."

"But I'm a suspect."

The marshal rubbed his chin. "I couldn't say you aren't."

The crowd lingered as the marshal stepped into the street
and beckoned to Blue. The two of them walked across the wide
street at an angle toward a small log building that sat by itself,

121

back from the sidewalk, between the Owl Café and the Argyle Hotel.

Hartley had known the building served as the town jail, but this was the first time he saw it used. He felt his spirit at a low ebb as he realized how easy it was for a person to be accused and jailed for a serious crime.

Hartley pulled in a deep breath and turned his attention to the crowd again. Al Wisner and Ned Farnsworth had left. The Hudsons and Treece had moved to the front of the crowd, and Treece was talking in a matter-of-fact way to a bearded teamster who leaned forward at the waist and nodded. The Hudsons kept to themselves, not standing still but shifting and turning as they spoke back and forth and passed a pint bottle. Treece finished his conversation with the teamster and transferred his heavy weight from one foot to the other as he rotated to face his cousins. He motioned with his head. The bottle went out of sight, and the three of them moved forward. The crowd parted, and Treece led their small group to a stop in front of Hartley.

In a loud voice, Treece said, "You seem to be everywhere there's trouble."

"I might be a witness."

Treece's sallow face tensed, and his eyes narrowed. He reminded Hartley of a painting he had seen of Mongolian invaders. "What do you mean?"

"I saw you fling the beer the other night, and then you took a poke at Blue when the bartender told you to leave."

"You've got a smart mouth. One of these days I'll push it in for you."

"When nobody's looking?"

"Don't tempt me right now."

One of the Hudsons stepped up, swaying his elbows. He had a slur in his voice as he said, "Look here, mister. We don't like you. All this trouble started since you came around."

"So did the rain."

Hudson peered at him with dull eyes, as if he needed glasses. "What do you mean?"

"Two things happening in sequence doesn't mean the first one caused the second."

"You do have a smart mouth." Hudson moved closer. His chest went up and down with his breath, and Hartley smelled whiskey. "Here an innocent girl has been killed, and you're as sarcastic as a—"

"As a what?"

"A shithouse mouse."

Hartley stood with his feet planted. "You're not making any sense. Maybe you should have another drink."

"Don't make fun of me, you buster." Hudson's hands came up as he leaned forward to push Hartley in the chest. His eyelids drooped, and his open mouth expelled more of the odor of whiskey.

Hartley raised his hands, pushed Hudson's hands to the sides, and gave the man a square shove in the chest.

Hudson stumbled back, caught one spur on the other, and fell in the street. The crowd moved back.

Treece stepped forward as the other two Hudsons helped their brother to his feet. "That's enough," said Treece. "Can't you see the man's upset? Have you got no respect for the family?"

"He crowded up and tried to shove me. All I did was defend myself."

"You started the argument."

"No, I didn't. Anyone here can tell you. He came up to me and said all this trouble started when I came around."

"Well, it's true. Once you came over to camp in our neighborhood, like a saddle tramp, the cattleman's men have come by to bully us. Then one of their men turns up dead, not far from you, and it turns out you had a grudge against him. And now this."

Hartley had a full awareness of being in public. "You've got things twisted up, maybe because you want to. But I didn't cause anyone to harass you, and I didn't have a grudge against Ben Stillwell. He was my friend, and I'm not afraid to say his name. And as for 'now this,' your upset and inept cousin started it."

"I didn't mean just this."

"What else is there?"

"That's what we're going to find out."

Treece turned to his cousins and signaled with his arm. As they walked away, the remaining men in the crowd began to mutter among themselves. A larger sense of the moment came to Hartley, and he did not think that any of them, himself included, had done much good to Nancy's family.

CHAPTER NINE

Hartley walked along the main trail south, keeping the eastern end of Decker Rim in view. He needed exercise and a quiet place to sort out his thoughts, and he did not want to run the chance of incurring suspicion by walking the streets of Jennet. Out on the plains, he heard only the occasional song of a bird and the trudge of his own footsteps.

The farther he walked from town, the better he felt. He knew he needed to overcome the feeling of being fed up. First, Miner's men had bedeviled him with accusations of fraternizing with the nesters, and to a lesser degree, of having had something to do with Ben Stillwell's death. Then came the nesters, who treated him as an agent from the enemy and as a remote cause for anything else that went wrong. He reminded himself that to some extent, the antagonism on each side was caused by jealousy of his acquaintance with Muriel, but the core of the conflict came from a larger motive that both parties shared. *Cupiditas* was the old-fashioned term for it. *Radix malorum est cupiditas.* The root of all evil is the desire for wealth. They went about it in two different ways, or with two different premises— Miner with the idea that he was here first and that might made right, and Treece and the Hudsons with the belief that they had a right to take what they could get, and because they were at a disadvantage, the end justified the means—but both sides had the same objective, and it was not his.

He was tempted to walk away from it all, but he knew he

125

could not retreat to a shady grove and ponder a cool, babbling brook. If he went somewhere else, he would be met by more systems or factions, and there would be machines. Besides, as he sorted them out in his isolation, he had two reasons to stay. One was Muriel. He needed to see if he had a prospect there. The other was the situation in town. No one was being held to account for the first killing, and a man he did not care for very much had a chance of being railroaded for the second one. Neither of those cases was his problem, but if he didn't do what he could to oppose injustice, he was going along with it. And if he did something, he would have to be prepared to defend himself. The thought made him queasy, but he knew he had to screw his courage to the sticking place. He smiled. Lady Macbeth did not have very good motives, either, but she had some good lines.

When he felt he had walked about half an hour, he came to a stop, took a full look at the rim, and turned around. Although each step now took him closer to town, he did not begin to lose his sense of well-being. He had thought things out and had gotten his ideas in order. He had a course to stick to.

As he walked, he realized he had a tune running through his head. All the way back to town the day before, as he rode from Muriel's, he had played in his mind the last two stanzas of the song she had sung, in which Sweet William and Barbara were buried in the churchyard and the choir, and out of their hearts there grew a red rose and a briar, which became entwined in a true lovers' knot. Now the melody came back, but instead of the final two stanzas, the portion of the song he heard consisted of only two lines, and it bore a different image. *In the month of May the green buds were swelling.* Hartley began to have an idea of why those words came to mind now.

Shadows were stretching well into the street when Hartley

returned to Jennet. As he passed the Great West Grain and Livestock office, dark inside, he heard the sound of metal clanging on metal. Across the street, the large door of the blacksmith shop was open. The marshal must be thinking things through in his own way.

Down the street past the post office, Hartley turned and kept to the left side of the street. More than halfway down the long block, he came to the Wisners' house. A boy with whitish-blond hair sat on the doorstep, wielding a small kitchen knife to cut on a length of stove wood in his lap. Hartley stopped in front of him, and the boy looked up, straining his eyes and wrinkling his nose.

Hartley said, "I'd like to talk to Al Wisner."

The boy showed narrow, gapped teeth as he said, "He ain't here."

"Can you tell me where I can find him?" Hartley hoped the boy wouldn't say the saloon, as Treece and the Hudsons had headed that way over an hour earlier.

"I don't know." The boy gouged at the wood and pulled with the knife in such a way that it made Hartley flinch.

"You know, you ought to cut away from you. If you cut toward yourself, you could—"

The boy turned his head and hollered over his shoulder. "Ma-ah!"

Footsteps sounded inside, and the door opened. A lean woman with mouse-colored hair and dull blue eyes appeared in the doorway. She spoke to Hartley.

"What is it?"

Hartley took off his hat. "I'd like to speak with Mr. Wisner. I'm sorry for the sadness in your family. But I'd like to talk to him."

"He ain't here." The woman's eyes wavered and came back. "You ought to be able to find him at the crusher."

"Thank you. And please convey my sympathies to Mrs. Wisner."

"I will." The woman closed the door.

Hartley glanced down at the boy. "Thanks."

The boy paused with his knife and looked up with a sullen expression. He said nothing and went back to gouging at the piece of wood in his lap.

Hartley preferred not to walk past the saloon, so he stayed on the shady side of the main street, crossed in front of the Argyle Hotel, and cut through an empty lot to the next street. He came out north of the lot where the crusher and rock piles were located. As he approached the site, he began to feel queasy again. It was the last place he had seen Nancy alive.

The machinery, the piles of rock, and the heap of crushed rock all lay under a film of dust and cast their own low shadows. At the back of this lifeless area stood the stable-like building he had noticed on his previous pass by. The door was open. There being no fence or gate on the property, Hartley walked onto the premises where there was the least amount of rubble in the way.

He found Al Wisner sitting on a crate inside the open doorway. The man had his dusty, short-brimmed hat on his knee and a whiskey bottle between his feet.

"Mr. Wisner?"

The gray-haired man turned and raised his head. He had a sad, lost expression on his face, and his eyes were swollen and bloodshot. "Al is good enough. Who are you?"

"My name's Reese Hartley. I can't tell you how sorry I am for what happened."

"Who are you with?"

"If you mean which side am I on, I'm not with either one. I used to work for a cow outfit, but I parted ways with them. And in truth, your kinfolk don't care for me very much, either."

"Then what are you here for?"

128

Hartley hesitated. "As simple as it sounds, I want to help you find justice for your daughter."

Wisner's face hardened. "We've got an old saying where I come from. If someone you don't know says he wants to help you, run the other way."

"I don't blame you."

"You don't blame me for what?"

"For being cautious with someone you don't know."

The old man's lower lip trembled, as if he had a thought he couldn't bring out, and then he broke down and sobbed.

"I'm sorry." Hartley kept himself from saying more, from talking too much. He wondered if the mention of blame had touched something off.

Wisner raised his head. Tears fell from his bloodshot eyes. "You didn't know her, mister. She was a headstrong girl, and she did things we told her not to, but I never thought it would come to this."

Hartley nodded.

"Her mother and I both. We tried and we tried. But she did what she wanted to do. If we'd had more kids, maybe things had been different. But it took a long time to get her, and we weren't able to have any others after that."

"You can never tell what would have happened."

The old man sniffled. "And now we feel like it's our fault."

"You can't blame it all on yourself."

Wisner put on his hat, reached for the bottle, and held it chest high. "I just hope they find the son of a bitch that did this, and hang him slow with a new rope." He uncapped the bottle and took a drink.

Hartley watched the man's eyes relax. After a long moment, he said, "Do you think they've got the right man in jail?"

Wisner shook his head. "I don't know what to think."

Hartley said, "I don't believe they do. But I don't want to try to convince you just for the sake of agreeing with me. Here's one way to look at it. Why do you think someone would do something like this?"

Wisner looked straight at Hartley, and his filmy eyes turned hard. "Men do filthy things every day of the year, somewhere. Sometimes they do it just to be doin' it."

"That's true. And this fellow Blue might be the kind that goes from one place to another, doing things like that." Hartley paused. "But it might be someone closer to home."

Wisner breathed with his mouth open. "I hope you don't mean the postmaster. He's right around the corner. But he's as good as a preacher to me."

Hartley shook his head. "I would never have thought of him. And I wouldn't want to narrow it down to one person right away. If we can get an idea of why someone did it, we might have a better chance of figuring out who."

Wisner took another drink. "You say 'we.' Why doesn't the marshal do this?"

"I think he's trying, but there are some things, let's say avenues of investigation, that if he makes them public, some people will want to stop."

Wisner's eyes narrowed. "Like what?"

"Let me lead up to that. First, I'm going to ask you a couple of questions that I don't want you to hold against me. I'm not doing this for myself."

Wisner studied Hartley for a moment. "Go ahead. If you ask somethin' I don't think you should, or that I don't want to answer, I'll just quit and tell you to go to hell."

"That's fine with me." Hartley tried to give a smile of assurance. "Now, to begin with, I gather that you had an idea, or at least a hint, that your daughter was sneaking out at night."

"I didn't say that, but I guess I didn't hide it." He shook his head. "I never thought it would come to this."

"And you may have had a hard time saying anything to her."

Wisner stared at the ground, and his voice was slow. "Like I said, we tried. We warned her about men. But Betty was sixteen when we got married, and Nancy knew it. She could always say, you did it, too. To tell you the truth, mister, I thought she would end up gittin' married, and that would take some of the starch out of her."

Hartley waited a couple of seconds for his next question. "And she started sneaking out, how long ago? A few months? Six months? Longer?"

Wisner tipped his head to the side. "I couldn't say. A few months, at least."

Hartley hesitated, then decided to follow through. "Long enough for her to be with child, and know it?"

The old man sagged in his seat and stared at the bottle he held between his knees. "I thought of that before today, of course. Like I said, we was more or less expectin' it."

Hartley let the silence grow until Wisner looked up. "I'm not expressing an opinion or a judgment, just thinking of what we can do. So here's my suggestion, and you don't have to take it if you don't want to. But before much time goes by, I think it would be worthwhile to have a doctor make an examination and determine whether that was the case."

"If she was . . . with child, as you say."

Hartley met the man's eyes. "Yes, and I think, in order to protect the truth, it would be best not to let the cousins, or the postmaster, or even the marshal know about it."

"Why not let the marshal ask the doctor?"

"For one thing, he might not want to spend the money. For another, as I said, he might tell someone and let himself be talked out of it. I was not comfortable with how quick he was to put this stranger named Blue in jail. Once it's done—well, depending on the outcome—there would be no reason not to tell the marshal. If there's nothing to report, then of course there's no need to tell anything."

Wisner stared at the bottle again. "I suppose we could do it. I know a doctor we could send for. It'll cost money, of course."

Hartley took a steady breath. "I'll put up the money. I'll leave it to you to deal with the doctor. I've got no business in that part. But we can't botch it, and we can't leave it to what someone else will call hearsay. We need to get a written report if things turn out the way we think." Hartley paused. He thought he sounded too quick and efficient. "I know this is personal," he said. "I won't ask to see the result unless we need it to . . . pursue justice at some point. Meanwhile, you can keep it under your hat."

Wisner made a slow nod. "I'll send for the doctor in the morning. We're plannin' for the burial in a couple of days. No one has to travel very far."

Hartley nodded, still trying not to rush. "Do you think ten dollars will cover it?"

"I think so."

"Here's this." Hartley laid two five-dollar gold pieces in Wisner's palm.

"Thank you, mister." The old man held his finger against his gray mustache, and tears came to his eyes again. "Not many people would go out of their way to help a poor stiff who's never had a dime."

Hartley rested his hand on the man's shoulder. "I'm not rich. I'm doing this because I think someone should."

"I know. I'll keep it under my hat."

Hartley was sitting in his room waiting for the call to supper when a knock sounded on the door. No voice came. The knock sounded again. Hartley rose from his seat, crossed the small room, and opened the door. Marshal Jock Mosby filled the doorway with his hat, vest, badge, pistol, and mule-ear boots.

"Come on in," said Hartley, stepping aside and then closing the door.

The marshal took off his hat. He was wearing a clean white shirt as well as his other attire. He fixed his dark eyes on Hartley and said, "I'm here as part of my questioning about what happened this morning, or last night."

"Go ahead."

"I want to know if you ever met the victim."

"In an odd sort of way, yes. She showed up out of nowhere one day when I was riding near her family's property."

"Out in badger country."

"I didn't know they called it that."

"Anyway, what was the nature of your contact?"

"No contact at all, and I'm glad of it. I was glad at the time, also. She jumped out of some bushes to try to scare me. I didn't think she should be wandering out of her parents' supervision and talking to men she didn't know. I told her she should go back to her parents and not be spooking horses."

"What else did you talk about?"

"I told her I was going to visit her cousin, and she told me she used to live there."

"Did you touch her?"

"Not at all. I didn't get down from my horse."

"And did you ever see her on any other occasion?"

"Once, when I happened to ride by the family business where her father works on the rock crusher. Her father and that swamper named Cletis were feeding rocks into the machine, and she was talking with her cousin Mr. Treece."

"You didn't hear what they said?"

"Not with all that racket."

The marshal paused in his questioning, but he did not signal that it was over. Hartley's gaze drifted over the man's receding hairline and pale forehead.

"What do you know about this man we have in jail? Mr. Blue."

"Only what he told me, that he was on his way to Sacramento and ran out of money to travel on. Or needed more, at least."

The marshal nodded. "Anything else?"

"I saw him in the saloon the night he came to town. He was standing by when Mr. Treece was evicted, or ejected, for throwing the contents of a beer glass at a man named Whittaker. On his way out, for no apparent reason, Treece threw a fist at Blue and almost hit him."

"Do you have any reason Treece would have a grudge against Blue?"

Hartley shook his head. "Nothing that I know. But it seemed as if Treece took a dislike to him and was more than willing to point the finger at him this afternoon. He seemed to be exerting undue influence."

The marshal's face twitched. "I'd prefer to stick to what you know and have seen."

"I understand. But if we're going to stick to facts and details, I don't think there's much real evidence against Blue."

With his face now rigid, the marshal said, "Gathering evidence is not like fitting a shoe on a horse. With a horse, you can trim the hoof and shape the shoe until they fit perfect. With evidence, you don't even know if you've got it all there. But we try to do things right. Meanwhile, I recognize your objection."

A rapping echoed on the panel of the door, followed by a voice. "Supper."

"Thanks," Hartley called.

"I don't think I have anything more," said the marshal.

"Neither do I, at the moment."

The broad main street of Jennet lay in afternoon sunlight, with shadows stretching out once again from the buildings on the west side. The shadows were cast from the east when Hartley rode out that morning. In the meanwhile, the sun had crossed over. The dog that was barking now would have spent most of its day following the shade. The majority of the townsfolk would not have ventured beyond the edges of town. Mike Ackerman would have gone out on his triangular routine, like the deer in farm country that moved from shelter to feed to water and back to shelter. Others, like Ben Stillwell and Nancy Wisner, would move no more.

Hartley brought his horse to a stop in front of the post office and took his time as he let himself down from the saddle. He found the ground with his feet, flipped the reins around the hitching rail, and loosened the stiffness in his legs as he walked toward the building.

Inside, Ned Farnsworth appeared at the postal window, neat as always in his gray suit and bow tie. He took off his spectacles and smiled.

"Long day?" he asked.

"I must have ridden twenty miles and back. Stopped in at two places asking about work. No luck."

"That's too bad. Something will come up, though."

"I hope. No mail today, I suppose."

"Not for you, but I did receive this notice." Ned unfolded a sheet of paper that was printed like a handbill. "I told you we received these once in a while. It's a notice about a tract of land they're opening up on the first of September. North of Lusk at a place called Hat Creek." Ned turned the paper around.

Hartley observed a smudged map that designated such places as Rawhide Creek, Rawhide Butte, Lusk, Old Woman Creek, and Hat Creek. Fort Robinson was the only place name in Nebraska.

"North of here," said Hartley.

"Yes. Two days' travel or more."

"I would think a fella should go up there ahead of time, take a look at things, and be ready when it opens up."

"That's the way many people do it. Some go out of curiosity, just to see what's going on, but others are serious and competitive. From what I've heard."

Hartley nodded as he let his eyes wander around on the map. He saw other names such as Castle Butte, Running Water, Van Tassell, and Crazy Woman Creek. "I'd like to make a little more money, but right now would be the time to go, and look for work again when I come back. Take about a week. I could still work the month of August."

"Wheat harvest will be over by then. Or at least they'll have the crews filled up by the time you get back."

"I don't care all that much about working in the wheat. I'll have to think it through."

"Of course. If there's anything I can do to help, let me know."

"Thanks. I suppose you need to keep this paper."

"Yes. I should post it on the board."

A lull followed for a couple of seconds until Hartley said, "Anything new happen in town today?"

Ned put on a thoughtful expression. "Not that I know of. The marshal let his prisoner out of jail. He said he didn't think he had enough evidence."

"That sounds fair of him. By the way, I thought you did very well with the speech you gave yesterday."

"A small thing, but thanks. I was glad to do my part."

The sorrel horse was dozing on its feet when Hartley stepped outside. One more task remained. Hartley unwrapped the reins from the hitching rail and led the horse to the livery stable.

Once there, he pulled off the saddle and set it on a stand. Next, he lifted the double saddle blanket from the horse's back and laid it, damp side up, on top of the saddle. Holding the reins, he brushed the horse on both sides, then turned the horse into the corral and took off the bridle. The horse headed for the water trough, and Hartley returned to the shadowy interior of the stable. As he was settling the bridle and looped reins on the horn of his saddle, a man approached on his left.

"Hallo," said the man.

Hartley turned and recognized Blue. "The same to you. I'm glad to see you out on your own again."

Blue's face had a dull shine, as if he had not met up with a bar of soap for a day or two. "The marshal said you put in a good word for me, though he would have let me out anyway."

"I believe he tries to be fair."

"I didn't have that impression when he marched me off yesterday. Being stuck in this town is bad enough, but that calaboose gives a man a hopeless feeling. On top of that, the only thing to read was an old newspaper from last November, telling of the execution of Tom Horn."

"People keep editions about memorable events. The death of Queen Victoria, the blowing up of the *Maine.*"

"Well, it didn't improve my sense of the hospitality of this place."

"I'm sorry to see you stuck here like this. If you'd like, I could stake you to a few dollars, help you make it as far as Cheyenne, at least. You could find work there, and it's on the U.P. line to take you to Sacramento."

Blue gave a light laugh. "Thanks for the offer, but I have a few shekels left, and I think I'll be going to Cheyenne before long."

Hartley felt a small wave of relief. In his mind he kept a tally of his own resources, which were dwindling. He had already resolved that this would be his last night in the boardinghouse for the time being.

"But I would accept the offer of a drink," said Blue.

Hartley demurred. "I'll tell you what. I don't want to miss the evening meal at the boardinghouse, but I could meet you at the saloon a little later. Say, at about eight. I don't want to stay out late anyway. I've got some travel myself tomorrow."

"Good enough," said Blue. "I'll see you then."

The Strong Water Saloon had not changed in any visible way since Hartley's last visit. The lamps were lit, casting a faint glow on deer antlers and steer horns where they hung on the walls. The woman with golden hair continued to look out upon the field of wheat, while below the painting, Fred the red-faced bartender stood with both hands on the bar.

"A glass of beer for right now," said Hartley. He did not take a full view all around, though he caught a glance of Buck Whittaker slouching at the far end of the bar.

As Hartley took his first drink of beer, the front door opened, showing the dusky light of the evening outside. A man with no hat appeared in silhouette. The door closed behind him as he walked toward the bar where Hartley stood. His face was not quite as shiny as before, and Hartley imagined he had found a basin or a bucket of water.

"Evening," said Blue as he held out his hand.

Hartley shook. "Good evening."

Blue raised a hand in signal, and Fred brought a bottle and a glass. He poured three fingers of whiskey without any show, tipped up the bottle, and pushed the glass toward Blue. Hartley laid a two-bit piece on the bar.

Blue raised his glass and took a sip. "This is not so bad, for being in the middle of a wasteland. Thanks."

"You're welcome."

"Curious thing, that newspaper. Gives an idea of how the world comes to places like this."

"Oh, there are telegraph lines all over. And then there's what they call the sagebrush telegraph. Word of mouth. Someone gets stabbed or shot on Crazy Woman Creek, and everyone knows about it the next day."

"You've got some good place names here. My favorite is the Stinking Water."

A voice barked on Hartley's right. "Why don't you leave, then?"

Hartley turned to see Buck Whittaker standing away from the bar with a glass of whiskey at waist level. His hat was tipped back, and he held his chin up as the corners of his mouth turned down. His prominent eyes were bleary. The belligerence of his tone and the swaying of his body suggested that he had had a few drinks.

Blue did not sound daunted. "It's what I have in mind," he said.

"The sooner the better." Whittaker drank from his glass, licked his upper lip, and focused his bulging eyes on Hartley. "And you. I don't know why you want to pal around with a drifter like this—and a murder suspect, I might add."

Blue's voice maintained a light tone. "And I might add that I'm not a suspect, else the marshal wouldn't have seen fit to set me free."

"Free. And there's an innocent girl layin' dead in her mother's house."

Blue held up the palm of his hand. "I'm sorry for the girl and her family, but I dare say I didn't have anything to do with it. There's no point in suggesting that I did."

"You dare say. I'd like to wring your neck. That girl didn't do no harm to anyone, but there's so many men in this country that's got a hard like a hoe handle that things like this happen. They should be strung up, every one of 'em."

"Maybe you should find out who did it, then, and do just that."

"I might. Get a few men together. I've known it to be done."

Hartley had an ugly feeling in his throat. "It's not good to talk that way," he said.

"There you are, stickin' up for him. It's bad enough that you fraternize with nesters, and now this."

Hartley recognized the echo of Dick Prentiss's diatribes. "Oh, leave it off."

Whittaker raised his eyebrows and wagged his head. "At least there's somethin' to sniff after there. Dick seems to think so."

"You had better leave that alone, Buck."

Whittaker seemed to take warning. Making ungallant mention of a decent woman in a saloon was a recognized wrong in itself. He shifted his attention to Blue again. "I just don't like drifters. And I don't like the idea of a girl bein' snuffed out like a candle when she had so much to live for."

Blue said, "You keep coming back to that, pairing me with it."

"So what if I do?" Whittaker took a drink and wavered on his feet. He stared at the bottom of his glass, which had only a spider of liquid, and turned up the glass to drain it. He let out a sound like "Bahh" and set the glass on the bar.

Blue continued to keep his calm. "You're drunk. You ought to hold your tongue."

Whittaker lunged forward. "Don't tell me—"

Hartley stepped in front of him and held up his right arm sideways. "Lay off, Buck. You're just causing trouble."

Whittaker tried to shove Hartley's arm out of the way, but in so doing, he pushed himself off balance. His feet went out from under him, and he landed on the floor next to a spittoon. His face had gone red, and his prominent blue eyes blazed with anger. "You didn't have to do that," he said.

"I didn't do anything but try to keep you out of trouble."

Whittaker made it to his feet and pulled himself together.

"You knocked me on my ass. People don't do that to me and get away with it."

Fred the bartender appeared and took the empty glass from the bar. "You've had enough for tonight, Buck. I don't want to have to throw you out, so just leave."

Whittaker hung his head. He had a sour expression on his face as he said, "I don't forget things like this." He wiped his hand across the bottom of his nose and walked out into the night.

When the door closed, Blue said, "Well, he has a lot of interesting things to say."

"Never mind him," said Hartley.

"I have to give you my thanks again. You shouldn't have gone to so much bother on my behalf. I'm leaving anyway, you know."

Hartley wanted to say he hadn't done it all on Blue's behalf, but he thought there had been enough talk already. "I know," he said.

CHAPTER TEN

The sorrel horse picked up its feet after a good night's rest. Hartley felt the energy brimming in the animal, but he kept in mind the need to use the horse well. He estimated a week for this trip, and he could not afford to wear out the horse at any point. He was traveling light, hoping to buy provisions as he needed them, but he was adding miles the first day by taking this detour to Muriel's place.

The morning sun was warm already, and the air was dry. The scent of sagebrush mingled with the arid essence of dust. On his ride the day before, he had seen the dark green leaves and purple blossoms of alfalfa where a seed had dropped here and there, but he saw no alfalfa over this way. He saw pale green Russian thistles, as big and round as pumpkins at this point in the summer but on their way to becoming airy tumbleweeds.

He had known of tumbleweeds, had read of them, when he was growing up. Since coming west, he learned that they had first come with the wheat. Now they were everywhere, piled up on fences, bushes, windbreaks, and old abandoned wagons. Wherever the ground was broken, by plow or wagon wheel or horse hoof, the scattering tumbleweed seed took root.

As he approached Muriel's little house, he was struck, as he often was, by the quietness of this part of the country. He still expected to hear dogs barking, chickens crowing, sheep bleating, or children shouting. As he slowed his horse and listened to the footfalls, he heard the opening of the door, a squeak and a scuff.

Muriel stepped outside and shielded the left side of her face from the bright sun. Her dark hair hung loose at her shoulders, and she was wearing a sand-colored dress that he thought she was wearing the first time he had seen her.

"Good morning," she said. "I didn't expect to see you this early. You look like you're packed and ready to go somewhere."

"I am." He dismounted, walked the last ten yards, and positioned himself so he wouldn't have to look into the sun.

She had her eyebrows drawn. "Are you leaving?"

He took off his hat. "Only to come back."

"Did you find work?"

"Not yet. The postmaster told me about a tract of land that is scheduled to be opened up for homesteading on the first of September, and I decided to go up and take a look while I had the time."

"Up?"

"About a hundred miles north of here, not far from where Nebraska and South Dakota come together."

She raised her eyebrows and smiled. "Far enough away from here."

"That thought occurred to me."

"I hope it's good land."

"It's hard to say until I've seen it. Even at that, it might not look the same way every year. I've heard of people coming out after a season of good rainfall, seeing the grass growing up to their stirrups, and thinking they found paradise. A year or two later, the grass isn't an inch tall."

"But the land is still good, if it grows grass."

"Yes. You just need a lot of it to raise livestock. To tell you the truth, I'm not interested in becoming a wheat farmer anyway."

She gave him a skeptical look. "Do you expect to accumulate

land like some of the people around here do?"

"I have to admit I don't have a definite plan. I want to have my own land. That's a basic idea. I want to see what it's like to be independent, or self-reliant, to use a popular term. If I can acquire more land, you can bet I want to do it in an honest way. If I have to work for someone else, I'll still have my own place. Call it an experiment in living if you'd like."

She waved her arm outward. "It all is. And, of course, that's a great part of the reason I came out here. I just didn't know what I was getting into with my relatives. By the way, you heard of the terrible thing that happened, didn't you?"

"About your cousin Nancy? Yes. I was in town at the time. I am still trying to make sense of it."

Muriel shook her head. "You'd like to think that things like that happen only in the cities. But all it takes is one evil person. Does anyone have an idea of who it might be?"

Hartley moved his head in the negative. "I haven't heard anything definite."

"And it was not so long ago that your young comrade was found. Does anyone have a theory about the two being connected?"

"I haven't heard anything about that, either."

Her gray-green eyes settled on him. "Do you have any ideas yourself?"

As he gazed at her eyes, his foremost idea was that he would like to kiss her, but he kept to her topic. "This is not like the Wild West stories, and it's not like the detective stories. But when one reads the detective stories, he learns not to start with an idea or theory and try to make the evidence fit it."

"Does that mean you don't have an idea, or that you don't want to state one, for fear of prejudicing your own thoughts?"

"Somewhere in between. I hope someone can do something about it, of course. And when I say 'it,' I mean both deaths, though I realize they may be separate."

"You seem somewhat aloof."

He took a breath and exhaled. "I'm rather weary of being badgered by both sides. Miner's minions, as I've thought of them to myself, continue to needle me about fraternizing over this way, while your cousins pester me about my earlier alliance with the cattlemen, as if I had an alliance, and now they say I've brought my trouble with Miner over to them. Then both sides, with little success, try to intimate that I had something to do with Ben Stillwell's death. I'll tell you, these two factions can squabble about property and material goods all they want among themselves, but it's not my fight. I could walk away from the whole mess with very little provocation." He saw her eyes widen. "But I'm not going to. Not yet. I'm coming back to see you, and if nobody has done anything about these . . . crimes, I'm going to nose around some more about that."

"Some more. Does that mean you've done something?"

"Very little, and nothing to speak of at the present. But I don't believe in sitting by and doing nothing. I don't want to get back into another lofty speech about citizenship, so I'll keep my comments on the level of cattle and pumpkins."

Muriel pursed her lips as she nodded.

Hartley said, "You look as if you have something to add."

"I don't want to stoke your fire any more."

He smiled. "Go ahead. Give me something else to brood on during my long ride."

"Arlis said you picked a fight with him and knocked him down."

Hartley laughed. "He was drunk and tripped on his own spurs. And I didn't know which one he was, so it was nothing personal."

She gave a light laugh. "I thought there was more to the story."

145

A slight breeze passed through the yard, moving her dark hair and rippling the light-colored dress.

She said, "I had better not keep you too long. I know you have a long trip ahead of you. Thank you for taking the trouble to come by and see me on the way."

"It's no trouble. This is the one place where I don't have any conflict. Unless someone else comes by, of course." He held out his hand, and she laid her hand upon it. She did not withdraw right away, so he closed his hand and drew her to him. With his other hand holding back the horse, he met her in a kiss.

They released and stood apart.

"I hope you have a good trip," she said. "This horse will take you the whole way?"

"I hope so."

"What's his name?" She reached out to pat the horse on the forelock.

"He didn't come with a name. I've been thinking about calling him Sandy for a while now. I don't know why. He's not the color of sand like your dress is, for example."

She patted the horse's neck. "He doesn't have to be. I think that's a nice name."

"Maybe I'll call him that." He met her eyes and did not want to leave, but he knew he should. "I think I need to get going."

She nodded. "Be careful."

"I will. And I'll see you when I come back."

He led the horse out, checked his cinch, and swung aboard. As he turned to wave, he had a perfect picture of her standing on the prairie, waving back.

As Hartley soon came to know, he rode through a country of trails. He followed the Texas Cattle Trail, or Texas Trail as the cowpunchers called it, until he reached the North Platte. After spending the night several miles east of Fort Laramie on a grassy spot above the river, he crossed the Oregon Trail and continued to follow the Texas Trail. In the afternoon of the second day, near the Jay Em Ranch, he struck and followed the old Cheyenne-to-Deadwood stage line, which brought him to the Rawhide Buttes. The stage line had varying routes, and here it had gone on both sides of the buttes at one time and another. He kept to the east side. Again he spent the night camped on the landscape, where he watched a flaming orange sunset as it cast shadows on the timbered slopes of Rawhide Mountain, the tree-spotted flanks of two lower grassy buttes, and the bare, faceted surface of a butte composed of rock the color of a light ruby.

In late morning of the third day, he rode into Lusk, a small town that sat next to a trickle called the Niobrara River. When he bought provisions, he learned that the river was once called the Running Water, or L'Eau Qui Court by the French trappers. The town of Lusk had formed where the Running Water Station lay on the stage route. Now it was Lusk, named for a man who settled there. The road that intersected with the stage route, running west from Fort Robinson and on to Orin Junction, Douglas, and Casper, now had its parallel in the form of a railroad. An engine sat chugging in the station, south of the river.

The sound carried to the spot where Hartley sat next to the thin-running Niobrara, a quarter-mile downstream. The Niobrara was more like a slough than a river at this spot, with cottonwoods and alders rising above tules and reeds. As Hartley lunched on the cheese, bread, and canned tomatoes he had just bought, he realized that Lusk would be the base for this part of his journey.

The chugging persisted. The sound brought to mind another machine almost a hundred miles away. Hartley wondered if Al Wisner was back on the job, producing crushed rock for the roadbeds of other trains. Nancy would be buried now, or maybe she was being buried at this moment, with a few people at least to mourn her. In other parts of this vast nation, Hartley reflected, people were dying every minute and being buried every day. Machines carried on, oblivious to any requiem or dirge that was struggling to be heard in a nearby church.

Hartley brushed away the crumbs and led his horse to drink.

At a little after noon, he found the office of a land locator on a side street north of the main crossroads. The office consisted of a room twenty feet square with only a desk and two cane-back chairs. In one of the chairs sat a man with slick, graying hair and a mustache to match. He held an open sardine can near his mouth and was feeding himself. He set down the can, rose from his chair, and offered his hand.

"H.R. Winston. In what way can I help you today?"

"I'm interested in the land that's going to be opened up for homesteading on September first."

"Very good. Lots of people are interested, of course." Winston sat down.

"What I'd like to do is go out and look at the country first, see if it appeals to me."

"Good idea. Doesn't cost a penny. If you like what you see, I can show you a map. You can pick out the parcel you'd like to request, and I recommend having a first, second, and third choice. I'll help you submit, and when you're assigned your claim, I'll help you find the boundaries. That way, you don't make improvements on someone else's claim. Ha-ha."

"I'd like to find two claims together."

"You can have only one for each head of household, you know."

Hartley nodded. "I understand that. I'm looking for another person as well. A friend."

"Fine, fine. Just tell him what I tell you."

"Somewhere there's a charge in here, I'm sure."

"Oh, yes. You pay me the filing fee and the locating fee. Comes to a hundred dollars altogether. Twenty-five now, which is the equivalent of the filing fee, and the rest later."

Hartley was almost rocked back in his boots. "I see."

"Might seem like a lot of money. You could wait for a relinquishment, but it'll cost you about the same."

"How about those who have been here all along?"

"Squatters? They have to legalize their claims, so they have to pay, too. No one gets anything for free. Just seems like it to people who don't know." Winston picked up the can and forked a sardine out of it. When he had the fish down the hatch, he said, "Railroad makes it easy. You can get everything shipped to here—tools, wire, furniture, even a premade piano box shack that you put together yourself. Your minimal shack is ten by twelve, but twelve by twelve is common, and if you go a little nicer you can build a twelve by fourteen or even bigger. You look like the kind of fella who likes to do things himself."

"When I can."

"Well, if your friend's any good, he can help you and you can help him."

Hartley nodded, transforming the image. "So the first thing for me to do is go out and take a look."

"That's right. I'd give myself a day to go there and back. You can go to Hat Creek Station, and they can direct you from there. Remember, of course, that the station is on Sage Creek. There isn't a Hat Creek there. It's just the name of the area. Comes from the original Hat Creek over in Nebraska."

"I see. The area itself where the land is located is called Hat Creek."

"That's right. You should have no problem."

Hartley found the Northern Star Saloon where he had seen it

earlier in the day, on the north side of a cross street. Light was streaming out the open front door on an otherwise dark street that dead-ended two blocks away on the west side of town. He went in and ordered a whiskey.

Having put up his horse at the livery stable and having had a bath and a meal at the Silver Bell boardinghouse, he thought he might pick up a little more information about the area. Therefore, he showed interest when a man stood next to him and struck up a conversation.

The man was of middle height, perhaps fifty years old, with a streaked face and a beard running to gray. He had a swayback and a corresponding belly, clothes that were neither new nor clean, and a sweat-stained hat. He began by asking Hartley where he was headed and what his interests were, and when he found out, he began to talk.

His name was Jack Clell. He knew the country. The Hat Creek area was a good one. Not like it used to be, when the stage line first ran through here. Indians burned the first Hat Creek station right after it was built. They attacked the stages and freight wagons. And road agents? Clell made a fluttering blubbering sound with his lips. They robbed and killed. People still talked about Stuttering Brown, the driver who was shot up one night and taken to Hat Creek Station and died before he could tell the superintendent who killed him. Some said Indians, but Indians don't attack at night, and Persimmon Bill had a grudge against him. Bill was well known for stealing horses and mules, and he had killed an army officer.

Talk about Indians. There's the story of Rawhide. Back in the early days, a fellow in a wagon train bragged that he was going to shoot the first Indian he saw, and he did. An Indian girl. Her people went on the warpath, threatened to massacre the whole wagon train, until they handed him over. The Indians skinned him alive. That's the story.

Back to homesteading. That's for people who can still do it. Takes a lot of work. Five years to prove up. Half the people don't make it. And a man's got to look out for sharpsters, like land locators. That's for people who come from the city and don't know the first thing. A man can do it through the land office. It's in Cheyenne, but it doesn't charge what these parasites do.

If a man wants to find work, that's another thing. The big outfits have steady work for a season. There's the Converse, the Seventy-Seven, the Double L—one of the biggest is the Node Ranch, but that's a little farther away from you. Node. The original brand was a knot. There's all kinds of brands, but a man learns to read them.

Clell might have talked until midnight, but he paused at the sound of a fiddle being tuned up. He took a slow turn, as he had just ordered another drink and was taking care not to spill any.

Two musicians stood against the east wall of the saloon. They looked like brothers, both in middle age with thinning hair and full waistlines. They wore white shirts and dark green vests. One held a fiddle, and the other had a mandolin like Muriel's.

"Oh, good," said Clell. "They'll play 'Cowboy Jack.' That's my name, Jack, and whenever they see me, they play that song." Clell raised his voice and said, "Hey, boys. Good to see you in town again. You know what your first request is." Clell turned to Hartley and said, "They're good."

Hartley could not disagree. The duo launched into a series of traditional ballads and love songs, including "Cowboy Jack." Most of them were sad and sentimental but done in a consistent style, at once stately and wistful. After half a dozen songs, the mandolin player said, "Thanks so much for your appreciation, folks. We all love these songs. And every once in a while, we try to slip in a tune we worked up ourselves. Here's one now. We call it 'Great Lonesome.' The hardest part for me is remembering all the words. It's kind of long, but it goes like this."

On the great lonesome plains of Wyoming
Where the winters last six months or more,
In a grave that is marked with wild roses
Lies a cowboy who died with his horse.

From the easy green pastures of summer
To the snow-crusted hard winter range,
With a horse and a song for companions,
Rode a puncher named Johnny Moraine.

In the country out north of Van Tassell
Lived a ranch girl that Johnny knew well.
She was sweet as cold water in August,
The raven-haired Josie O'Dell.

It was thirteen long miles from the bunkhouse
To the homestead where Josie's light burned.
Leaving early on cold winter Sundays,
By moonlight he made his return.

On a cold day in middle December,
For winter came early that fall,
He picked out his best red bandana
And took his wool chaps from the wall.

With the lariat of rawhide he'd braided,
And a hatband of horsehair he wove,
He whistled a tune to the buckskin
As out of the ranch yard he rode.

At a frost-covered pane in the bunkhouse
Stood a man who had hate in his heart.
He scratched with his thumb for a peephole
As he watched the young cowboy depart.

How deep runs the malice in some men
Over things that will never be theirs,
For this puncher he had a sick fancy
For the girl with the raven-dark hair.

The musicians went into an instrumental interlude. Clell turned to Hartley and said, "This is a good song. I've heard them play it a few times before."

The interlude came to its end, and the mandolin player resumed singing.

When Johnny left Josie's that evening
As the moon was beginning to rise
And reflected on snow that had fallen,
He could see all the stars in the sky.

He found the trail easy to follow
For the night was as clear as the day,
So his thoughts drifted back to the ranch house
As homeward he traveled his way.

He went down through a draw where he startled
An owl from its perch in a tree,
With the branches so stark in the moonlight
Every twig and small fork he could see.

Through the cold, thin air of the rangeland

Came the blast of a gun loud and clear.
As the buckskin horse shuddered and crumpled,
The rider jumped into the clear.

But a second shot ripped from the rifle,
Sending Johnny facedown in the snow.
Then the silence returned as the moonlight
Spread over the still forms below.

In the morning the other hands found him,
With his angora chaps stained in red,
And his arm draped over the buckskin
On a blanket of snow for their bed.

Well, the puncher named Cline was among them
When they brought Johnny back to the Node.
And they buried him there on a hillside
Overlooking the range that he rode.

Now the killer could not dare to court her,
For he lived every day with his fear,
While she planted wild roses on the hillside
And watered them all through the year.

And he might have gone on for a long while,
As he peeped out at life through the pane,
But a rider came down from Montana,
And he said that his name was Moraine.

And in less than a week from a trestle
Overlooking an old silver mine

At the end of a rope was found dangling
The remains of a puncher named Cline.

Then the brother went back to Montana,
And Josie at length settled down
With a rancher not far from Van Tassell
And the grave where they laid Johnny down.

Now they say on a clear night in winter
When the moonlight shines down with its glow,
There's a spirit comes drifting in silence
Wearing chaps that are white as the snow.

When the applause died down, Hartley tossed off the last of his drink. He shook Clell's hand and said, "I've got a long ride ahead of me tomorrow, so I had better turn in. Thanks for all your information."

"Glad to help you, boy. I hope you like this country well enough to settle here. I knowed her when she was young. We don't have the dangers we did then, but you still want to keep an eye on your backtrail."

"Good advice. Thanks."

The sun was rising when Hartley rode north out of Lusk. The road climbed onto higher ground right away, and within a short while he found himself in rolling grassland, with vast, treeless sweeps to the east and higher hills to the west. He followed the old stage route, well worn in the grass and sage, for about ten miles north and a little east. As he expected, he came to a pine ridge that ran east and west, and the trail led uphill. He was going into the Hat Creek Breaks.

The pine trees became thicker as the trail wound its way through sandstone and hard clay. A deer jumped up on his left, crossed the trail ahead of him, and paused in the next stand of pines.

He rode for about two miles across the ridge, or breaks as they were called, finding more pines on the north side than on the south, and greener slopes when he caught glimpses of the side of the ridge as it angled east. As the trail descended, it had frequent sharp, deep ruts, the product of recent thunderstorms.

He came out of the trees onto high, grassy hills. The road was still rutted, but the grass was drier than on the higher slopes or in the basin below.

A wide area, some ten or twelve miles to the north and perhaps fifteen miles wide, lay before him, bordered on the west and north by ridges. A long row of dark trees in the eastern half of the area ran toward the north and marked a watercourse. A shorter row, closer in below him, showed the tops of cottonwoods.

He arrived at a green, grassy draw with healthy box elder trees. It curved around to meet a creek, which had the cottonwoods he had seen as well as more box elders. He assumed this was Sage Creek, for when he crossed it and rode onto higher ground, Hat Creek Station came into view on the west of the road.

He could see at a glance that the station was still a vital place, with a two-story log building, low stables, and other outbuildings. The surrounding grass was grazed off but green, and an apple tree on the east side had a few green apples an inch in diameter.

Inside, he saw that the station consisted of a store, a post office, an eating place, and lodging. The aroma of fresh-baked bread drifted in the air. A man about forty, who wore a sweat-stained gray hat and looked as if he worked outside, said the owner and his wife, Mr. and Mrs. Falconer, had gone on a trip, but all services were available, including the blacksmith shop.

Hartley stated his purpose of looking over possible land claims. The man told him about some of the local landmarks and how to find the main trail that would take him east to Indian Creek and beyond. Hartley thanked the man, resisted the temptation to buy a fresh loaf of bread, and walked out into the warm morning. He could feel the humidity from the green undergrowth around the station, and he saw further evidence when he slapped a deer fly on Sandy's shoulder. He checked his cinch, mounted up, and headed for drier ground.

The trail took him through good grassland with here and there a mudhole or a small marshy area. This region in general, the edge of the western plains, was semiarid, and he was always struck by the frequency with which he saw standing water. Nevertheless, very few claims would have water, for most of the water sources were already staked out by people who had settled earlier. At one point he saw a small body of water, blue in the distance, that turned out to be a small reservoir on a fenced section. The nearby ranch building came into view as the intervening low hill receded.

Toward the eastern edge of the basin, he came upon a large draw, green in the bottom, with a grove of cottonwoods. Half the trees were dead, and others had dead branches. He crossed the draw and followed the trail as the land began to rise. He dipped into a small green valley with a marsh and pond, again fenced, with a house and barn tucked into a hillside on the upper end of the section. A buck and a doe antelope, well fed, sprang up from a swell in the land and trotted away.

Hartley turned around and rode back on the trail he had just followed. He found it interesting to see the country from the other direction, and he recalled Clell's advice to watch his backtrail. He hadn't looked back very much today, and he made a mental note to remember to do so. Not only would he look out for modern-day versions of Indians and Persimmon Bill, but he would learn the country better.

As he saw it now, it seemed rather even with good grass and occasional water. Bordered on three sides, it was isolated from the rest of the world, a great lonesome range of its own. He imagined it in winter, with a foot or more of snow on the ground, packed hard by merciless winds. Seeing this area on a sunny summer day was similar to seeing a region in a year when the grass grew up to the stirrups.

As he rode west, a couple of large rock formations came into view beyond the place where he had ridden through the breaks. One of them had the shape of a hat with a crease in the crown. Now that he thought of it, the man at Hat Creek Station had made a reference in passing to a location that sounded like Hat Rock. The landmark rose up from the lower, bare slopes of the breaks, and it was visible from at least ten miles. Had he watched his backtrail, he would have seen it earlier.

He stopped at a water hole to let Sandy drink. As he waited, he began to think about his return to Lusk. The distance from Running Water Station to Hat Creek Station had been quoted to him more than once as fourteen miles, and he had ridden at least another ten. The two miles or so crossing the breaks were the hardest, and they would come late in the day for Sandy. Even if he made it to Lusk tonight, he would have two long days of travel after that.

Rawhide Station, as he recalled, was sixteen miles from Running Water Station. He did not have to stay in Lusk. He could camp somewhere on this side of the breaks and try to reach the Rawhide Buttes by late afternoon of the next day. But he did not care to stay at Hat Creek Station. A room would cost money, and if he slept out, the mosquitoes would torment him. He decided to camp about a mile on this side of Hat Creek Station, water his horse well at Sage Creek, cross the breaks in the morning, and try to make it to the Rawhide Buttes in good time tomorrow.

Hartley acquired a new view of the Rawhide Buttes as he approached them from the north. Visible from fifteen miles away, or even farther when he had first seen them from the south, they resembled a small mountain range. Big Rawhide Butte was also called Rawhide Mountain, and so it seemed as he saw it again, dark and forested in the late afternoon shade. The round, bald butte that had looked like a pink rock a few evenings earlier again had the hue of watery red wine.

Hartley awoke with the dawn. He realized he had been half-dreaming about his ill-fated affair in Ohio. As he often did, in order to dispel the thoughts, he told himself that it was all for the best that it ended when it did. It dragged on long enough, and as he looked back, he could see that the uncertainty and the anxiety occupied much more of his life than the soaring moments did.

He rolled out of his blankets and sat up. As he did so, a huffing sound carried across the sage and grass. A hundred yards away, a buck antelope with midsized horns, and the usual tan and white body muted in color in the crepuscular light, stood looking at him straight on. Hartley stirred, and the animal huffed again. It cut to the left, ran twenty yards, and stopped. It turned around and ran back. Whoofing one last time, it took off on a straight line toward the buttes.

On the trail again, an hour later in the morning, Hartley remembered to look back. The bald butte had changed color. Where the morning sun struck it on the eastern side, dirt and dry vegetation showed. The small basin, a mile and a half by two miles, had an even tone of green, as the rangeland in Decker Basin had appeared about three weeks earlier. Counting as he returned his attention to the trail, he figured he had two days of travel ahead of him. By the time he returned, he would be gone a week.

CHAPTER ELEVEN

Sagebrush that did not reach the stirrups was casting three-foot shadows as Hartley followed the last half-mile of trail to the small house where Muriel lived. The sorrel horse, Sandy, was holding up all right and seemed to have perked up a little as the air cooled in the evening.

Muriel was standing in front of the shack as Hartley rode up to the yard and dismounted. He took a few steps to regain his ground legs after the long ride. He realized that he hadn't stepped down from the saddle since the crossroads that led to Winsome, almost four hours earlier. He took off his hat and swept it around to his left side.

"Welcome back," she said.

"Thank you. It was a long trip, but once it's over, it seems as if it didn't happen at all. Or if it did, it was all in a long moment that's a bubble now."

"I know what you mean. I went from Columbia to Fort Smith one time, and I had that feeling when I stood in my own house once again." Her gray-green eyes met his. "Tell me about your trip."

"Well, I saw a lot of country. It changes a little as you go along, but it's similar—grass and sage, plains and buttes. The area I went to see is like a world apart, though it's still a broad grassland. You'll see what I mean if you go there."

"As a tourist?"

He laughed. "I looked into claiming land, of course. To begin with, I met a land locator. He helps folks with making sure the details are all correct."

"Paperwork."

"That's the term I heard used. He will locate the claim and file for the land if I want to pay him to do it. In case I do, I expressed interest in two claims, side by side. I'm going to try to do it all myself, but I have to know how to avoid mistakes, both in the paperwork and in the locating. As he pointed out, you don't want to put your improvements on someone else's claim, and as it occurs to me, you don't want to leave yours open to being contested. I have to go to the land office and pick out land that hasn't been filed on yet, and then I have to make sure I settle there. I would pay the filing fee myself. For each claim, I would save the locating fee, which is seventy-five dollars, in addition to the extra seven dollars he adds to the filing fee. He didn't tell me that detail, but I found it out."

"I worry about the money."

"So do I. I had a modest sum in the bank when I came out here, and I've put a little by from what I've made in wages, but it goes fast."

"I've got a little, also," she said. "I haven't let my cousins know how much, or they would try to wheedle it out of me."

"How many of them are married?"

"Just Arlis. Brant and Crisp would marry immigrants if they could, to milk cows and plant spuds."

"By immigrants you mean—"

"Swedes or Norwegians or Russians. Foreigners, but white. These cousins could go back to Missouri to look for a wife, but most of those girls are set in their ways and don't want to leave their families. Or if they do, they won't like it here, like Betty."

"I thought you mentioned before that at least one of them had the idea of joining estates with you."

"That would be Mr. Treece. He has the strongest aspirations

to be a kissing cousin. I think he has let the others know that, and so they think along other lines. I try not to judge them or the women they end up with. Everyone has a right to be happy. But I feel sorry for a girl who feels she has to get married because her family's farm can support only so many, or because she doesn't want to live like a servant beneath her parents' roof. Some of these girls work in the fields like men, while others cook and churn and scrub from daylight to dark. And milk the cows."

"I haven't seen many families like that around here."

"I went and looked into settling on land in Nebraska before I came here. All the free land is taken up there and has been for a while. The families have been there long enough that now they have grown-up daughters."

"As the land locator told me, none of the land is really free. It all costs something."

"I believe that. And from what I've seen, there's a price taken from the human spirit as well."

"Yet you're willing to try it."

"Oh, yes. A person just has to be on the lookout to avoid going into bondage. That whole idea of raising a passel of children, as they say, so that enough will survive to work on the farm and take care of the parents in old age."

Hartley drew his brows together. "Are you opposed to having children, then?"

"No, not at all. Just not interested in having a passel. And until I turn thirty, I'm not in a hurry at all."

"Oh, that must be a long ways off."

"You didn't lose any of your gallantry on your trip."

"Forsooth. It was augmented by your absence."

Muriel glanced over her shoulder to the east. "You might want to put your hat on. That looks like two of them right now."

Hartley put on his hat and observed two light-featured riders he could identify as Hudsons. As usual, they wore dark hats and dark vests, but on this occasion, they rode a gray horse and a deep brown one.

"Which two are they?"

"I can't tell until they're closer."

Harley waited with Muriel without speaking as the two riders approached.

"It's Crisp and Brant," she said. "Crisp is on the gray horse on the left."

The Hudsons rode in with a cloud of dust and piled off their horses. They still looked identical to Hartley, with their whitish-blond hair, narrow noses, and close-set blue eyes. Crisp swaggered ahead of his brother, with the gray horse trailing by the full length of the reins.

"Looka here," he said. "We're gittin' sick an' tard of seein' you around." He peered at his cousin. "And Muriel, it's yer fault as much as his."

She maintained a calm demeanor as she held her head up and said, "Crisp, I'm a grown woman, free and white, and you're not going to tell me how to live my life."

A drumming of hooves sounded from the north side of the house. The Hudsons paid no attention, but Muriel and Hartley did. Within a minute, Treece appeared on a stout dark horse that gave out heavy breaths as it jolted to a stop. Treece swung down from his horse, dropped the reins, and strode up to the group. He took off his brown leather gloves and slapped them in his left palm. Glaring at Hartley, he cut the air with his voice.

"What the hell are you doing here?"

"There's a lady present," said Muriel.

Treece did not look her way. "Keep out of this. I asked him a question."

Hartley frowned. "What do you think? I came to pay a visit. Does it look like I'm selling sewing machines?"

"Maybe you should. Far away. No one wants you here." Treece turned to Muriel. "And you," he said. "You should leave outsiders alone. Stick with your kin like we were all taught."

In her even voice, Muriel said, "We grew up in different households and went to different schools. No one owns me."

Treece narrowed his eyes so that they looked like pig eyes. "We stick together as a family, and we work together for a common good. Me an' these boys work fourteen hours a day so we can get somewhere."

"I'm not opposed to work," she said, "but I'm not going to grub and bicker just to add to your material gain. I've seen how you do things."

"You haven't seen much. You sit here readin' a book while we're out workin' like—"

Hartley thought Treece did not finish the sentence because he had already been chided for his language use.

"You're not going to run my life," said Muriel. "I'm not going to be used."

Treece scowled. He turned to Hartley again. "It's bad enough that you can't hold down a job. But you come around here, where you're not needed, and you put ideas into her head. She didn't go against us like this until she listened to you."

"That's hogwash," said Muriel.

"Hold your tongue. I'm talkin' to him." Treece's eyes went flinty as he focused on Hartley. "Deep down, you're still one of them. You won't work in the wheat. You want to ride a horse. Sit on your britches and watch cattle graze. I wouldn't be surprised if you were over here as a spy."

"I worked for one of your neighbors for a week. Name of Eldredge."

Treece's face stiffened. He put his gloves in his hip pocket.

Hartley continued. "The last time you complained to me, you said I was bringing trouble because the cattlemen resented me. Now you say it's because I'm still one of them. Which is it?"

"Both."

"You don't make any more sense than your cousin did the day he tripped over his spurs."

Crisp's voice broke in. "Look here, mister, I was there, and I'm witness to the fact that you started that fight and then pushed him down."

"He pushed me, and I pushed back."

Crisp sniffed and said, "Everyone says trouble follows you around, and they're right."

"Is that why you're here today?"

Treece held his hand straight out with his palm toward Crisp, as if to push him back. He leveled his sullen gaze on Hartley, and his heavy lips moved. "You should have stayed gone. No one would miss you if you left now."

Hartley took a deep breath and did not answer.

Treece stepped forward. His nose was less than two feet from Hartley's. His large hands made a brief, almost imperceptible movement, and Hartley thought the man was going to push him or grab him. But the moment passed. Treece said, "I'm telling you for your own good. We don't want you here."

Hartley closed his hands to still the faint trembling he felt. He did not know whether Treece saw the movement, but the big man stood back.

Hartley glanced to the left. Muriel was taking in the scene with full attention. To his right, Crisp and Brant were peering in the odd Hudson way that suggested a need for eyeglasses.

Treece spoke to Muriel. "We're not done talkin' about this."

"We are today," she answered. "You might as well leave. I've invited him to stay for supper."

"This is not your place, Muriel."

"Then throw me off." She directed her attention to Crisp

and Brant. "Have you boys anything to say?"

"Not now," said Crisp. He and his brother led their horses around to face east. As they made ready to mount up, Treece followed them.

A minute later, the three horses were leaving in a fast walk that raised little puffs of dust.

Muriel smiled to Hartley. "Tell me more about your trip."

"I think I told you most of it. I did hear an interesting song while I was in Lusk. It was called 'Great Lonesome.' "

"Maybe you can sing it."

"Oh, it's too long. It must have twenty verses. I might be able to bring back the first one. Were you serious about supper?"

"Yes, I was. My only fib was in saying I had already invited you. But I was planning to. I hope you don't mind mutton stew."

"Not at all. Do the Hudsons provide you with meat?"

"Not much. I buy some food items from the neighbors over there." She pointed to the south. "Meat, potatoes, onions, and the like. By the way, they have cut all their wheat."

"Do they come around and keep an eye on you as well?"

She pursed her lips in a playful expression. "No. They mind their own business, and they come around only in the daytime."

CHAPTER TWELVE

Hartley and Muriel sat in the shade on the west side of the little house, drinking coffee in the cool of the morning. He had thought he should leave at dawn, but she convinced him to stay for breakfast. The cookstove heated up the interior of the shack, and now that they sat outside, he felt in no hurry to go anywhere.

"Do you enjoy the quietness?" he asked.

"Quite a bit. At first, after I lived here a while, I thought something was missing, but then I became accustomed to the scarcity of sound. There's a bird now. That's a meadowlark, isn't it?"

The five silver notes died away.

"Yes, it is," he said. "Beautiful sound."

"I hate to think it, but some day there will be farm machines coming right up to the door, making their beastly noises."

"And automobiles."

"They're not so bad. The noise isn't deafening. And they do good on a daily basis. For example, if a woman goes into labor, someone can take her into the doctor."

"That's a thought. I believe that in some places, doctors are already making calls in their horseless carriages." A thought passed through his mind. "By the way, I don't know what made me think of this, but when I was up north, I heard of a ranch called the Node. It was in the song, too. For the brand, or symbol, the ranch has a knot, like in a rope. But I think it also means a connecting point, as when a leaf joins a stem."

"I believe I've heard that, too. Also, there are such things as lymph nodes. I think I've heard them called lymph glands more often. They're those things that are found up in here." She pushed with her fingertip underneath the corner of her jaw. "Sometimes they swell up on a person."

"Ah, yes. That was the other use I had heard. I couldn't place it."

The long snuffle of a horse came from behind the shack.

Hartley stood up and drew his brows together. "Sandy does that when there's another horse around." Hartley had an image of his horse tied with a picket rope while his saddle, duffel bag, and bedroll were stacked against the back of the little building. Those details could tell on him.

He stood up to see if he could spot a horse and rider. Rising dust and a moving object caught his attention from the west. A buggy drawn by a single trotting horse was wheeling along, churning up a low cloud of dust. With no trees or bushes intervening, Hartley had a clear view of the vehicle as it approached the homestead. The details of the buggy and the horse did not interest him as much as the person driving.

A man in a gray suit sat perched on the seat. He was wearing dark leather goggles and a white straw hat with a black leather hatband, the kind called a boater, which men in Ohio wore on Sundays for picnics and lawn parties. Hartley had a hunch who it was. When the man stopped and took off the goggles and hat, he revealed the features of Ned Farnsworth. He rubbed at his eyes with a white handkerchief and put on his spectacles.

Hartley and Muriel stood together in front of the shanty. When Ned had put himself together and had smiled at Muriel, Hartley spoke. "Top of the mornin', Ned. What brings you out here?"

Ned had a serious tone to his voice. "There's quite a stir in town, Reese. People have been looking for you. Good morning,

Miz Dulse."

"Good morning."

Hartley said, "Huh. I've been out of the area. I went up north to look at the land you told me about, and I just returned last night. How does anyone even know I'm back?"

"I believe it came from Doyle Treece. He came into town this morning to start up the rock crusher. When the marshal was asking around for you, Doyle said he saw you yesterday afternoon or evening."

"Well, he's full of information, isn't he? What does the marshal want to see me about?"

Ned held his blue eyes steady. "Buck Whittaker was found dead this morning."

All of the cheer went out of the morning as Hartley felt a sinking weight inside. "Where did they find him?"

"At Earl Miner's little sawmill."

Hartley pictured the scene as he had last observed it—quiet and abandoned, almost haunting. "And the marshal thinks I had a hand in it?"

"I can't say what he thinks. But he has questions."

"I appreciate you taking all the trouble to come and tell me."

"I thought you should know."

Hartley took a deep breath and exhaled, then turned to Muriel. "It looks as if I had better go to town. There's no ground for suspicion, of course, as far as I'm concerned, but I can clear it up better this way."

She nodded. "If you don't mind, I'd like to go, too," She smiled at Ned. "Do you think I could ride with you, Mr. Farnsworth?"

Ned blinked. "I don't see why not."

"I won't be a minute," she said. "I need to put these things away."

As she gathered the cups and chairs, Hartley spoke to Ned.

"Thanks for letting her ride with you. And thanks for letting me know about this . . . development. It's got me puzzled, not to mention worried."

Ned gave a perfunctory smile. "Happy to be of help." He bent his attention to adjusting the strap on his goggles.

Hartley recalled that the evening before, he had felt a small displeasure, or irritation, at the thought of Ned gossiping about him, as in the case of his not wanting to work in the wheat harvest. But now he appreciated Ned's good intentions, and he thought that the postmaster would be safe company with Muriel. He said, "I'll be right along. I need to get my horse ready. I'll probably end up ahead of you by cutting across country, so don't worry if you don't see me."

Ned looked up and smiled. "That's fine, Reese. And good luck."

Sandy stood on his own shadow when Hartley tied up in front of the barbershop. A crowd was beginning to form in front of the post office next door. The marshal was standing apart, wearing his black hat, gray vest, and badge. Hartley walked up to him.

"I understand you wanted to talk to me."

The marshal's voice sounded even deeper than usual. "Gonna have a town meeting in a little while. We'll ask our questions then."

"All right." Hartley decided to stand at the edge of the crowd, halfway back. He felt several eyes on him, and he tried not to avoid people he knew, even if he thought they were prejudiced against him by now. He saw Dick Prentiss and Tobe Lestman, and he recalled seeing the two of them together at Muriel's place. He saw Fred the bartender, red-faced and without a hat, perhaps ready to testify about the small altercation between Hartley and Whittaker. Earl Miner appeared in the company of

Mike Ackerman and Bess. As they took their places with Bess between the two men, Miner laid his hand against Bess's back in a protective pose. Mike Ackerman maintained a posture of dignity, with the help of a black walking stick with a brass knob. Other townsfolk stood with patient expressions in the bright sun—the owner of the general store, the barber, the proprietor of the Owl Café, two women wearing aprons and carrying umbrellas for shade, and Ed Becker, the livery stable man. Al Wisner and Cletis, looking solemn and hangdog, sidled up to the front of the crowd not far from the marshal.

Movement caught Hartley's eye. The buggy carrying Ned Farnsworth and Muriel rolled up to the north side of the crowd. Hartley was sure he had passed them up when he cut across country, but they hadn't lagged. Ed Becker hurried over. After helping the occupants climb down, he led the horse and buggy to the stable down the street. Hartley caught Muriel's eye and smiled as she and Ned took a place not far from the marshal.

Hartley wondered if the marshal was waiting for someone. An answer presented itself when Doyle Treece and the three Hudson brothers came marching four abreast from the direction of the Argyle Hotel and the rock crusher beyond it. When they joined the crowd, the marshal spoke in a loud voice.

"Thanks for shutting down that machine so we can have our meeting. I think we can start now."

He took his place in front of the crowd and cleared his throat to the side. Holding his hands up at shoulder level, he began. "Folks, I thank you for taking the time, and dinner time at that, to come together. As I think you know, this is the third incident of this nature in less than three weeks, and we need to find answers. I'm goin' to begin with a statement of the case, and then I'll be willing to hear anything that anybody has to offer—within reason, of course."

He waited for a murmur to run through the crowd, and he

resumed. "As most if not all of you know, a man was found dead here in town this morning. His name was Buck Whittaker, and he worked for Earl Miner, first as a ranch hand and more recently at an interest that Mr. Miner has here in town. A little sawmill. That's where his body was found. He appears to have died from a blow to the back of the head."

Hartley winced as others in the crowd made comments among them.

"Now the question before us is this. Who would have a reason to do this, and does it have anything to do with either of these other two crimes? I'd like to hear first from Al Wisner."

Dick Prentiss interrupted. "Let's not put the cart before the horse. I want to know if anyone had a grudge against him."

Hartley felt an uneasiness spread through his body as his heartbeat picked up.

"I was going to come to that," said the marshal. "But we can ask that now. Fred, can you step up here and speak loud enough for everyone to hear?"

The short man with a low hairline and a red face took his place next to the marshal. "For those who don't know, I'm the bartender at the Strong Water Saloon. Mr. Whittaker came in just about every night since he started working in town."

Hartley caught a glance of Earl Miner, whose face wore an imperturbable expression.

Fred continued. "Some nights, he had quite a few, and he got kinda sarcastic. But the only time I saw him have it out with someone was a little over a week ago, when he got into a shoving match with Reese Hartley."

A muttering went through the crowd, and the marshal held up his hand. "All right. Let's hear from Mr. Hartley."

A movement from the back of the crowd distracted Hartley. A tall man with no hat had joined the group at some point.

Hartley blinked. He thought Blue had left town, but here he was.

Hartley shook his head to bring himself back to the moment. His mouth was dry, and he had a strange, detached sensation, but he found his voice. "That little scuffle wasn't anything. Buck Whittaker was drunk, and he was picking an argument with this man here, Mr. Blue."

A collective breath and rustle of bodies went through the crowd as heads turned. Hartley saw Muriel's face cloud up, and when the rest of the crowd came back to him, he resumed.

"I stepped between them to prevent anything further from happening. I didn't even shove him. I blocked him, and he fell down. If there was anything resembling a grudge, it was on his part. He said he wouldn't forget something like that. But I would imagine he saw things in a better light the next day. After all, we were friends of sorts. You can ask Tobe Lestman there. We worked together, and later, I helped them find Ben Stillwell. The last time I saw Tobe and Buck together, we were on friendly terms and had a drink together."

The marshal tipped his head from one side to the other. "This isn't all that uncommon, to have two different stories about a disagreement in a saloon."

Hartley said, "But I was gone for a week. I just came back yesterday evening, and I didn't come to town."

The marshal drew himself up with a breath. "Well, he was found at dawn. Lookin' at it from a practical point of view, you could have ridden in from your camp and gotten back to there by daybreak. It's possible."

"But I didn't."

"I'm saying you could."

Hartley held his tongue, not sure how to answer without saying the same thing. His pulse jumped when Muriel stepped to the front of the crowd. Mike Ackerman, who had been stealing glances, looked her up and down. A murmur went through the crowd and died.

Muriel's voice was clear and steady. "This may not reflect well on me, but I can tell you that Mr. Hartley did not ride into town. He came straight to my place when he returned from his trip, and he spent the night with me."

Pandemonium went through the crowd. Hartley watched and listened as townspeople chattered and exclaimed to one another, telling who Muriel was and what relation she bore to Hartley, Treece, and the Hudsons. Mike Ackerman's mouth hung open, Dick Prentiss was fuming, and Treece and the Hudsons were ranting among themselves. Earl Miner held his chin up in an attitude of dignity. Ned Farnsworth kept a calm, nonjudgmental expression as he did when he arrived at the homestead and found Muriel and Hartley in a tête-à-tête.

When the hubbub died down, the marshal spoke. "Well, I think we'll leave that line of questioning as it is for now."

"Excuse me, marshal," came a voice from the back of the crowd. Blue was raising his hand. "I'd like to offer an impression if I could."

"Well, I suppose so." As Blue began to make his way to the front of the crowd, the marshal said, "Does your impression of the scuffle in the saloon correspond to what Hartley has said?"

Blue waved his hand. "Oh, yes. I don't have much to say about that. He told it the way it happened. What I'd like to add right now is a few words about Mr. Hartley himself."

Blue paused for a couple of seconds, but not long enough for anyone to cut him off. Hartley thought that Blue was going to return the favor of putting in a good word, so he waited with optimism.

"You see, I have found out that Mr. Hartley, prior to coming here, had a failed affair of the heart back in Ohio with a woman who told him she would leave her husband but couldn't do it when it came to the crunch."

Hartley was stunned. All the time he was trying to help Blue and be fair, the man was gathering information on him, first here in town and then in Ohio. Hartley felt a compulsion to say that Blue was telling a slanted version, but he thought he could make things worse by talking about them longer, so he kept his silence.

Mike Ackerman spoke up. "See here, man. I don't know why you're taking the trouble, and the time, to tell this. A man's business is his own, especially when it's in the past and far away."

Blue gave a light shrug. "I mention it because the marshal said he would like to hear anything pertinent. And I think this sheds light on this man's moral character."

Hartley was sure that what the man wanted to do was discredit him with Muriel. He must have followed Muriel here, and he must have known Hartley had an interest in her. He would have understood Whittaker's slur about Muriel. And he took the trouble either to go to Ohio or to inquire by telegram from a place like Cheyenne, to find something unfavorable to disclose.

Muriel, who had stepped back to stand by Ned Farnsworth, now took a step forward. Her eyes were afire, and her voice cut like a razor. "You have nothing to gain by this. Nothing. You're going to a great deal of effort to be peevish and to make others look bad. You should have accepted long ago that things were over between you and me, but you pursue me and spy on me and spy on someone who takes an interest in me. This is cheap and perverse." She scanned the crowd. "And for anyone who is interested, his name is not 'Mr. Blue.' Not that his real name has any fame or infamy."

Blue shrugged. "I understand that people sometimes take a new name when they come west. Mine is Blue, but I don't have any criminal past to hide."

"Neither do I," said Muriel, "and please do not imply that I do. Or anyone else present, unless you have proof."

Dick Prentiss shouted, "Why don't you go back to where you came from?"

"Why don't you?" Blue snapped.

"Moocher!" came a voice from the crowd.

Mike Ackerman held his black walking stick by the brass knob as he rapped the stick on the hard ground. "Here, here," he called out. "This whole meeting has degenerated into . . . defamation and sarcasm. I don't care what your name is, Blue, but you're not doing any good. Marshal?"

The lawman had an unhappy look on his face, and Hartley thought he was at a loss for a way to bring the meeting back around to his purpose.

The marshal said, "I agree. This thing has fallen apart. If anyone has information to offer, and I do mean something pertinent, he can talk to me by myself. Thanks to everyone for comin'."

As the crowd began to drift away, Hartley caught Muriel's eyes from across the distance. Ned Farnsworth made himself scarce by heading for the post office door and unlocking it.

Hartley walked toward Muriel, not sure what to expect. "Should we talk?"

"I shouldn't have come," she said. "I had no idea that odious person was anywhere near here. Can you take me home?"

"I could ask Ned for the loan of his buggy. But I think we should talk."

"Oh, yes. As soon as we're out on the prairie again. I could scream."

"It won't do any good. And you might alarm someone."

"I know."

"I'll see about the buggy." Hartley thought, this was no time to worry about who told Blue what town in Ohio he had come from. The damage was done.

The brown horse pulled the buggy at a fast, even trot and put the town of Jennet behind. Muriel did not seem disposed to talk right away, so Hartley watched the sagebrush and grass roll by. As he looked around him, he had a strange feeling of vulnerability. He recalled the story of Stuttering Brown and Persimmon Bill. Driving a team of four or six horses at night required a great deal of skill, and a man had to have courage to drive through country rife with hostile Indians and cold-blooded road agents.

Those were the tales of almost thirty years earlier. The Indian wars had ended, but crime had not. Men still robbed trains and banks, stabbed each other in drunkenness, clubbed men in the back of the head, and shot other men in the back with cold, clear intent. Pure treachery existed in real life, not just in melodramatic ballads. One of the truths Hartley had acquired in reading was that in spite of advances that civilizations were pleased to credit themselves with, human nature did not change. People repeated the errors of past generations, and they reproduced the deceit and cruelty that had always lived in their blood. The idea gave him a queasy sensation in the middle of his back.

To put his mind on another track, he turned to Muriel, who was still keeping to herself. He said, "I suppose I can tell my story first."

With a faint smile, she said, "That would be fine with me."

He studied the trail ahead for a few seconds, took a full breath, and exhaled. "The episode that this man referred to is the one I mentioned to you a while back."

"I thought it might have been."

"With time, as I look back, I see that it did not last that long.

When I was in the middle of it, of course, it seemed to crawl on forever. As I told you before, it was the first serious relation I was in. I met this woman, and everything became—how shall I say—deep and narrow. Not broad and sunny at all. I didn't care about other people or things, and she didn't seem to, either. Perhaps that's one kind of love, but perhaps it became that way because of the terms she put our situation in." He glanced at the trail ahead. "That doesn't sound clear, even to me. Let me be more specific. She wanted to meet in out-of-the-way places and in nearby towns. She said it was because she was trying to get rid of a man with whom she had broken things off. But I came to learn that she was married. I was stuck deep. I couldn't let go. I was in the dark. Everything was on her side, if you see what I mean. If anyone knew how things sat or what was going to happen, she did. And I'm not sure that even she did."

Muriel said, "That sounds like a bad situation."

"Yes, and I couldn't end things just like that. When I tried—that is, when I told her I thought I should get out—she would ask me to wait a little longer. Things dragged out more. She said she didn't want to give me up. I thought it meant one thing, but I came to understand that it probably meant something else."

"I think you'll have to explain that."

He backed up to go through the idea again. "I thought she meant she didn't want to give me up because she wanted to be with me only, at some point. But after some time, I interpreted that she didn't want to lose me, but she didn't want to commit herself to me, either."

"She wanted it both ways."

"I think so."

"Well, that's not plausible at all."

"Of course not. But I couldn't see it. I was up too close, and in the dark. And I think you might understand how a person is kept there."

Muriel's eyes widened as she nodded.

"In the end, I told myself it didn't matter—that is, how or why she didn't want to give me up—because it was a bad deal from the start, even if I didn't know it sooner, and it was never going to arrive anywhere."

"You must have gotten some distance in order to see that."

"Oh, yes. It took a time of being shut out in the cold." He watched the progress of the brown horse for a couple of seconds. "So, as I told you before, that was one factor that helped me decide to come west and start over."

She nodded again, confirming, he thought, that she remembered.

Feeling as if a weight had been lifted, he said, "Now you know the worst about me."

"If that's as bad as it gets, I don't have much to fear at all."

Hartley did not have an answer. After a moment of hearing nothing but the hooves of the horse and the jostling of the carriage, he said, "This is a nice outfit Ned has. Good of him to lend it to us." He ran his fingers across the leather dashboard. "He must make more as a druggist than as a postmaster, and I don't suppose he was broke when he came here."

"He's a bachelor, isn't he?"

"Um, yes."

"Perhaps he has a nephew or a niece somewhere. Bachelor uncles are known to leave an inheritance."

"That's what they get for not being drawn into desperate love affairs. People who live their lives in turmoil don't sack away as much money," said Hartley. "I was thinking just a little while ago about how people repeat the same errors with each generation. I was thinking about war and crimes, but the same could be said about love."

"Sublunary love," she said.

"We hear stories, and we read stories, and still we go through the ordeals ourselves. Yet the stories sometimes help us understand the messes we find ourselves in. Speaking about myself, you realize."

"Of course." The vehicle rumbled on for a moment. "I suppose it's my turn to tell my story. I'm afraid yours is better— more like a French novel, at least."

He raised his eyebrows in a mild expression, as if to say he didn't know how good that was.

She said, "My story is shorter, or at least this part of it is. I told you the part about my quondam husband."

He laughed. He enjoyed her ability to keep up a light tone when she was about to tell a story that, as she would say, did not reflect well upon her.

After a pause of appropriate length, she continued. "Not long after I became a widow, I met this man who spoke today. He was a smooth talker, and I was what you might call disconsolate—sad and feeling somewhat lost or cut loose from my moorings. Things moved too fast with him, and I had to break things off. I assure you I did not string things along. But he did not give up easily, as you can still see."

Hartley had an uncomfortable feeling in his throat, as if he was choking on the idea that she had something to do with Blue, but he told himself he could not very well hold it against her if he had done something similar. Furthermore, their spending the previous night together was an act of mutual interest and consent.

"And that helped you decide to come west?" he asked.

"Not to the extent that I was running from my problems, as you said about yourself, but I did appreciate the prospect of putting a great deal of distance between us." She looked off to the side at the passing prairie and came back to Hartley. "I don't know how you see things between you and me at this point."

He glanced at her but kept his eye on the brown horse and the road ahead. "Nothing that isn't salvageable," he said. "The way I see it, we're two people, each with our own flaws. Not fatal flaws, but neither of us is perfect. I won't tell you about yourself, but for my part, in addition to having this episode in my past, I have my other imperfections. I don't like to be around very many people, and I tend to dislike them when they take on a group personality, especially in service to some opportunist. I've told you about that. In addition, I have a tendency to think I'm always right. That will come out sooner or later. So I'm not pristine and I'm not perfect, but some of that is the consequence of having made it to thirty. Some of it is my nature. Perhaps when you reach the distant age of thirty, you will see some of this yourself."

She smiled. "It's not so distant, of course, and thank you again for your courtesy. My imperfections, as you call them, may not be the same as yours, but I agree with your general idea of not being pristine or perfect." After a pause, she said, "Still, I think I come out looking worse, insofar as my error has been made public—not that yours hasn't—and because I am a woman."

Hartley shrugged. "I see things as being more equal."

"Just to be clear, you know. I wouldn't want to continue in a situation in which I would be regarded as inferior."

"I wouldn't worry about that," he said. "I'm not going to be guilty of upholding a double standard. And as you know, I don't let others decide for me."

"I've seen that."

He had an awareness of verging upon a bold moment. "You refer to yourself as a modern woman, and I want you to know that I am compatible with that. I will speak with frankness.

After last night, I would be quite a cad if I thought my conduct, past or present, was superior to yours. You haven't done anything that I haven't."

"You seem rather modern yourself."

"Perhaps it's because I've had what might have become superiority or condescension beaten out of me."

"From being in the dark."

He smiled. "It gives the story a happy ending, doesn't it? I'll tell you, there was a time, after being strung out for so long, that I thought that any ending would be a happy ending."

"I understand that sentiment," she said.

They rode along for a while without speaking. Left to his own thoughts, Hartley began to recall details from the broader world. The Hudsons or Treece could show up at any time. They could be waiting at Muriel's shanty. The marshal would be continuing with his investigation. Three people had died, and one or more killers were at large.

He spoke out loud. "I wonder if I should begin to wear my gun."

She turned to him. "I should say so."

"I didn't know if you were philosophically opposed to it."

She tipped her head. "This is not the Yale Club. People kill each other out here, sometimes in malice and sometimes in self-defense. Where is your gun? Is it a six-gun? I remember seeing a rifle."

"It's a six-gun, a regular Colt .45 in a holster. It's in my war bag, which is in a larger duffel bag. Right now they're in the livery stable, along with my rifle and my saddle." As he said it, he realized how unguarded he had been. "That will change as soon as I get back."

"Good." After a second, she asked, "Where will you be staying?"

"I think I had better go back to the boardinghouse, in spite of the cost. For one thing, it will be in my interests to have my whereabouts accounted for. For another, it would be all too easy for someone to come up on me in my camp, even if I never slept."

"I agree with you."

"Not wanting to make you worried, I don't like the feeling of being unarmed now. Not as much with you here as on the drive back." He glanced around at the landscape and was comforted at seeing nothing, but he recalled the vulnerability he had had earlier. "For a modern man who doesn't like machines, I wouldn't mind having a .45 with me. Are you worried for yourself at all?"

She shook her head. "My greatest worry, besides finding a mouse in my food supplies, is that my cousins will come and berate me for what came out at the meeting today."

"Would you rather not stay out here, then?"

"I'll be all right, for the time being, at least."

Hartley did not waste time letting Muriel off at her residence. He watered the horse and headed back toward town.

The sun was shining in his eyes, so he pulled his hat forward. The buggy rolled along as before. Thoughts of events from the day came crowding in again—the comments people had made and the way the meeting had ended. A sense of incompleteness nagged at Hartley until he pinpointed the cause. Early in the meeting, the marshal had said he wanted to hear from Al Wisner. That detail had gotten lost in the later chaos, and the marshal may well have forgotten it at the time.

Hartley studied the land around him and again wished he had at least his six-gun. He hunched his shoulders and relaxed them. His earlier line of thought came back to him, and he wondered what Al Wisner was prepared to say at the meeting.

CHAPTER THIRTEEN

The ringing, clanging sound of metal pounding metal carried out from the depths of the blacksmith shop as Hartley left the livery stable. He pictured Jock Mosby in his skull cap, leather apron, and leather gauntlets, heating metal until it was red and making the yellow sparks fly. When he passed the open door, the noise died for a moment. He did not look in but rather kept his eyes on the buildings ahead.

He crossed the wide street before reaching the Argyle Hotel. Shadows stretched a third of the way, darkening a palomino horse that stood tied in front of the general store. As he passed the horse and the hitching rail, he noticed that the animal was tied with a neck rope made of hemp. The sight took him back about a month earlier, when he was braiding jute twine as the other bunkhouse hands were playing cards. Two of those men were dead now. Hartley wondered if any of the causes of their deaths had been set in motion already at that time, and if so, how aware either of them was as he studied his cards and laid them down.

At the post office, Hartley waited outside as Fred the bartender finished his business at the postal window. Rising voices signaled the end of the transaction, and footsteps thumped on the board floor inside. As Fred stepped through the doorway, wearing no hat, his low hairline and red face came into view. He looked up, and all expression left his face.

"Hullo," he said.

"The same to you."

Inside, Ned Farnsworth greeted Hartley with his usual equanimity. "Did everything go well?"

"Yes, and thank you. A comfortable ride, and no trouble at all with the horse."

Ned's voice had an even tone. "He's very good."

"And here in town—any news?"

"Nothing, really."

"I heard banging in the blacksmith shop, so I imagine the marshal is thinking things over."

"That seems to be his practice. I see you're wearing a pistol. Other men in town have taken to doing the same. With good reason, one would think."

"Didn't seem as if it was doing me any good in my war bag."

"That's more or less what others say. It's a strange feeling to think that there's someone in your midst who would do such a thing. Common theory is that it's one man behind all three. What do you think?" Ned peered at him and wore a faint smile.

"It's my belief as well. Even though we found Ben Stillwell out on the range, I've thought all along that he was killed in town. Not a shot fired in any of the three cases."

"It's a terrible thing." Ned shook his head as if they were talking about ants in the kitchen.

After a few seconds, Hartley said, "Where do you think I can find Al Wisner?"

"You might find him at the crusher. He's been going there of an evening."

"Have Treece and the Hudsons gone back to badger country?"

"I believe so. Mike Ackerman said he saw them leave the saloon and head out of town less than an hour ago."

"I'll give it a try, then. Thanks again for the use of your horse and buggy."

"Any time. Good luck, Reese."

The shadows seemed to have lengthened in the short time that Hartley was in the post office. He crossed the street, walked down the block to his right, and cut across the empty lot on the south side of the hotel. Across the street on the next block east, the steam engine and crusher sat in silence beneath a coat of dust. As on his earlier visit, he found a path through piles of rock and rubble and arrived at the open door of the stable-like building.

Al Wisner sat inside, wearing his dusty, short-brimmed hat. A brown cloth vest hung loose on a gray work shirt, and his wrinkled denim trousers had dust ingrained in them. He had one leg hiked over the other and a whiskey bottle on the floor in front of him.

"Good evening, Al."

"Likewise to you." The old man looked up with the same sad, lost expression as before, but his eyes were not as swollen and bloodshot. Hartley saw that they were light brown. "Hartley, isn't it?"

"Yes. I was at the meeting today."

"Yeah, yeah. Just gettin' the name straight."

"I was gone for a week. Came back yesterday evening."

Wisner nodded. "I followed that."

"I was taken off guard by the news of what happened to Buck Whittaker."

Wisner's eyelids had begun to lower, and he blinked to keep them open.

Hartley continued. "I can't help thinking, like anyone else, I suppose, that it might have had something to do with either of these other two . . . deaths."

"Everyone says the same."

"Then maybe they've asked you this question. But I haven't." Hartley paused until Wisner looked at him. "Did Buck Whittaker

187

know your daughter?"

Wisner reached for the bottle, squeaked out the cork, and took a drink. He brought his hand down over his gray mustache and said, "To some extent. Not much, I don't think."

"Is there any more to that? You understand, I'm asking this for all of us."

Wisner steadied the bottle on his lap and made a small, smacking sound with his lips. "He had eyes for her. But I don't think he got very far. She said he told her she thought she was the Queen of Sheba. I don't think she would have told us that if he'd gotten anywhere with her."

"How long ago was this?"

"Oh, a month or two. When the days were longest. We told her she could stay out until dark, and he would come around. Nothin' new in that. Others did."

"She must have been amused by the line about the Queen of Sheba."

"Oh, she was tickled. She made fun of him with it, to her mother and me."

"But not to him, you don't think. Not enough to send him into a rage."

"Oh, no. I don't think so. He was like a puppy dog with her, as far as I know."

Hartley had an image of a female dog sitting down when she wanted to shut out an eager male. "Well, it's too bad," he said. "I didn't have anything against him. He liked to talk crude sometimes, but he never mentioned your daughter."

"He better not have."

"And it doesn't figure that someone would do him in out of jealousy." Hartley waited for a comment, but Wisner stared at the bottle and said nothing.

Hartley ventured his next question. "Do you know of anyone who would have had reason to be jealous?"

The dusty hat moved back and forth as Wisner shook his head. "Not enough to say." He exhaled through his nose into his mustache, then leaned to the side and took a sack of Bull Durham from his vest pocket.

Hartley would have liked very much to ask whether the old man had gotten a report from the doctor, but he stood by his assurance that he would ask for the information only for the sake of bringing someone to justice. His sense of what was proper told him to wait.

He said, "I went on a trip up north to see new country. I might go back, but I'd like to see all of this cleared up first."

Wisner peeled out a cigarette paper and kept his eyes on his work. "I don't blame you. Some people still say you had a grudge against Whittaker, in spite of what came out at the meetin' today."

Hartley felt as if he had been pushed back a step. He had just told Wisner he wanted to see all of this cleared up, and he had said earlier that he was asking for all of them, and here the old man was treating him as if his main interest was in protecting his own name. Hartley told himself not to take it ill. He expected he would want Wisner's cooperation again.

"Well, thanks for your impressions," he said. "I'll move along and leave you alone."

"No bother. I'm always here. Or somewhere."

Hartley found the Strong Water Saloon almost empty, though night had fallen. Counting the days and recalling where he had been on which day, he realized that this evening was Tuesday.

Fred of the low hairline and red face appeared in front of him. "What do you need?"

"I'd like a whiskey."

"Glass or whole bottle?"

"I'll start with a glass."

Hartley took a sip when his drink came to him. He kept an eye on the mirror and did not care to observe the painting this evening. He wanted to keep his wits about him, and at the back of his mind he had the question of why Fred had become antagonistic.

Movement in the mirror and a voice at his elbow did not startle him.

"Could you stand an honest man to a drink?"

Hartley turned and observed Cletis, who had been loitering at the end of the bar. The man had bleary eyes and two or three days' worth of stubble.

Hartley said, "Beer or whiskey?"

Cletis's voice had a strange, nervous quality. "I prefer whiskey, but beer's cheaper. Whatever you'd like, boss."

"I'm drinking whiskey. If it's good enough for me, it's good enough for you, I'd think."

Cletis's eyebrows went up. "You bet."

Hartley ordered a glass of whiskey for Cletis. When the drink came, he said, "What do you think of sitting at a table over there?"

"Sure."

When they had a seat, in dimmer light, Hartley found Cletis almost grotesque in his appearance. Bald and toothless, with his remaining hair cropped short and his neck rising out of his neckless, sleeveless shirt, he looked as if he could have been a convict or a roustabout for the circus. Two sips of whiskey put a leer on his face, and he waited for Hartley to speak.

"This is a hell of a thing that has happened," Hartley began. "You know, Ben Stillwell and Buck Whittaker were my friends. You saw me in here drinking with them."

"That I did."

"Someone has tried to make it seem as if I had a grudge against either or both of 'em, and I don't like it. I need to find out what I can."

Cletis shrugged.

"And I have a hunch you know as much as anyone in this town."

"I'm just a dummy." Cletis took a sip.

"I know better. Buck Whittaker used to joke with you all the time. He knew you knew some things."

The leer returned to Cletis's face as he dipped his head to either side.

"So I want to know. Do you think Buck ever got anywhere with this girl who died?"

"You mean did he frig her? Nah, he never so much as got his finger in the pie."

Hartley was taken aback by the man's bluntness, even though he had seen his lack of inhibition before. Keeping his composure, Hartley said, "How about Ben Stillwell? He was kind of a sly one, I think."

"He was. He would've done it if he could. But all he got to do was watch."

"How did he know where to watch? You showed him, didn't you? You knew where."

Cletis's toothless mouth came into view as he grinned.

"Ah, then who was doing it with her?"

"That would be shit. I can't tell you. He'd kill me." Cletis took more than a sip from his glass.

"He doesn't know you saw, or he would have killed you already. Isn't that right?" Hartley narrowed his eyes. "He never caught you, did he?"

Cletis smiled with his mouth shut as he shook his head.

"I won't ask you, then. I won't ask you who, or what he did, or what you did when you watched. Buck Whittaker asked you those questions, but I won't."

"He frigged her hard. More than just diddlin'. He got rough

with her. He choked her and pulled her hair and kept his hand over her mouth."

Hartley felt a revulsion in his stomach. He had wanted Cletis to say the name, not what he had seen the man do. "I don't want to know any more," he said. "You can forget I asked you." Noticing a detail he had seen earlier, he asked, "How did you get that little white scar on the side of your head?"

"Right here?" Cletis touched his skull above his left ear.

"Yeah."

"My old man hit me with a bottle. Threw it at me from about five feet away."

"What for?"

"He said I was exposing myself."

"Were you?"

"Not really."

"What time do you clean this place out in the morning?"

"About nine." Cletis took another drink, as if he was afraid Hartley was going to take his glass away.

"And you go to work at the crusher after that?"

"When there's work."

"Well, that's good. Like they say, keeps you out of trouble. Speakin' of which, I've got to get up early in the morning. Let me buy you another drink, and I'll cash in for the night."

"You bet. Thanks, boss. And don't worry. I won't peep a word of this to anyone."

CHAPTER FOURTEEN

Hartley sat on the front porch of the boardinghouse as he watched a white chicken walk into the morning sunlight. On his way home from the saloon after his conversation with Cletis, he had again felt dread, a creeping sensation between his shoulder blades, as he imagined someone sending a bullet his way. Now in the light of day, with his back to the wall, he did not feel as uneasy, but he knew there was someone out there who killed to protect himself.

Hartley tightened his shoulders and neck as he recalled the haunted feeling from the night before. He had wanted to talk to Al Wisner again, but the house down the street was dark, and he did not know how appropriate it would be to rap on the door of a bereaved family at night anyway. Now the urgency was stronger. He did not know at what time Wisner went to work at the rock crusher or if he worked there every day.

A different kind of uneasiness passed through Hartley as he recalled flashes of the visit with Cletis. He was appalled by the man's depravity—the ease with which he talked and smiled about things he had done and seen. Hartley had heard, in diatribes against the evils of alcohol, that the fiend intemperance brought men to the level of brutes. He wondered to what extent the alcohol debased the human, and to what extent a given human might have a predisposition toward low behavior. Excessive drink would then lower the barriers that otherwise held the brute in check. Hartley had read the story about Dr.

Jekyll and Mr. Hyde not long after it came out, and although he knew it was pure allegory, it helped him think about the impulses that people had latent within them.

Hartley flinched as the door of the house he was watching opened. Al Wisner stepped out onto the doorstep, dressed in an undershirt and trousers, and shook a plate. Scraps fell to the ground, and a flock of half a dozen chickens, some brown and some white, came scurrying out from the sunny side of the house. Wisner coughed and went inside.

Hartley pondered. He fidgeted. If he waited too long, someone else might show up—Treece or one of the Hudsons. He needed to talk to Wisner before the old man talked to anyone else today or listened to the babble of Cletis. On the other hand, each step he took drew him in deeper.

To hell with it, he thought. He was already in. It was too late to sit back. He had talked to Cletis, and if his hunches proved out, he was going to try to talk to him again. But he needed to talk to Al Wisner.

Resolved, he stood up and took a deep breath. He settled his hat on his head and walked out into the morning sun, feeling like a target.

Al Wisner answered the rap at the door. His eyes were dull, and his face showed worry. "What is it?" he asked.

"There's something else I'd like to talk to you about. It won't take but a minute or two."

Wisner looked up and down the street. "Meet me at the back step."

Hartley walked around the west side of the house, at once avoiding the chickens and keeping to the shadows. The back step had a porch-like structure consisting of an overhang and two walls built onto the main part of the house.

Al Wisner appeared in the dark doorway and stepped out. He was wearing an unbuttoned flannel shirt over his undershirt.

194

His trousers hung on his waist, and he stood in stocking feet. He beckoned to Hartley.

The dim enclosure, about six feet square, had a washtub and washboard hanging on one side with galoshes below. A shovel, hoe, and rake stood against the other wall, and a worn slicker hung on a nail. Hartley stood within three feet of the older man.

"Keep your voice down," said Wisner, pointing with his thumb. "She doesn't need to hear all this."

"It's just as well. And by the way, it would also be best not to repeat any of this to Cletis."

"I know that much."

"Good." Hartley met the man's tired eyes and said, "I think it's time I asked about something I said I wouldn't press you about right away. But I need to now. It's about the doctor."

Discomfort showed on Wisner's face as he raised his head and breathed in through his nose. "The marshal asked me about it. He knew I had the doctor here, and he wanted to know why. I told him I couldn't tell him."

Hartley kept his voice down. "I don't think it would have done any harm for him to know at this point, once it was done, but that's all right. What did he say? By the way, when was this?"

"After the meeting yesterday."

"Oh. Do you think he was going to ask you in front of everybody?"

"I think so. We didn't have anything worked out ahead of time, though he did ask me about Whittaker and I told him a little of that."

"I see. What about the doctor, then?"

"The marshal said he would go talk to the doctor himself. He said he would leave the first thing this morning. He had to go to Winsome."

"We could have saved him a trip. And time."

"I said I would keep it under my hat, and I did."

"That's fine. No harm done at all." Hartley paused as he observed the sad eyes and worn face in the close, dusky atmosphere of the little porch. "What is there for him to learn from the doctor?"

"What he told me." Tears started in the old man's eyes, and his lower lip trembled. "Same as what you said. She was . . ."

"With child?"

Wisner nodded but did not look up. He sobbed, then coughed and cleared his throat.

Hartley patted him on the shoulder. "I'm sorry."

"She was just a girl. And for some son of a bitch to do that—"

"I know. But the marshal's on his trail, and we'll do what we can to help."

Wisner sniffed and brought his hand down over his mustache. "Hangin' is too good."

"Well, there are laws. And we need to be sure of who it is. I've got my hunch, but I don't know if some people will want to protect him."

"I don't care who it is. And if it's who I think it is, he's no blood kin of mine."

"All right," said Hartley. "We'll see what the marshal can do. And if I can find out anything else in the meanwhile, so much the better." He held out his hand. "Thanks, Al."

The old man blinked, and his mouth trembled, but he held up. "Thanks to you," he said.

Hartley walked up and down the main street to wear off some of his nervousness. Businesses opened, but the blacksmith shop remained closed. Hartley wished he knew where Cletis lived. Ned Farnsworth would know, but Hartley did not want to ask him.

The sun climbed fast, as it did in the first part of the morning. The shadows in the street receded. Hartley knew he could pop into the post office and ask the time, but he preferred not to live by the clock, and he had some idea of when nine o'clock came around. He walked the cross streets and kept an eye on the Strong Water Saloon. When he saw the back door opened inward, he headed in that direction.

He stood by the open door and listened. He picked up Cletis's voice but could not make out the words. A lower voice responded with short comments. Hartley imagined that Cletis was moving around in the saloon and chattering to Fred behind the bar.

Hartley did not like to be seen lingering around the back door of a drinking establishment in the morning, but he did not want to go in and be rebuffed by Fred. He made himself wait.

At length he heard scuffing footsteps, and Cletis emerged into the sunlight, leaning against the weight of a bucket of water he was lugging. He came to a stop, swung the bucket once with his body in motion, and stopped short as he pitched the contents. His face was sweating, and the pink interior of his mouth showed as he spoke out.

"Good mornin', guv'nor. What's on your mind?"

"Workin' hard?"

Cletis smiled with his mouth closed. "That's my middle name."

"Can you take a break to talk for a minute?"

Cletis's neck, face, and head glistened as he looked over his shoulder. "I don't wanna catch hell."

"It won't take a minute. I'd buy you a drink, but I don't think he'd let you have one this early in the morning."

"You're right about that. He's a tit."

"But here's somethin' to buy yourself a refreshment later

on." Hartley laid a half-dollar in the palm that opened to receive it.

"Never turn it down," said Cletis. "Let's walk over on the north side, where there's a little shade."

With the rest of the town out of view, Hartley felt more comfortable, but he knew he didn't have time to lose. He brought his attention to bear on Cletis, who raised his chin and stretched his neck.

"Just a small thing," Hartley began. "I got to thinking about what we talked about last night. We didn't say who did, but I think we concluded that Buck Whittaker didn't ever do anything with that girl."

"That's right."

"But he found out someone else did, and he was jealous as hell. Maybe even offended."

Cletis's bare shoulders went up and down as he shrugged. "I guess so."

"And he found out from you that Ben Stillwell had seen it."

"I don't know."

"Oh, come on, Cletis. He either did or didn't find out from you. I suppose he had to pump it out of you, but he did, didn't he?"

Cletis took on a stubborn countenance. "If you say so."

"Not if I say so. He did or he didn't, and I know he could get things out of you."

"Maybe he did."

"And maybe he knew what condition she was in. Because you heard that, too, didn't you? Between her and the person whose name we don't say."

Cletis had begun to shake, both in his hands and in his upper body. Hartley could tell he was afraid and wanted a drink.

"It was all a good joke as long as Whittaker was buying drinks and laughing. But you told him more than you should have."

Cletis's lips were trembling as he opened and closed his mouth. At last the words came out. "Look here, mister. You could get us both killed."

"I'm not going to. And you're not going to, either. Here's what I'm going to do. I'm going to go in and buy a bottle of whiskey, and I'm going to leave it right there." Hartley pointed at a sliver of shade against the bottom of the building. "You won't have to wait the rest of the day to brace yourself up."

"Thanks."

"But for God's sake, keep your mouth shut about all this until the time comes."

"I will."

Hartley shook his head as the swamper walked away. Cletis was not as dangerous as Mr. Hyde. He was not going to descend into a demonic rage and bash in Mike Ackerman's head with his walking stick. But he could cause trouble with a milder form of unrestrained behavior. The bottle of whiskey that was supposed to keep him quiet might loosen his tongue.

Hartley walked along the east side of the street, taking advantage of the shade. It had not shortened much in the time he had spent with Cletis, but he felt as if he was sitting on a powder keg with a building in flames all around him. He told himself he needed to stay calm and appear normal until the marshal returned.

To be sure that the marshal was gone, he walked past the blacksmith shop again. Seeing it closed, he ambled on toward the livery stable. He took two minutes to check on his horse, and he stood in the street once more.

A thought occurred to him. He crossed to the east side of the street and went into the Great West Grain and Livestock office.

Bess sat up to attention at the sound of the bell. Hartley took off his hat.

"Good morning, Reese."

"Good morning to you, Bess."

Her blue eyes traveled to the pistol at his side and then came back to him. "Is there anything . . ."

"Nothing in particular at the moment. I was out walking, and I thought I'd drop in to see how you're doing."

"That's thoughtful of you. I'm doing all right, I suppose, considering all that has happened."

"Oh, yes. It's hard to comprehend." Silence hung in the air for a few long seconds. "One wonders, of course, if these things are related."

She blinked her eyes and rubbed her lower eyelids. "I don't know what to think."

"Neither do I sometimes. But here's a question that occurred to me. Did you ever notice anything unusual about Ben? That is, anything secret, or even furtive, that he might have known or done?"

She shook her head. "Oh, no. I think he was . . . as you saw him. I don't want to say simple, but ours was a simple courtship that didn't last long. That's how I see it."

Hartley did not have a comment.

She continued. "I'm sorry he came to the end that he did, and I hope someone can find out why."

Hartley inferred that she was wrapping up the interlude in her life and putting it away. He said, "It looks as if you're headed toward a safe situation now."

Bess's features tensed. "It always looks like something from the outside. To me, it seems as if I had one chance at true love, and it passed me by. He was taken unjustly, and at times it seems as if I never knew him. It lasted so short a time." For a second she had a faraway look in her eyes, but she came back. "Perhaps you think I'm settling for something less, but I'm not. It's not settling. It's just something different."

"Is it what you want, then?" He was tempted to tell her what kind of a man he thought Miner was, but he knew that such a comment might be repeated someday, out of a sense of duty or in a moment of dispute. So he said no more.

She regained her composure. "I think it's the best choice I will have."

For a moment she seemed like a woman of thirty-five or forty, rather than twenty-five. Perhaps she felt trapped in a small town, with a widowed uncle she would have to take care of in later age. But he saw the truth of what she had said a minute earlier: it always looked different from the outside. He could not know, and it was her life.

"I wish you well," he said.

"Thank you, Reese. And I wish the same to you."

In that moment he wondered how she might see him, given the comments she had heard at the public meeting the day before.

The doorbell jingled, and Mike Ackerman walked in. "Good morning," he said.

Reese smiled. "The same to you. How are you doing?"

"All right, I guess." Ackerman tapped the floor with his black walking stick as he held it by the brass knob. "I think my gout is coming back."

"I'm sorry to hear that."

"So am I. And the doctors are so severe. They want to take away everything."

"Is your doctor in Cheyenne?"

"There's one who comes around. They're all the same. Snatch the wine glass from your hand."

Hartley reached for the doorknob. "Well, I hope it gets better. So long to you both."

Ackerman raised his eyebrows. "Not leaving town, are you?"

"No, just out walking for exercise."

"Ah-hah. Well, good for you."

Hartley stepped outside and decided to cross the street again. A strip of shade was worth the effort. As he was halfway across, however, he saw a wagon drawn by two horses and accompanied by a horse and rider. The group was approaching the corner on the cross street coming from the east. Al Wisner sat hunched on the driver's seat, and Cletis's head showed from the box of the wagon. Doyle Treece rode a stout dark horse alongside.

Treece spurred his horse, and the animal shot out ahead of the wagon and turned onto the main street. The heavy man pulled to a stop a few yards ahead and swung down. Leaving his horse to stand alone, he strode forward, swinging his arms and his heavy hands.

Hartley stopped. His stomach tightened. From the corner of his eye, he saw the wagon roll forward and come to a halt. Cletis jumped down and gathered the reins of Treece's horse. Al Wisner gazed away to the southwest.

Hartley made a move to his left, and Treece spoke in a commanding tone.

"Stay where you are. I have something to say to you."

Hartley stood his ground. Treece could not shoot him or choke him to death in full view like this, but he could do something.

The big man settled into a stance two feet away. He held his chin high, and his broad features were as hard as chiseled rock. His pig eyes flamed. "I don't like you, and I don't like what you're up to."

Hartley felt his pulse in his throat, in his ears. He was trying to think of something to say when Treece punched him once, twice. His head rocked with the impact, and the ground came up to meet him. He heard horse hooves moving away, the creak of wagon wheels.

Mike Ackerman's florid face loomed close, with a distant

blue sky in the background. "Are you all right, man?"

Hartley sat up. He had a sharp, steady headache, and he heard a ringing sound, like birds chirping. "I think so."

"What did he do that for?"

"He doesn't like me."

"Well, I don't like him, but that doesn't mean I can knock him down in the street. Can you stand up?"

"I think I can." Hartley rose to his feet. His head had a constant ache, and his legs were unsteady, but he could walk. "I need to go to the boardinghouse and lie down." He pulled in a breath and took the hat that Ackerman handed him. It was his own hat. He put it on. "I can make it," he said. "I just need to lie down for a while."

A knocking sound came from somewhere. He felt as if he was in the bottom of a deep, dark house. Or at the bottom of a pool, where he could breathe and hear. *Knock, knock, knock.* It wasn't water. Maybe he was in a ship, and someone was knocking on his cabin door. He was on the floor and couldn't move enough to tell whether he was chained.

Knock, knock, knock. "Mr. Hartley! There's a lady here to see you. Mr. Hartley!"

He floated up out of darkness. He was not on a floor. He was on his bed. Light was streaming in through the window. He did not know if it was morning or afternoon.

"Mr. Hartley!"

He rolled over and swung his feet off the side of the bed. He had his boots on. He had all his clothes on.

He stood up and staggered to the door. He could not unlock it. The little lever on top of the latch would not move. It was not locked. He turned the knob and opened the door.

Mrs. Mead stood in the hallway in her apron and pinned-up gray hair. "Are you all right? I thought I was going to have to have someone go in there with me."

He blinked his eyes and moved his head. "I'm up. I was out pretty cold. Deep down. Dark." He rubbed the back of his neck. "Sorry."

"That's all right. You were pretty woozy when you came in. Said someone hit you."

A word came into his mind for no reason. *Wimple.* He frowned and pushed it aside. "Yeah. Someone hit me."

"Well, you're on your feet, and there's someone here to see you. Out front."

"Okay. I'll be there in a minute." He left the door open and took a few steps inside. He didn't know if he should wear his hat. A wash of fatigue swept through him, and he lay on the bed with one foot hanging over. *Wimmering.* He opened his eyes. What kind of a word was that?

"Mr. Hartley!" Mrs. Mead was still standing in the hallway.

He sat up. "I'm on my way." He put on his hat and followed her. He said words to himself that made sense. *Wisner. Persimmon. Whittaker. Winsome.* It was as if he was setting the words apart, one by one, like little wooden figures. *Willomene.*

"Here you are," said Mrs. Mead, standing aside to let him walk into the little front room.

A woman stood up from the couch. It wasn't Willomene. This woman had dark hair. Muriel.

"You look like you're in a daze. Are you all right?"

He blinked his eyes. "I think so. I got hit pretty hard, and I was out for a while."

"Knocked out? Did something hit you on the head?"

"Someone hit me. On the street. Knocked me down, but I got up and came here. I fell asleep." He put his hand on the back of his neck and stretched.

"Who hit you?"

Hartley couldn't find the name. All he had was an image.

"The fat son of a bitch."

She coughed. "Do you mean Doyle Treece?"

"Yeah. That's him. Sorry. The words just came out."

"Well, sit down. I had something for you to do, but I can see you're not quite yourself."

"I'm coming back. What time of day is it? Morning or afternoon?"

"Afternoon. It's about two."

He thought he could hear a clock ticking. "Same day. Wednesday."

"Yes."

"How did you get here?"

"I borrowed a horse from the neighbors. I told them I wanted the gentlest, most docile animal they had. His name is Bob."

"That's good." His head was clearing. "What did you want me to do?"

She held her lips mum for a few seconds. "Move my things."

"Move? Like move out of the shanty?"

"That's right. My cousins won't leave me alone. The Hudson brothers nag, nag, nag at me about you, about this wretched Mr. Blue, and everything else. They think they should take shifts watching over me. And your antagonist Mr. Treece, when he's not busy pummeling you, looks at me in the most lewd way, as if there's no reason why I shouldn't favor him. Rather brutish, but normal for him. At any rate, I'm very uncomfortable with the idea of him taking a shift to keep an eye on me."

Hartley could feel himself coming back to life. His head ached, but his blood was circulating. "How much stuff do you have? Can we move it with two horses, or should I try to borrow that buggy again?"

"I have two trunks. Portmanteau style. One of them folds out, and the other is a dresser trunk, the type in which the front part folds up on top to make a straight-back dresser."

He opened his eyes wide. He remembered it, covered in leather with brass trim and latches. "We'll need at least a buggy. Two people, two heavy trunks. A buckboard with two horses might be better for time as well. I'll talk to the stable man."

Dusk was closing in when they returned to town with the buckboard and Muriel's belongings. In addition to the trunks, she had a wool overcoat, a heavy lap blanket, a handbag with food items, and her mandolin in a black leather case.

Hartley had the impression that Mrs. Mead had talked to someone in the meanwhile, for she treated them with reservation.

"No guests in the room, you know. You're not to go to her room, and she's not to go to yours. Not even if you were brother and sister. I've had them here before, you know. Or so they said. If you want to visit, there's the front room and the porch."

Hartley nodded. Muriel smiled, but she did not melt the landlady's cold exterior.

Hartley said, "We're going to take the wagon to the stable. We'll walk back. I expect to be gone for half an hour or so."

"Do as you wish," said Mrs. Mead.

They returned the wagon with no incident and walked toward the center of town. The main street was lit only by faint moonlight, and Hartley felt as if there could be an eavesdropper in any dark doorway. During the whole time that he and Muriel had driven out to the homestead, loaded up her belongings, and driven back, he had expected an encounter with at least a couple of the Hudsons, but he saw nobody. He assumed that Treece and his helpers had gone to gather rocks, but they would have returned by now. Hartley could imagine the big man lurking, and not just to eavesdrop.

After walking past the blacksmith shop, which lay in silence and darkness, Hartley led Muriel across to the west side of the street, where the light from the rising moon was brighter. Once there, he still feared the presence of some dark form in the shadows between the buildings.

"Let's walk in the middle of the street," he said.

She held his arm as she kept pace with him.

Once there, he surveyed the whole street and saw nothing out of order. His head had cleared up, and he could make sense. In a low voice, he said, "I have an idea of how things have happened. The marshal should be back tomorrow, and if he sees things anywhere near the same way as I think I do, he should be able to wrap things up. But whatever happens, we're on our own, you and I. With the exception of the marshal and perhaps the postmaster, everyone is looking out for his own interest. Not that anything has really changed, but there's not very much for either of us here, and no one's going to go out of his way to help us or stick up for us."

"I can see that."

"If the marshal can collar a culprit, things will settle down. These two sides will go back to taking what they can get. In various ways. As for the culprit, I'd just as soon not mention a name until tomorrow."

"You're being reticent now."

"To say the least." Realizing he sounded as if he was making a pun, he said, "That is—"

"I know what you mean." She pressed his arm, and they walked on together.

CHAPTER FIFTEEN

Ned Farnsworth was sweeping debris out the front door of the post office when Hartley turned the corner onto the main street. The morning sun glinted off the postmaster's glasses as he stepped outside, turned, and waved.

"Beautiful morning, isn't it?"

"It sure is." Hartley had a residue of his headache from the day before, plus a sense of dread for the day at hand, but he could agree that the cool, fresh air and bright sunshine were agreeable.

Ned lingered with his hand on the broom. "Something this morning?"

"Just out for a walk. I was wondering if you had any idea of when the marshal would be back."

"I talked to Mart at the close of day yesterday, and he said he received word that the marshal was staying over at Winsome and would ride back this morning."

Hartley noted the neatness with which the postmaster framed his words. Mart Keithley had the telegraph office in a corner of his general store, two doors down, and so he had access to some information before Ned did, which seemed to be a small source of envy. Also, the postmaster did not refer to the reason for the marshal's trip.

"Anything pressing?" Ned asked.

"Nothing that can't wait. I would just like to see some things resolved."

"Oh, I think we all would."

"I have the feeling that there's going to be more trouble."

"I wouldn't be surprised."

The tone of the postmaster's voice suggested that he had knowledge to share. Hartley said, "Is there something afoot?"

"There may be. Dick Prentiss is in town, and he has apparently gotten word that Cletis has information to be gotten out of him."

"How did he come to know that? Prentiss, I mean." Hartley was sure he hadn't heard it from Treece.

"I believe the bartender, Fred, was aware that Cletis was sharing information."

"Ohhh. That makes sense. I was wondering why Fred was being curt with me, not to mention what he was willing to say out front here."

"Yes, I wondered at that myself."

"It seems as if he has picked his side." Hartley realized that Ned liked to stay as neutral as he could, so Hartley did not wait for him to make a comment. He continued the conversation by saying, "So, is Prentiss going to interrogate Cletis?"

Ned raised his eyebrows and tossed a glance up the street. "I believe he's doing that right now."

"In the saloon? I thought Cletis didn't get there until nine."

"Fred might have fetched him a little earlier."

Hartley made an effort to suppress the agitation that was rising up within him. "I wish Prentiss had waited. I can't picture him being very subtle or discreet."

Ned shrugged.

Hartley assumed that Ned knew who else had been questioning Cletis, even if he himself had been discreet. "I don't know if I should go over there."

"The worst they can do is not let you in."

"I suppose. Well, thanks, Ned."

209

"For what it's worth. Good luck, Reese."

"Thanks." Hartley set off for the Strong Water Saloon, feeling as if the eyes of the town were upon him with his gun at his side.

He decided to go around back rather than rattle the front door, which he was sure would be locked.

The back door opened when he tried it, and light flooded into the dim barroom. Dick Prentiss turned in his chair where he sat at a table across from Cletis, who raised his head like a prairie dog.

Prentiss squinted against the light and spoke in a rough voice. "What are you doing here?"

"I could ask the same question of you. This man's a potential witness, and I don't want any harm to come to him before the marshal returns."

"What are you, a deputy?"

"I'm someone who wants to see things done right."

"Just stay out of the way, and they will."

Hartley stepped inside and closed the door. The interior darkened, as only a couple of lamps were lit.

Prentiss rolled his shoulders as he leaned back in his chair and took out his white sack of cigarette makings. "Why don't you leave?"

"Fred hasn't told me to. Meanwhile, I might tell you that I know at least as much as anybody else in this room does. Cletis, have you had a drink?"

Cletis pushed out his lips in a way that only toothless people could do. "Just one," he said.

Prentiss went to work at rolling a cigarette. Hartley noticed that the man had more dexterity than one would expect from such large hands.

Prentiss did not look up from his work. "You think you know so much. You think you're smart."

210

"You told me I acted like a dummy before."

"It all pays the same. That is, unless you don't have a job."

"I'd rather not have a job than not have a set of ethics."

Prentiss stopped with his fingers and thumbs on the half-made cigarette. "Well, look who's talkin'. What was the name of that woman in Ohio?"

"Guinevere. Does that help you solve any current problems?"

"Like I said. Always smart. Let's just say I know a couple of other things that could solve problems."

Hartley let the comment go by.

Prentiss said, "You can leave any time."

"I'm in no hurry." Hartley drew a chair around so he could sit with his back to the wall and see both doors.

Fred went about his busy work of adjusting bottles beneath the mirror.

Prentiss tapped the seam of his cigarette, struck a match, and lit up. He blew smoke toward the ceiling.

Hartley took advantage of the silence and worked his way through a succession of thoughts. Prentiss seemed to have pumped a satisfactory amount of information out of Cletis, in which case he would know that Hartley hadn't done anything to cause the death of Ben Stillwell or Buck Whittaker. Prentiss's lingering resentment, then, was based on their initial disagreement about land and on Hartley's closeness with Muriel.

Fred's voice broke the silence. "Do you need anything, Dick?"

"Not now. I don't drink this early in the day. We'll get Cletis something in a little while."

Prentiss smoked his cigarette down and ground the snipe with his bootheel. Relaxed in his chair, he let out a long breath and said, "We've got enough information to hang this son of a bitch as it is."

Hartley said, "I don't think you want to do that on your own, even if you could."

211

"I've heard of it done. It put Big Nose George Parrott out of business, finally. Hung him from a telegraph pole in Rawlins. Then they skinned him, and the guv'nor made a pair of boots out of the hide. After that, someone used the top of his skull for a souvenir."

"Yeah, yeah," said Hartley. "That's an old story from twenty-five or thirty years ago."

"It wasn't the only one. The hangin' part, anyway."

"I don't think much of vigilante justice. Especially now. Maybe in territorial days, when there was little or no law. I wasn't there. But even then, people sometimes had crooked motives when they took the law into their own hands."

"Takes a handful of men."

"Even if you had a vigilante group, you'd have his cousins to deal with."

"My God, what does it take? That girl was his cousin, and theirs, too."

"You never know how far along people will stick with someone who's plumb rotten."

"Like I say, it takes a few men. As soon as Tobe gets here, we've got a start. Doesn't sound like we can count on you. You don't have the guts for it. If you had any decency, you'd go along. But no matter. Can't get blood out of a turnip."

Hartley began to wonder if Prentiss had had something to drink after all or if he was feeling elevated by his sense of command. The barroom went quiet again except for the occasional clink of Fred arranging bottles and glasses.

A burst of light was accompanied by a thump and scrape as the back door flew open. A man with no hat appeared in silhouette and rushed in. At the same time that he recognized the man, Hartley laid his hand on his gun. Prentiss already had his drawn.

"What the hell?" Prentiss barked. "You could get shot. Close the door."

Blue closed the door and turned around, blinking his eyes.

Hartley wanted to ask him what errand of philanthropy brought him here, but he watched without speaking.

Prentiss said, "If you're here to bum a drink, you're too early."

Blue gave a condescending glance and smile. "I'll buy my own, thanks, when the show is over. I came here to tell you that Doyle Treece and the Hudson brothers are outside in front. They're pulling up a wagon to hide behind, and I think one of them is coming around back."

"Well, lock the door, you damn fool. Go!" Prentiss waved his pistol and stood up. "Fred, go look out the front door and tell me what you see."

Fred walked with light steps, lifting his feet like a chicken. He came to a stop next to the door. He eased the bolt aside, opened the door a crack, peeked out, and closed the door.

"There's a wagon out there, and old Wisner is taking the horses away. Treece and the Hudsons are behind the wagon, and I saw at least two rifles."

"Well, the fat's in the fire now," said Prentiss. "What time is the marshal supposed to be back?"

Blue said, "I have no idea. And as far as that goes, I'd just as soon leave the way I came."

"You'd better go before they put someone guardin' the back door. Fred, do we have a rifle at all in here?"

"Just a pistol and a shotgun."

"Blue, why don't you see if you can bring us some rifles?"

"Sure." Blue wasted no time unlocking the back door and taking off at a soft run, straight away to the east.

Fred closed the door. "You won't see him again."

"At least he's out of the way." Prentiss turned his ear toward the front door as a voice sounded from the street.

Prentiss made a stealthy approach to the front door. Hartley followed. Prentiss said, "What are you doing?"

"You're going to open the door and answer, aren't you?"

"Yes, I am."

"Well, if they shoot you, I want to be able to close the door."

"Is that all you can do to help?"

"You wanted me to leave earlier."

"You've got a gun. Are you going to help, or what?"

"I'll see what happens. This is your fight."

Prentiss stopped at the door as Fred had done and opened it three or four inches. "What do you want?" he hollered out.

Treece's voice came back. "The old drunk. Cletis. Send him over."

"Don't kid yourself, Treece. He's not goin' anywhere."

"Send him out, or we'll come and get him."

"You'll never do it. Every last one of you'll get a bullet in the guts."

Treece's voice rang clear. "I'm telling you again, send him out."

"Won't do it." Prentiss closed the door and slid the bolt.

A hail of bullets rat-tat-tatted on the thick planks of the door, and a few splinters pushed through.

Prentiss opened the door, laid his pistol across his forearm, and shot three times. Another volley hit the door as he slammed it. He opened again and fired three more shots.

"I think I hit one." He stood back a few paces and began to eject empty casings from his pistol. "Get down on the floor and look out while I open the door again. Tell me what you see. Just a minute. Let me get this loaded."

Hartley drew his pistol, took off his hat, and lay flat on the floor. As Prentiss opened the door and two shots sounded, Hartley peered through the empty space beneath the wagon. Two Hudsons were bent, kneeling, while the third lay with his full head of whitish hair reflecting the sunlight.

"There's one down all right. A Hudson."

Prentiss closed the door and slid the bolt. "Maybe that'll slow 'em down." He turned toward the bar. "What are you doing?"

Cletis, standing, held a spittoon above his knees and was using it as a urinal. "I'm sorry. I couldn't hold it anymore."

Fred said, "He wanted to go in the corner, but I wouldn't let him."

Prentiss shook his head. "We've got men trying to kill us, and here you are." He held still and turned his ear toward the street. "They're quiet now. Maybe they'll take that wounded fellow somewhere. I think we wait now."

The marshal returned at a little before noon. In the meanwhile, the wagon had been taken away from the middle of the street. Fred went out and brought back news that the Hudsons and Treece were forted up at the rock crusher. Brant Hudson had lost blood from a wound to the shoulder, but he was not dying. Hartley kept his place to make sure nothing happened to Cletis.

At last the marshal showed up, dressed in his black hat, charcoal-gray vest, and long black boots with mule-ear pull tabs. He was wearing his badge and pistol as well. He sat at a table in the saloon and told Fred to leave the front and back doors open so he could see who came and went and not have any surprises. As the others gathered, he pushed back his hat, revealing his pale forehead and receding hairline. He looked around at the group, which now included Al Wisner as well as Cletis, Fred, Prentiss, and Hartley.

"I have an idea of what I want to do next," the marshal said, in his unhurried voice. "But before I do, I want to make sure I have everything straight."

Prentiss said, "I think we should lay hands on this son of a bitch before we do anything else. He's a danger. He tried to shoot me. All of us."

"Let's start with the details."

Cletis and Wisner both looked at Hartley, so he took the lead.

"Here's the sequence as I've put it together. I may not have everything in perfect order, so I'm willing to be corrected on that as well as on any details."

"Go ahead," said the marshal.

"It starts with Buck Whittaker, although it revolves around the girl, whose name I am not going to say in a place like this, out of respect for her, and her father." He nodded at Al Wisner, who gave him a somber stare from beneath his dusty hat. "At about the time we came back from spring roundup, but it might have been sooner, Buck Whittaker took an interest in the girl. Like many young men, he wanted to do something with her, but she brushed him off. To his credit, he took 'No' for an answer. Unbeknownst to him, she didn't say 'No' to everyone. Doyle Treece was taking advantage of her, and I use that phrase because of her age, his age, and his status as a family member. I do not know when Treece began, but at about the time my version of the story begins, Cletis knew about it and had observed it. Am I right, Cletis?"

Cletis kept his eyes lowered as he shrugged.

"Next came Ben Stillwell. He might well have liked to do some mingling himself, but he was either turned down or didn't get that far. Through Cletis he learned how he could watch. Unfortunately, Treece found out. I suspect that he caught Ben watching, and that was the end of one witness."

"How do you know?" asked Prentiss.

"I don't, except that it's the only reason I can imagine someone could have, and there's only one person who would have that reason and would kill the witness with his bare hands so no one would hear."

"Whew!" said the bartender.

Hartley resumed. "So a little time goes on, not long, as we know. The girl discovers that she is with child, which has been confirmed by a doctor, *post mortem.*" Al Wisner gave a faint nod, as did the marshal. "Then it stands to reason that if she was far enough along for the doctor to determine it, then she would have known. And I believe Cletis heard her say as much to the opportunist."

Cletis again did not look up, but he tipped his head side to side as if in agreement.

"My guess is that she said more on at least one other occasion, when Cletis was not around, and her opportunist, who had the habit of being rough with her, silenced her for good. I'm sorry."

Al Wisner, Fred, and Cletis were all looking at the floor. Dick Prentiss was staring out the door toward the street where Treece had stood. The marshal was studying the group.

"Comes now Buck Whittaker. He knows two people have died, and like anyone else, he wonders if there is a connection. Moreover, one of the people was his friend, and the other was a girl for whom he had, by now, sentimental feelings. So he pressed Cletis with questions, which he was in the habit of doing, and he found out his friend Ben Stillwell had seen some things." Hartley took a breath. "And here my trail thins out a little. I don't know whether Whittaker let Treece know what he knew or whether Treece found out some other way. But as with Ben Stillwell, there was only one reason someone would want to do him in, which was knowing too much, and there was only one person who would have that reason."

The marshal pushed out his lips, and his large mustache went up and down. "Does anyone have anything to say that would disagree with this version of things?" He fixed his attention on each man until he received a shake of the head. "Well," he continued, still at his deliberate pace, "it all hangs together, which is sometimes a flaw in a story, when it hangs together too well. But it all makes sense, even if some of it is what you could call conjecture." He paused as the last word settled. "But we have enough to start with, between the doctor's report and what Cletis has seen, to call for the arrest of Mr. Doyle Treece."

Prentiss gave a sharp look. "You say, 'call for.' What does that mean?"

"Go tell him he's under arrest. And if he's not at the crusher, go out to his place and bring him in."

The marshal had a small crowd at his heels as he walked down the back street toward the lot where the rock crusher was located. In addition to Prentiss, Fred, and Hartley, the group had picked up Tobe Lestman, Blue, the owner of the Owl Café, and the barber. Al Wisner and Cletis stayed to keep an eye on the saloon, with strict orders from Fred not to touch the merchandise.

At the crusher, Hartley counted three horses tied next to the stable-like structure. A Hudson lounged in the doorway, leaning his shoulder against the doorjamb and resting his loose hand on the belt of his six-gun. The marshal led the way through the dusty piles of rock and rubble and came to a stop at about five yards from the building.

He said, "Good afternoon. Are you Arlis?"

"I am. I don't know what's so good about it. My brother's shot."

"We'll deal with that later. You can send for a doctor in the meanwhile. Right now, I've come to arrest Doyle Treece."

"He ain't here." Arlis stood away from the doorframe and called over his shoulder. "Crisp."

The second Hudson emerged from the shadows to stand by his brother. Arlis raised his chin, and with a saucy tone, he said,

"What do you want him for? You take him in, you'll have to take us all."

The marshal continued with his deliberate rate of speech. "I'm not talkin' about the skirmish in the street. I said I'd deal with it later. Right now, I want to arrest Doyle Treece by himself. I've got witnesses and evidence to show that he took advantage of your cousin, Nancy, got her with child, and stifled her."

The Hudson brothers' faces fell together. Arlis said, "I don't know anythin' about that. It's new to me. No wonder he lit out of here."

The marshal said, "What caused him to do that?"

Arlis pointed at Blue. "That fella there came and told him somethin'."

Hartley felt as if he had his breath taken away. He took a close look at Blue. The man must have eavesdropped through an open door and then made an attempt to gain favor with Muriel's family.

The marshal turned and spoke to Blue. "I don't know what your game is, but there's a law against aiding and abetting. We'll deal with you later, too." Back to Arlis, he said, "Which way did he go?"

Arlis pointed to the west. "That-a-way. Like you was goin' to the rocks."

"And what kind of horse was he on?"

"A big white one with spots."

"I think I know the horse."

Arlis peered with his close-set blue eyes. "Are you goin' after him?"

"It's my idea."

"I thought your jurisdiction was just here in town."

"Not when I'm pursuin' a fugitive who did somethin' in town. Do you want to stand in my way?"

"Oh, no." Arlis turned to his brother, and they both shook

their heads.

The marshal drew a breath and addressed his gathering. "All right. We'll have a meeting in front of the post office in ten minutes. I need some men to go with me, and we've got no time to lose."

The crowd consisted of all men until Muriel arrived. She was wearing a gray dress and had her dark hair pinned up. She stood by Ned Farnsworth and scanned the group. Hartley was glad that Blue had made himself scarce again. Al Wisner stood not far from Muriel. Fred had stayed at the saloon. Hartley imagined Cletis sleeping under a wagon somewhere.

The marshal cleared his throat and spoke in a loud voice. "Let's not waste time. I'd like three or four men to go with me to bring in this fugitive."

Dick Prentiss spoke from the front of the crowd. "I'll go."

"Ahem," said Earl Miner. "Let me say something. If this man is headed west toward my ranch, I need to keep my men close by. And I don't know but what his cousins might come to help after all, or to cause trouble on my place."

"I don't think they will," said the marshal. "But it's your say."

Mike Ackerman spoke up. "I can't go. There was a time I could, but I'm past that now. I'm too old and heavy, and my gout is acting up. But I'll be glad to contribute to expenses."

"Every citizen does his part. Appreciate it, Mike."

One by one, the other business owners said they could not go. When it came to Tobe Lestman, who stood ready with a rifle as well as his sheath knife and cross-draw pistol, he said, "I'd go, but the boss won't let me."

"It's all right," said the marshal. "Anyone else?"

Al Wisner spoke up. "By God, if no one else'll go, I will."

The marshal laid his hand on Al's shoulder. "With all respect, Al, I don't think I could let you. It's gonna be hard ridin', and you've been through enough already. You can help hold things together here in town." Turning to the crowd, he said again, "Anyone else?"

Hartley swallowed. His mouth was dry, and his heartbeat was picking up. He heard himself say, "I'll go."

"That's good," said the marshal. "Now, if we could get two or even three more to join us—"

Dick Prentiss stepped forward. With a roll of the shoulders and a glance toward Muriel, he put his thumb on his belt and raised his chin. "I want to go. I wanted to get him before he had a chance to take off, and I want to help run him down now."

Miner shook his head. "I'd rather you not go, Dick. I've already lost two men. You know I'm short-handed."

"That's just it. We've lost two men. We've got a stake in this."

"I wish you wouldn't."

"Let me do it. The marshal just said he needs at least two more."

Miner raised his hand and made a backward wave. "All right. Go ahead. I hope nothing goes wrong."

Prentiss squared his shoulders. "Oh, we'll get him."

The marshal took over again. "All right, men. I've got two to ride with me. One or two more would be good." He waited a long minute as men shifted their feet and muttered. At length he said, "I guess that's it. Three of us. Thanks anyway to everyone else. Now, you two, here's my plan. We take two horses each. He's got a start on us, but with a change of horses, we'll gain on him. And he's a heavy rider, even for that speckled horse."

"I can get another mount," said Prentiss.

"Good. I'll rig up two for me. Hartley, I suppose I'll have to arrange for a second one for you."

"That's right."

"I'll take care of it, and I'll put together some grub. Let's meet at the livery stable in fifteen minutes, ready to go."

As the group was breaking up, Earl Miner said, "Are you going to deputize them?"

"I already did."

Hartley found Muriel with his eyes and took quick steps her way. She fell in with him as he kept walking toward the boardinghouse.

"I need to pick up my rifle and my jacket, and then I have to hoof it to the other end of town to saddle my horse. Sorry I'm in a hurry."

"I heard him. I know." She was walking fast and having to take an occasional extra step to keep up with him. "You haven't done something like this before, have you?"

"No, and I don't know if the marshal or Prentiss has, either."

"This is very dangerous. I don't think I need to tell you that."

"No, but thanks." Hartley pictured Treece riding away on the speckled horse. "He's on the run. He's got only one horse, and as the marshal says, that horse is going to tire out." He decided not to say any more, but he could imagine Treece wanting to acquire a fresh horse.

At the boardinghouse, he paused at the door. "We'll have to make this quick. No time for poetry."

She held her face up and met him in a kiss. "Come back," she said.

"I'll do all I can."

"Don't hesitate when you're out there."

"I won't."

He gathered his rifle and scabbard, his jacket, and, on a well-spent second thought, a box of shells. Walking faster than before, he headed for the livery stable.

Ed Becker had Sandy tied and waiting. Hartley gave the horse a quick brushing, combed out its mane and tail, and slapped on the double saddle blanket. He swung the saddle up and settled it in place. Reaching under the horse's chest, he caught the cinch while it was still swinging. He ran the latigo one, two, three times, pulled it tight, and put the spike of the buckle in a hole. An image came up of Treece pointing a rifle, and he pushed it away. Next came the rear cinch, which he did not have to leave very tight if he was not roping. From there he moved to the head of the horse, where he slipped the headstall over Sandy's ears and settled the bit in his mouth.

He led the horse by the reins and walked out into the sunlight. Prentiss was waiting with his long-legged bay saddled. At the end of a neck rope he had a sorrel that Hartley recognized from Lestman's string. Prentiss did not speak. He smoked on a cigarette and gazed off to the west.

Ed Becker came walking out of the livery stable with a buckskin on a halter and lead rope. He handed the rope to Hartley and said, "Jock wanted a second horse for you. This one should do all right."

"Thanks." Hartley looked over the buckskin. It was a solid horse, a little over fifteen hands, blocky in the hips and shoulders.

A minute later, the marshal appeared, leading two horses. The one in front was a chestnut bay, redder than Prentiss's horse and with a glossy black mane and tail. It carried a shiny double-rigged saddle with oxbow stirrups wrapped in leather, rounded skirts, and a breast collar, very modern to Hartley's eye. The second horse, a plain brown animal but well-muscled like the first one, had a lightweight saddle with a canvas pannier draped over it and lashed up snug. From the looks of it, the marshal did not plan to have many meals on the trail.

"That's our grub," said the marshal. "I don't know if anyone had a chance to eat, but we'll grab a bite when we stop to rest the horses."

"I'm not hungry," said Hartley, fudging the truth.

Prentiss dropped the butt of his cigarette and ground it out. "Neither am I."

"Then I think we're ready." The marshal led his horses away from the others.

Hartley did the same. He tightened his cinch another notch, held the lead rope clear, and mounted up.

Prentiss's spurs jingled as he heaved himself up onto the big bay. "I guess we're gonna see how the cow ate the cabbage," he said.

The bit on the marshal's horse sparkled in the sun as the lawman touched his spurs to the animal and stepped out ahead. After a few yards, he picked up a lope. Prentiss followed.

Hartley fell in third, leading the buckskin, as the group rode out of Jennet.

CHAPTER SIXTEEN

From a distance, Hartley had a broad view of Decker Rim. It had the appearance of a wall of bluffs that began at a point due south, curved west and north for about fifteen miles, and then ran north for another fifteen miles or more. The bluff-like aspect was accentuated by the sunlight reflecting off the upper one-third or one-fourth, which in most places consisted of bare, light-colored clay and sandstone. The lower part, or skirt, was characterized by steep slopes varying in cover from grass to sagebrush to dark trees like pine and cedar.

Hartley knew, however, that the rim was not that simple. He had gathered some familiarity with the area in his work as a range rider, which brought him within a mile or so on several occasions and up to the rim itself on a few. He knew that Decker Rim contained a long series of crevices, enclaves, and canyons, some of which reached back in and forked into grassy, timbered side canyons and sheer rock gorges.

As the rim came closer in view, Hartley wondered why Treece chose to flee this way rather than to the east, where he lived in badger country, or, deeper down, which was the direction of his home in Missouri. With more time and deliberation, Treece might have done so, or he might have gone south to Cheyenne so that he might go west on the train and then north to some place like the Yukon. But Treece had left on short order, and this route offered him a hundred or a thousand hiding spots along the way.

The small posse had ridden about ten miles when the trail approached the base of the rim where it curved northwest. The bluffs were steeper in this spot, and a great deal of light-colored rock lay about. The marshal brought the group to a halt, and the three riders dismounted. Hartley took his first few steps with care as he regained a normal feeling in his legs. When he felt steady, he led his two horses to join the marshal and Prentiss.

The marshal's bushy mustache moved up and down as if he was shaping his words first. "This is the place where they come for rocks. He would know this part of the trail like his own backyard. I don't know how well he knows the rest of the country."

Prentiss said, "This here is your old stompin' grounds, isn't it, Jock?"

"I don't know how much I stomped. But I hunted and trapped along the rim quite a bit when I was younger. Some fifteen, twenty years ago. Some of these places have grown over and aren't like they used to be. But some things haven't changed. Until you get to the hills 'way around on the north, there's two ways out. That is, there's two trails that a wagon or a regular rider on horseback could go over. They're both long climbs, steep in some places. One's way south of here, and he didn't go in that direction. The other's around to the north, on the western edge. Other than that, it's cow trails and game trails. And the cow trails are more like game trails, the way they go between rocks and along ledges. If a man knows which one to take, there's ways out of here, but he'd better know, 'cause there's some places he couldn't get off his horse, much less turn around. This fella's trail isn't difficult to follow so far, so it shouldn't be too hard to tell if he takes a turn."

Prentiss pulled out a white tobacco sack with yellow drawstrings. Casting an intense look around, he said, "Two heads are better than one, Jock. I know some of this country, too."

"Well, I wanted to stop here to see if there was any sign. I don't notice anything except the messes they left before."

"Neither do I."

The marshal sniffed and pinched his nostrils. "Let's give these horses a chance to catch their wind, and on the next stop, we'll change mounts."

"Good idea." Prentiss began to roll a cigarette. As he did, he shifted his stance and gave his back to Hartley.

"We'll grab a bite to eat, then, too," said the marshal.

Hartley kept to himself. He felt as if he was being ignored, more by Prentiss than by the marshal, and he wondered if he should have taken the trouble to ride with them. He lifted the canteen from the near saddlebag and uncapped it. On reflection, he knew why he had come along. He wished one or two others had joined in as well, if only to change the balance of men present.

The sun was beginning to slip in the afternoon sky. Hartley figured they had about four hours of daylight left, but the shadows would reach out sooner up against the rim. Although there were several main-traveled trails across Decker Basin, Treece had chosen the one that ran along the base, where the land was not as hilly as it was a mile or so into the basin.

The group moved on, loping for a mile or so, slowing to a walk, and loping again. Hartley had developed good riding legs while working for the Pick, and he had done an ample amount of riding since then, but continuous, fast travel was harder. He recalled stories of men riding fifty miles across country in one push, sometimes at night. And there was the story of Portugee Phillips's legendary ride of more than two hundred miles from Fort Phil Kearny to Fort Laramie, through a blizzard. Hartley told himself that this ride would not go on forever. It would have an end.

When they had ridden about fifteen miles out of Jennet, they drew rein at another rocky area. Large gray and salmon-colored boulders lay about, with smaller, broken pieces scattered over an area of an acre or more.

The marshal said, "I believe he came this far on some occasions with the wagon. This is a better kind of rock. But he didn't stop here today."

"Doesn't look like it," said Prentiss.

The marshal continued. "There should be a windmill about another mile ahead. We'll have our rest stop there."

The windmill came into view a little while later. It was a stark-looking structure, standing by itself on a bare, trampled area. The men slowed their horses and took the last quarter-mile at a walk. At the tank, they dismounted, loosened their cinches, and let the horses drink.

The marshal dug out a can of tomatoes and two biscuits for each man. They opened the cans with their pocketknives and made a short meal.

Prentiss said, "Should we keep these cans to boil coffee?"

"Sorry about that," said the marshal. "I meant to bring coffee, but they didn't have any ground, and I was goin' to pick some up at my house, but I had too much on my mind. And I did buy a can of tin cow."

"Airtight," said Prentiss.

"I didn't bring that much grub. I figure if we don't catch him by nightfall, we'll lose him. Once he gets onto the main trail that leads up out of here, by those columns of rock, you know, he'll be up on the flats where he can go in different directions to Uva, Bordeaux, or Chugwater."

Prentiss had his thumb on the front of his belt as he squared his shoulders and leaned back. "We'll have to sleep out, then. No matter. I can shoot a deer in the morning."

"Just don't fire any shots now. We don't want him to know how close we are—or how far back."

"Yeah." Prentiss drank the juice from the can, shook it, and tossed it on the ground. He wiped the tip of his nose where it had touched the lid of the can.

"I try not to leave those things around," said the marshal.

"Worried about leavin' a trail?"

"Not so much that. It's the trash. Even when I hunted out here as a kid, I didn't like seein' sardine cans, round cans, even whiskey bottles."

"One don't hurt."

"I'd just as soon you picked it up. Leave the place clean for whoever comes next."

"I didn't see where the nesters left things clean. They didn't even cover up their messes."

"That's them."

Prentiss picked up the empty can, rinsed it in the water tank, and tucked it into the open pannier.

The marshal gazed at the trail ahead. "I don't have a sense of whether we're gainin' on him or not, but we must be."

"I'm sure we are." Prentiss drew out his cigarette makings.

The marshal turned to Hartley. "We can get started changin' mounts."

Hartley rubbed down the buckskin with a folded piece of burlap he carried in his saddlebags. The horse had presented no trouble at all so far, and it stood still as if it knew the saddle would follow. Hartley pulled the saddle and double blanket from Sandy, flipped the blanket to turn it dry side down, settled it onto the buckskin's back, and swung the saddle up and onto the blanket. The horse did not flinch as the stirrups flopped into place.

So far, Hartley had done all of the work while holding the reins and the lead rope. Now he pondered how to switch the

229

bridle and the halter on the two animals. Even if he tied one of them to the windmill, he would have to leave the other loose for a few seconds. He glanced at the other two men, and each of them was working alone, so he decided he should do the same.

He knew and trusted Sandy, so he slipped the bridle off first, let his good horse stand alone, and made the transfer onto the buckskin. With the halter and lead rope in hand, he turned to see Sandy walking away. He hurried after the sorrel, grabbed him by the mane, tossed the lead rope around his neck, ducked under, and pulled the halter up onto the horse's head—all while hanging onto the reins holding the buckskin.

Prentiss and the marshal paid him no attention. He led the two horses away a few paces and checked the rigging on the buckskin, including the straps that held on the scabbard and rifle.

A few minutes later, the horsemen mounted up and moved out. Hartley pulled his hat brim down to block out the late afternoon sun. After a hundred yards of warming up, the marshal put his brown horse into a lope, and the pursuit was on again.

A mile later, the group slowed. Riding behind the other four horses, Hartley had not been able to see the trail ahead for most of the afternoon, so he did not know the cause for the slowdown until the others came to a stop and he rode around and came up next to them.

A husky white horse with dark gray flecks lay on its side, motionless, with no saddle or bridle.

"I believe that's the one," said the marshal.

Hartley nodded. "I'm quite sure I've seen him riding it."

The marshal pushed out his mustache as he scanned the bluffs a quarter of a mile away. "Gotta think about this," he said. "I don't see any horse tracks leadin' away, so I don't think he put his saddle on another horse. But he might want us to think he did. My guess is that he stashed it some place." The marshal stared down at the dead horse. "Looks like he used up one bullet. Finish it off to keep it still so he could pull off the outfit. I didn't hear a shot, but a pistol held up close won't carry all that far."

Prentiss had put on his intense, searching expression as he studied the rim. "He's not gonna go very far or very fast carryin' a saddle. My hunch is he's holed up."

"Could be," said the marshal.

"Do we shoot on sight, then?"

"I'd rather give him the chance to surrender."

"Puh. I say, what's good for the goose is good for the gander. He didn't give anyone else much of a chance."

"I'd like to arrest him if I can. Let him give himself up."

Prentiss heaved a breath. "What you say. But if he shoots first—"

"Oh, then everything changes." The marshal let his gaze travel across the short, drying grass on his left. "Hard to pick out footprints, but it looks like someone walked off in that direction." He raised his head and scanned the bluffs again. "I think we're goin' to change our method. Hartley, we're goin' to let you hold all the extra horses. Wait here, out of range. He needs a horse, and we don't want to give him one. So you stay here. Me an' Dick 'll ride closer to the bluffs and see if we can find where he left the saddle, if he did."

Hartley dismounted, took the ropes for the other two horses, and added them to what he already held. Standing with two horses on each side, he watched as Prentiss and the marshal rode toward a rocky canyon that opened out onto the level of the rangeland. Hartley felt nervousness build within him as the two riders arrived at the mouth of the canyon and turned left, disappearing behind a rock wall.

A couple of minutes later, they rode into sight. Prentiss waited on his horse while the marshal rode into the deeper part of the canyon on the right. A few minutes later, he rode out, trotted his horse toward Prentiss, and exchanged a few words. They turned toward Hartley and the spare horses, and they took off on a soft lope.

They slowed to a trot and drew rein a few yards away from Hartley and the horses.

The marshal cleared his throat and said, "I found where he left his saddle, or at least someone did in the last little while. It hasn't been there a day. Empty scabbard, no rifle." He nudged his horse around to face the canyon. "He needs a horse, and I don't think he cares how he gets it. Meanwhile, he might be movin' along on foot, or he might be holed up like Dick says, not far away."

"We need someone up on top," said Prentiss.

"I don't know anywhere we can get up there with a horse."

"I'll go up on foot. Hell with him. I'll pin him down like a rat in a grain barrel."

"You can't see as well as you think from up there. I know that from hunting. There's always nooks and crevices you can't see into."

"If he's holed up, we can't get close enough from down here."

"I know. What we need is more men, and I don't know where we can get 'em."

"This is a hell of a fix. If I can get up on top, I might be able to see where he is. If he's moving along through this stuff, I should be able to catch up with him, and if I can't get a shot at him, I can point him out to you." Prentiss heaved a breath of impatience. "We can't just sit here."

"I know. If we had even four men, we could have two coming from the north, and the two of us here, one on top and one down below going both ways."

"But we don't. And if all we do is have a stalemate, he'll slip

232

away in the night." Prentiss gave a hard stare at the canyon.

"As long as he's holed up, if he is, he's got an advantage. It would be too easy for him to see you."

"I'll stay back from the edge where he can't see me."

"In order to look down into some of those places, you have to stand right on the edge. You skyline yourself for him."

"I think I can get him. We can't just wait and sit him out. If I don't see him, I'll come down, and we can try another plan."

"All right. We'll try it your way for an hour. He may have slipped away already." The marshal motioned with his head to the right of the canyon, where the rim continued to the north.

"Good. Let's ride over there, and you can bring my horse back."

"Just a minute. I've got to do something first." The marshal dismounted from the brown horse. "I've got to pull up my stocking in my right boot. It's been bothering me." He handed his reins to Hartley and sat down. With some straining, he pulled off his stovepipe boot and shook it out. He pulled the wrinkles out of a long, gray wool sock and then used the mule-ear straps to put his boot on again. He stood up, pressed down on his heel, and seemed satisfied.

"One other thing." The marshal's face was clouded as he looked at Prentiss and Hartley in turn. "I know we don't want to think about this, but we have to. If he gets two of us, whoever is left has to keep all these horses out of his hands. That means go back to town. It's a long walk out of here for a man his size, but if he gets a hold of one or more of these horses, then all we did was help him."

"He's not goin' to get anyone," said Prentiss.

"I hope not. We just have to do our best." The marshal took his reins from Hartley and mounted up.

The two horsemen rode across the flat to the mouth of the canyon. Prentiss slid down from the saddle and pulled the rifle from his scabbard. He handed the reins to the marshal, raised his hand in farewell, and walked into the canyon. The marshal rode back to the spot where Hartley stood with the horses.

He dropped the reins into Hartley's hand. "I told him the canyon on the right was pretty steep, and if he didn't see a good way up, he could come out and try the part on the left. As soon as I see him up on top, I'll start workin' along the bottom. Just like huntin' deer. You can walk around a rock wall and there they are, or they can be long gone and you never know it." The marshal clucked to his horse, turned it around, and headed again to the opening of the canyon.

Hartley prepared himself for a long wait. The world went quiet as the brown horse swished its tail and walked toward the rim, carrying the rider with a gray vest and black hat.

Prentiss emerged from the right side of the canyon, waved and pointed, and walked into the inlet on the left. The marshal took his time and slowed to a stop.

The minutes dragged on. Prentiss appeared on the level, grassy area on top of the rim. He held his rifle below his waist with both hands, then raised his left hand and waved. The marshal raised a hand in response. His horse must have become restive, for he reined it to one side and the other and backed it up a couple of steps.

Out of nowhere, the blast of a rifle shot ripped through the afternoon and echoed along the rocks. The marshal's horse lurched, reared, turned to the left, and fell to the ground with great force, jarring the rider and sending his hat several feet away.

From the ledge, Prentiss fired twice with his rifle. To Hartley's surprise, he was shooting down into the left side of the canyon where Prentiss and the marshal had ridden in about fifteen minutes earlier and where Prentiss had walked in and begun his climb. Hartley's thoughts raced. All the time they had assumed

Treece was ahead of them, he had let them pass him up. He must have been hiding there, patient, thinking of a plan and waiting for the right moment. Four quick rifle shots sounded from down in the rocks, and Hartley was able to place them now. Prentiss returned fire, kneeling. He fired twice. Another shot blasted from the canyon, and Prentiss dropped his rifle on the grass and grabbed his shoulder. One more shot flattened him.

All this time, the marshal was squirming, trying to pull his leg free from underneath the fallen horse.

Shots continued from the canyon, not as forceful or piercing in their sounds, and a couple of them kicked up dirt beyond where the marshal lay. Hartley took them for pistol shots.

The marshal pulled free, rolled over, and settled into position lying down behind the dead horse. He drew his pistol and began firing. After a few seconds, all the noise stopped.

Hartley could not count the pistol shots back and forth, but he thought they must have been close to a dozen. He did not know whether the ambusher had run out of cartridges, was reloading, or had been hit. What he did know was that the marshal needed help.

Not much more than a minute had passed since the shooting began, and Hartley had had plenty to do in holding the horses together and figuring out how the gunfight was taking place. Now he had to clear his mind and decide how to do things. The marshal had been emphatic about not letting any horse fall into Treece's hands, but Hartley was going to have to let go of the three remounts if he was going to bring a saddled horse to the marshal. That was a risk he was going to have to take.

He dropped the three lead ropes, pulled Prentiss's horse away, held the reins clear, and swung up onto the buckskin. He started at a trot and moved into a lope.

No shots sounded. The marshal remained prone until Hartley

was twenty yards away. He pushed himself to his knees, then onto his legs, teetering and limping. Hartley came to a stop.

"I've got to get on the other side," said the marshal. "This leg's no good."

Hartley bailed off, held both horses by the reins, separated them, and put his shoulder against the marshal's buttocks to push him up. He handed him the reins, swung onto his own saddle, and rode close as the marshal hung onto the saddle horn and jolted along.

Out on the flat, Hartley helped the marshal ease out of the saddle and sit down.

"What about Dick?" the marshal asked.

"I think he's done for."

The corners of the marshal's mouth went down. "That's too bad. And Treece was waitin' for us all that time, like a rattlesnake. We passed him right up."

"Do you think he's out of ammunition?"

"Sure seemed like it. That's what he gets for leavin' in a hurry. I did remember to bring a box of shells."

"So did I."

"But mine are in my saddlebag. And my rifle's stuck underneath my horse."

Hartley's eyes went to the dead horse, lying out in the open. "I bet he'd like to get his hands on that rifle."

"He sure would. And then a horse."

"Yes, and I need to round these up. Can you hold this one?"

"Oh, yeah. I don't know if I can climb into the saddle by myself, but I can hold the reins. Bring my bay horse first. He's carrying that light saddle and panniers, which someone could jump onto, and he's a good strong horse. So was the other one, damn it."

Hartley mounted up and rode away. The chestnut bay horse had wandered toward the rim, but it was not skittish. Hartley rode up beside it, leaned over, and grabbed the lead rope. He led the horse to the marshal and set off for the other two.

He hadn't gone twenty yards when he heard the marshal's voice, quick and clear but not very loud.

"Hey! Look here!"

Hartley cut the buckskin around and located the area in front of the canyon. The brown horse still lay in a heap. From the rocky area on the left, a bulky figure in dark clothes was running. He did not move his arms and elbows very much, and he did not bound up and down. He reminded Hartley of a locomotive, but there was no doubt that the figure was Doyle Treece, running to get hold of a rifle. In that instant, Hartley wondered if Treece had shot the horse for that reason to begin with, making sure the rifle didn't get away while he finished off the marshal. He just didn't count on running out of rifle and then pistol shells.

The man kept running on a straight line toward the dead horse. Hartley thought of everything at once—horses to keep together, the marshal in his condition, and a desperate man running to lay hands on a loaded rifle and, if he thought of it, the extras shells in the saddlebag. Hartley kicked the buckskin into a lope.

He did not know if he could hold Treece at gunpoint. But he had to get there first. He leaned forward as the horse's hooves drummed on the dry earth.

Treece was covering the ground faster than he had seemed to when he started out. He was going to reach the horse first. Hartley had no idea how much the man might have to struggle to pull the rifle free.

The bulky man moved like a figure in a kinetoscope. He jumped over the body of the horse, jerked around, reached forward, and grabbed the two legs lying on the ground. He pulled on the dead body, rocked it, and threw all his weight backward. The horse's feet went straight up. Treece sagged back and pulled again, and the horse flopped. Without straightening up, Treece leaned forward and reached for the rifle in the scabbard.

Fifty feet short, Hartley pulled the buckskin to a stop and held onto the reins as he jumped off. He had to use the horse as a shield, even as he knew that Treece would not scruple to shoot another horse.

The buckskin stutter-stepped side to side as Hartley held the reins close up to the bit with his left hand and pulled at the rifle with his right. Hunched behind the horse, he let the reins go and levered in a shell. He hit the horse in the ribs with his left elbow, and as the horse lunged forward, Doyle Treece came into view. He had a rifle to his shoulder and was looking for a target. Hartley aimed and fired.

The buckskin squealed and grunted as it took off with a pounding of hooves. Doyle Treece's pig eyes opened wide as he dropped the rifle and pressed both hands against his full midsection below his chest. Blood appeared between his fingers. He coughed, and a watery red vomit leaked out over his lower lip. A strange, guttural sound rose from his throat, his knees buckled, and he fell next to the dead horse.

A red sun was burning above the crest of the rim when Hartley finished dragging Dick Prentiss's body next to those of Treece and the marshal's brown horse. The marshal sat nearby, holding the five horses by the reins and lead ropes.

"What else?" asked Hartley.

"I'd like to pull my outfit off that horse before he goes stiff and put it on my bay horse."

Hartley winced. He had noticed that the saddle had become scuffed and bloodstained, with a bullet hole in the skirt in front. "Are you planning to ride all the way back to town?"

"I think it's too much to ask of you to load up two dead men, look out for them and the rest of the horses, and have to deal with a cripple as well, all through the night. I don't mind stayin' here until you can have someone come with a wagon."

"Don't you think it would be better if you came with me? We can still send someone out to pick up these two."

"Nah. I don't care who it is. I'd rather not leave his body to the magpies and coyotes if there's a way not to. If you saddle my bay horse and leave him here, I won't feel stranded."

"Are you sure?"

"Yes, I'm sure. I could ride if I had to, but I'll be all right this way. My leg's broke and my hip hurts like hell, but I'm not leakin'."

"I hate to leave you alone. I'll try to get a wagon started this way tonight."

"Don't worry about me. I've had to do a lot of things alone. Stayin' out like this is not that hard. I'm sorry about what happened to Dick, but I'm glad to have the help I did on this trip."

Hartley surveyed the wreckage, including the marshal, sitting with his legs straight out. He might never walk the same again in his stovepipe, mule-ear-strap boots.

"None of this had to happen," said Hartley, "except for the sick will of someone who wanted to get his hands on things."

"Well, it's done, and he is, too. Sometimes you wish you could punish someone more than once."

CHAPTER SEVENTEEN

Hartley and Muriel were sitting on the porch of the boarding-house and studying a map when a buckboard with a dark blue canopy stopped in the street. Hartley recognized the buckboard and the driver at the same time. Earl Miner raised his hand in greeting. On the other side of him, in the shade of the canopy, sat Bess Ackerman.

Miner's voice carried across the short distance. "I say, Hartley, do you have a minute?"

"I suppose so." Hartley let Muriel hold the map as he stood up. He settled his hat on his head and walked down the steps into the sunlight. He crossed the yard with a small tree on each side of the walk, then slowed to a stop next to the carriage.

Miner looked down on him from the shaded driver's seat. The man was dressed in his characteristic dark suit and black hat, white shirt, and silver watch chain. Gray hair showed at his temples, but his slender build, clean shave, and clear dark eyes showed a man of energy and authority. Miner brushed at a fleck on his coat sleeve and said, "We just dropped in on Jock Mosby. He's doing all right."

"That's good to hear."

"I want you to know how much I appreciate what you did, in spite of our loss."

"Thank you."

"From what Jock told me, you showed your mettle."

Hartley shrugged. "I did what I had to do."

"All the same, it was well done, and I want you to know you have my gratitude."

"It's good of you to say so."

As if with the same breath, Miner said, "I'd like to have you back as a hired man."

Hartley gazed at the side of the buckboard, where the Pick brand was burned into the wood and painted over with the rest of the body. He was trying to think of how to work his answer when Miner spoke again.

"You know, I've had some losses. Three good men. I need to build back up."

Hartley's eyes traveled to the dust at his feet, then tensed as he looked up into the bright sunlight. "I thank you for your offer, sir, but I'd rather follow my own trail."

Miner's face showed little expression. "As you wish. But you know, it's harder when you try to make a go of it on your own."

Hartley met the man's eyes and caught a glimpse of Bess in the background. He said, "I believe you, sir, but I think I'm more suited for it."

"Good enough." Miner gathered the reins. "I wish you luck."

"Thank you, and the same to you."

The buckboard wheeled away as Hartley walked back to the porch. Muriel met him with a reserved smile.

"He offered me a job."

"I overheard."

Hartley shook his head. "I couldn't do it. I've seen how he does things, and that's why I left in the first place. I don't care for it." He motioned toward the map. "This is a much more interesting prospect. Where were we?"

"As if you don't remember. I was telling you what I had said before, that I wasn't going to take up a claim and then turn it over to a man in marriage before I had the deed in my name."

He stared at the map without seeing details. "But you don't

mind having claims side by side."

"Not at all. Each claim is a household."

He met her eyes. "So you live in your hut, and I live in mine. Two households, as they say in the opening of *Romeo and Juliet,* but not at war."

She smiled. "I've read a little about this, and as I told you before, I've seen and heard some of it for myself. One thing people can do is build on the property line, with the two houses adjoining."

His spirits picked up. "That would be a good solution."

"Efficient."

He seemed to be seeing her anew, with her gray-green eyes, tanned complexion, and dark, flowing hair. "It would make the great lonesome plains not so lonesome." A second thought presented itself. "Are you not afraid of the distance?"

"If it's the distance that separates us from the things we hope to avoid, not at all."

"Like the farm machinery coming up to the door."

"That, and all of it." She waved her hand. "We'll get away with it for as long as we can."

He took her by both hands. "You know, I could fall in love with you if I hadn't already."

Her smile was playful. "When did you know it?"

"About a minute ago, when you talked about building two houses together. And you?"

"When you rode away with the other men. I was afraid I would never see you again. When you came back, I knew for sure. I knew I could learn to ride a more spirited horse than Bob, and I knew I could tend the node."

ABOUT THE AUTHOR

John D. Nesbitt is the author of more than forty books, including traditional western novels, crossover western mysteries, contemporary western fiction, retro/noir fiction, nonfiction, and poetry. He has won the Western Writers of America Spur Award four times—twice for paperback novel, once for short story, and once for poem. He has been a finalist for the Spur Award once, as well as for the Western Fictioneers Peacemaker Award three times and the Will Rogers Medallion Award four times. He has also received two creative writing fellowships with the Wyoming Arts Council (once for fiction, once for nonfiction). John has had a distinguished career as a college instructor, most notably for thirty-nine years at Eastern Wyoming College. He lives in the plains country of Wyoming, where he stays in touch with the natural world and the settings for his work. He writes about lifelike people in realistic situations, people who deserve justice and a fair shake in life. Recent works include *Castle Butte*, a young adult novel, and *Dusk Along the Niobrara*, a frontier mystery, both with Five Star.

The employees of Five Star Publishing hope you have enjoyed this book.

Our Five Star novels explore little-known chapters from America's history, stories told from unique perspectives that will entertain a broad range of readers.

Other Five Star books are available at your local library, bookstore, all major book distributors, and directly from Five Star/Gale.

Connect with Five Star Publishing

Visit us on Facebook:
   https://www.facebook.com/FiveStarCengage

Email:
   FiveStar@cengage.com

For information about titles and placing orders:
   (800) 223-1244
   gale.orders@cengage.com

To share your comments, write to us:
   Five Star Publishing
   Attn: Publisher
   10 Water St., Suite 310
   Waterville, ME 04901